THE KILLER IN THE HOUSE

THE KILLER IN THE HOUSE

LAUREN REDING

THOMAS & MERCER

This is a work of fiction. Names, characters, organizations, places, events, and incidents are either products of the author's imagination or are used fictitiously. Otherwise, any resemblance to actual persons, living or dead, is purely coincidental.

Text copyright © 2026 by Lauren Reding
All rights reserved.

No part of this book may be reproduced, or stored in a retrieval system, or transmitted in any form or by any means, electronic, mechanical, photocopying, recording, or otherwise, without express written permission of the publisher.

Published by Thomas & Mercer, Seattle

www.apub.com

Amazon, the Amazon logo, and Thomas & Mercer are trademarks of Amazon.com, Inc., or its affiliates.

EU product safety contact:
Amazon Media EU S. à r.l.
38, avenue John F. Kennedy, L-1855 Luxembourg
amazonpublishing-gpsr@amazon.com

ISBN-13: 9781662532818 (paperback)
ISBN-13: 9781662532825 (digital)

Cover design by Damon Freeman
Cover image: © Steve Peet / ArcAngel Images; © Viktor1, © itim2101, © OSTILL is Franck Camhi / Shutterstock

Printed in the United States of America

THE KILLER IN THE HOUSE

CHAPTER 1

1125 Linden Avenue was a large brown Victorian with two columns of bow windows that made it look like a partly unrolled scroll. It stood on a shaded street in Richmond's Fan District, shoulder to shoulder with other elegant row houses, some brick, some painted blue or beige, some with bronze plaques proclaiming their status as historic homes. Renee, broom in hand, paused in her sweeping of the front steps and took a moment to be amazed by the ritziness of the neighborhood and the fact that she was there at all.

She hadn't expected to be offered the job as live-in housekeeper to the Weatherup family. In fact, three months of no interviews had made her think the whole thing had been a mistake: the thing where she paid seventy-five dollars for a video training course in high-end house-keeping, the thing where she was trying to get a stable job and finally move out of her parents' house at twenty-eight. Clearly her résumé, with its catalog of part-time jobs awkwardly gapping and overlapping, painted too accurate a picture of a life that had been stalled since high school. Nobody had wanted to bring such an obvious downer into their fine home.

Until Kim Weatherup invited her for an interview. "You'd be joining us at the perfect time," Kim had said as they exchanged information on the phone. "Our homelife is about to get more complicated, and we really need somebody to help me keep everything together."

Renee had scheduled the interview and then made the hour's drive from her parents' house in rural Cumberland County all the way to the Weatherups' downtown neighborhood. But first, of course, she'd done the requisite internet searches. By the time she'd parked in front of 1125 Linden Avenue, she'd already known what the house looked like and already known the very worst thing that had happened there.

It was a long, sad story told in more news articles than she had the patience to read. Richmond Attorney Found Murdered . . . New Leads in Julie Weatherup Investigation . . . Husband Indicted in . . . Money, Infidelity, Divorce Possible Motives in . . . Julie's Coworkers Speak . . . Headlines scrolled for pages, but one article published in the *Richmond Tribune* just two weeks ago summed up the story.

> Edward Weatherup will be released from prison this month after he was exonerated for the murder of his wife, Julie Weatherup, a prominent Richmond attorney, who was found brutally slain on the rooftop of her home in 2018. Later that year, Mr. Weatherup was indicted by former Commonwealth's Attorney Raymond Prescott, who argued that Weatherup murdered his wife in a fit of rage after she suggested ending their fifteen-year marriage. A jury convicted Mr. Weatherup of first-degree murder in 2018.
>
> Since that original conviction, the Prosecutor's office has come under scrutiny, which resulted in Prescott's firing. Weatherup was granted a new trial, after which he was acquitted of all charges.
>
> The Weatherup case has become a true crime sensation, thanks to the podcast *Innocent Blood*, which brought the tragedy to the popular consciousness. The podcast's host, Mariah Cusmano, in a statement

> earlier this week, said that she is honored to have been a part of Weatherup's exoneration. "There are so many reasons that Ed shouldn't have been convicted in the first place. There was no evidence that Ed knew Julie was considering divorce; no murder weapon was found; and, most notably, he wasn't even in the state when Julie died. That's motive, means, and opportunity, all missing from the prosecution's case."
>
> The Office of the Commonwealth's Attorney has said that they are unable to comment because the murder of Julie Weatherup is once again an open investigation.

Two pictures accompanied the article, the first of Ed, a tall man with salt-and-pepper hair looking somber in a brown suit and standing, flanked by lawyers, on the courthouse steps. The second was a picture of Julie, a candid snapshot of a smiling woman in white shorts and a baby blue T-shirt. She was in her late thirties or early forties with honey-brown hair teased up just enough to identify her as a child of the eighties. She sat in a youthful, carefree pose on the end of a picnic table, trees behind her, a warm smile on her face and a charming tilt to her head. The photo had a golden, hazy feel that might have been because of the sunshine, or it might have been the light nostalgic wash that news outlets seemed to favor for photos of murdered women.

In the comments section, CrazzyCrissty lamented: It's such a shame. How could someone do that to such a beautiful woman?

> Shamrockyhorror: Yes, let's make sure only the ugly people get murdered.
>
> Benjamin35: Five seconds later and the lib is trying to make it about political correctness.

xxthedizzxx: I just wish that husband had fried. He literally got away with murder.

1990Bananafan: I don't believe in the death penalty, but I'd make an exception for this bastard.

Shamrockyhorror: He was wrongfully convicted. He's the victim here.

CrazzyCrissty: God forgives everyone. He just has to let Jesus into his heart.

Shamrockyhorror: Isn't anyone going to yell at her for bringing religion into it?

1990Bananafan: He does look good in a suit, tho.

During Renee's job interview, Ed and Kim had sat her down and explained everything again, Ed making what sounded like a prepared statement, Kim with her hand on his arm as though warning him or urging him on. But the details were mostly what Renee had already read in the news: Julie's gruesome murder, Ed's conviction, the hit podcast, his exoneration.

"Our baby was born while I was incarcerated," Ed had said. "My older two kids have been living with their grandparents for the past five years. All I really want is to put it behind me and try to make up for lost time with the people I love."

"Of course," Renee had said. She knew that sometimes innocent people went to prison, and some of them were lucky enough to get out again. They, too, had families who loved them and deserved good lives. She thought of Enid Salinas of *Today's Housekeeping Essentials*, who narrated each lesson in pearls and makeup fit for a Broadway stage, and she echoed one of her de facto mentor's favorite reminders. "I'm here to make your life less complicated in whatever way you need."

They had offered her the job on the spot.

"But think about it," Kim had urged. "Talk it over with your family."

Afterward, back at home, Renee had made the mistake of showing Mama some of the news articles. She'd been excited to recount what she'd learned about the Weatherup story, assuming it would make a juicy topic of conversation, but she'd instantly regretted it.

"I don't like it," Mama had said, rasping her peeler over a russet potato. "I don't want you getting mixed up with people like that."

"People like what? Anyone can be accused of a crime they didn't commit. It says right here: He's innocent in the eyes of the law." Renee jabbed a finger at her laptop screen. The courts believed in Ed's innocence. The media believed. Why didn't Renee get to believe it, too, and let her life be just a smidge easier as a result? "You know this was my only offer," she added. "I need a job sometime, and they seemed like perfectly nice people."

"I know, baby." Mama plopped the potato in a pot of water and picked up another. "But it's so dangerous in the city. There's gangs and all kinds of crime, you know. I don't see why you can't get a job closer to home. You don't have to take the first offer that comes along."

Enid Salinas had said the same thing, and Renee knew it was common sense, but hearing it out of her mother's mouth just made her think of all the times she'd heard *I don't see why you can't* in all the arguments of all the past twenty-eight years. She gazed blankly at the wood-veneer cabinets and blue-and-cream floral wallpaper that had been the backdrop of her entire life. She'd practiced writing her letters here, had eaten countless breakfasts, and had washed her mother's everyday dishes until their tulip pattern had worn pale. There had been many joyful moments, she supposed, but she couldn't think of any of them just now.

"You know I've worked hard to get to the point where I can do this," she said. "I've been looking forward to it."

Mama pursed her lips. "I know, baby, but don't you think this just isn't the right time? After everything that happened? Should you really be making big decisions?"

After everything. And here she was, invoking Brandon without speaking his name.

"Am I supposed to sit in the house wearing a black veil the rest of my life?" she demanded, feeling her temperature rise.

"Don't be like this, Renee," her father said, having come in from the living room, probably, Renee thought, at the sound of her unreasonableness. "You know Mama just wants what's best for you." He was dressed in wide-leg jeans that hung off him more than they used to. He'd put on his boots, ready to head out on the tractor as soon as this had blown over.

"I'm just saying," Mama went on. "This man might be a murderer and you want to go live in his house."

"He's innocent!" Renee cried, her voice getting louder than she wished. She hadn't meant to find herself defending Ed, a man she'd only met once, but so many of her arguments with Mama ended with Renee yelling about not quite the right thing.

Mama folded her arms over her ribbed brown sweater. "Still," she said. "Everybody says he did it. You have to wonder if someone like that can ever lead a normal life."

Renee felt a familiar sick feeling in her chest. "I don't think this is even about him," she said. "Deep down, you don't think *I* can ever lead a normal life. You don't think *I* can be forgiven for what everybody says *I* did."

Her mother was silent, perhaps searching for a way to explain, or maybe just looking for a new avenue of attack. But either way, the silence went on long enough. Renee pulled on her boots and went outside to walk the perimeter of the farm.

The Beale Christmas tree farm was located off rural Route 13 in Cumberland County, and from the road, the only sign of it was a rutted track disappearing into the woods. During the pre-Christmas season, the entrance to the farm would be decorated with red bows, battery-operated lights, and a blow-up Santa, but in September, it looked like a whole lot of nothing. Beyond the house, down one hill and up the next, stretched the acres and acres of Douglas firs planted in neat rows, each carefully trimmed to grow in the perfect cone shape. Daddy and Mama had planted trees on those acres every year of Renee's life, and those trees now ranged in size from the ones that would dominate living rooms this December to those that would take their turn the next year or the year after, marching over the hills toward all the Christmases in decades to come.

The truth was that she could keep living here indefinitely. Mama and Daddy didn't charge her rent, and her expenses were next to nothing. If she gave up the job search, her parents would probably be happy that she'd come to see their side of things. She might never have to leave at all. Which was exactly the problem.

Cumberland was a quiet place, flat and piney, smelling of drying hay and fertilizer. It was a fine place to be a child, building forts in the acres of Christmas trees and riding her bike along miles of dirt tracks, nothing to worry about except sunburns and tick bites.

But it was a hard place to be a young adult. Farms, which had been a mainstay of the local economy for as long as anyone could remember, now faltered and failed on an annual basis. For Renee and the eighty-odd members of her graduating class, there were just a few options for how to proceed. Some did their best to go to college and not come back. Of those who stayed, the lucky ones got jobs at family-owned businesses like the hardware store or, more grimly, the prison. The rest worked part-time at the dollar store, the ABC liquor store, the gas station—or they went to prison themselves.

Renee hadn't meant to stay in Cumberland permanently. She hadn't meant to do anything, except lead her life, but her life hadn't led her anywhere. She'd cobbled together an income from part-time jobs and helping during the farm's busy season. She'd toyed with going to community college or getting some kind of certification, but she'd never felt excited about any of those things, and there was always something else to worry about, a vehicle to fix, a family health scare to lose sleep over. When she was twenty-two, her little brother, Aaron, had joined the marines and gone overseas, and it had become even harder to contemplate leaving. If something happened to sweet, funny Aaron, and she wasn't there for her parents . . . it was unthinkable.

In the last year or so, Brandon had come along, and the clouds had seemed to part. But that hadn't ended well. Suddenly, here she was at twenty-eight with nothing but a high school diploma and a lot of not much to show for herself. Except, of course, the grief and universal condemnation that followed everything that had happened with Brandon.

Yes, technically she could wait for another job to come along, but she had no idea how long she'd be waiting, or how long she could survive before the walls of her childhood bedroom closed in and suffocated her.

When she'd reached the little hill at the back of the property where there was better signal, she'd called Kim and accepted the job.

And less than a week later, there she was, sweeping two or three prematurely fallen leaves off the front steps of her new workplace, her new home, this enormous house among its enormous brethren on this beautiful street, all patinaed in wealth. Bad things had happened in this house, she knew that, though she tried not to think of them. But people had to move on from bad things. The thing to focus on was that it was a lovely, mild late-summer morning, and it was a fresh start for Renee, for all of them.

CHAPTER 2

Renee had only been on the job for one day and was still just catching her bearings among the many cupboards and discreet, trendy appliances, but already everything was about to change. As she was unpacking her small number of belongings in the spare bedroom and signing her official contract of employment with Kim, Ed was driving to Virginia Beach to embrace his children for the first time as a free man and help their grandparents move them back to 1125, a home they hadn't seen in five years.

Now, on the afternoon of the children's return, Kim stood in the grand parqueted foyer with baby Willow on one hip and her phone in hand. She was a little older than Renee and had delivered the baby just nine months ago, but she moved with the grace of a woman who knew she looked good, her body smooth under her mauve workout attire, hair tastefully highlighted, manicure glossy fresh. From what little Renee knew of her so far, she cared about what others thought of her, wanted them to think she was doing a good job as a wife and mother, as a woman in the world.

"They're half an hour out. Ed says they're bringing so much stuff," she said apologetically. "There's all the seasonal clothes and sports equipment. We're going to have to find places for all of it. Don't worry," she added in a rush. "In general, the kids will have to put away their own things. It's going to be some adjustment for them after living with their mother's parents, but both Ed and I really care about them being self-sufficient. You know how it is."

Renee did not know how it was, but then, she suspected, neither did Kim. The woman had gone from zero children to three in less than a year, and she was very nervous about it, if the sheer fact of Renee's presence in the household was anything to go by. But she couldn't blame Kim for the nerves. It was a momentous thing to become a mother figure to two children who had good reason for skepticism or outright distrust. In another lifetime, Renee would have been in that position herself, a thought that gave her an ache somewhere near her solar plexus. But in this lifetime, all she could offer was platitudes.

"I'm sure everyone will do just fine with a little time," she said and escaped into the kitchen.

She was finishing up some dinner prep, stowing chopped vegetables in the cavernous stainless steel fridge, when the front door opened and a boy with straight brown hair charged in, a fast-food bag clutched in one hand.

He halted in the foyer, his brown eyes scanning the space in narrow assessment. The last time he'd been here was right before or after his mother died, Renee realized. Five years was half a lifetime for a ten-year-old, and she wondered what memories, if any, he had of this place.

A pair of retirement-age people came in behind him. They were the Lauderbachs, Julie's parents, dressed somewhat formally for a road trip, Debra in a brocade shawl and Dale in pleated brown slacks.

Oliver turned to them and crinkled up his nose. "It smells funny in here."

Debra put a hand on his shoulder. "I'm sure it's just different from how you remember it smelling," she said.

The boy's eyes got very wide, and Debra hurried on. "But your room is still upstairs. Want to go see it?"

Kim bustled in then, along with Willow and a flurry of words. "Welcome, everyone! Oliver, this is your new baby sister. What do you think? Oh, and can everyone please do me a huge favor and take off your shoes?"

The Lauderbachs gave her a quiet hello and smiled politely at the baby, but Oliver simply looked blank, and after a moment, Debra ushered him up the stairs, shoes and all. Even after they disappeared from view, Renee could still hear the grandmother's voice saying something in low, comforting tones. A chill touched her neck when she imagined what it must be like for the Lauderbachs to return to the house where their daughter was murdered. She had an impulse to follow and express her condolences, but on second thought, it was better to keep quiet and let them focus on the child. She'd just found out about their tragedy this week, but they had been living with it for years.

A crestfallen Kim stood in the entry. "I guess it wasn't a shoes-off household before," she said to no one in particular.

The mood lightened when Ed came in next, folding Kim and the baby in his arms as if he'd been gone for weeks. "I'll never get tired of coming back to you two," he murmured into Kim's hair. He was about ten years older than his wife, a tall man in jeans and a polo shirt, and his hair, though streaked with gray, was thick and wavy. He was on the handsome side of average, good looking enough to make it plausible that a woman Kim's age would choose him.

"It's good to be home!" he added. "Isn't that right, Catherine?" This to the last person to enter the house, a teenage girl with sharply asymmetrical hair and a Nirvana T-shirt.

"Caz," she said by way of response as she marched up the stairs with a backpack, a suitcase, and a stoic expression.

"She's going by Caz now, did you know that?" Ed said to Kim, who shrugged. "Don't worry, Baby," he crooned to Willow. "Your sister and brother have been through a lot, but they'll get to know you soon enough. I'll be the first to admit," he added to Renee, "we have our challenges as a family, but at least we're honest about them. No secrets."

Who needed secrets, Renee wondered, when the reasons for everyone's trauma were so obvious. Caz had been twelve when her mother died, old enough to have firm memories of what home had been like. Returning to the house had to be bittersweet for the girl, if there was room for any sweetness at all.

After setting out some lunch options for anyone who hadn't already eaten, she went upstairs to check on the unpacking. Caz had gotten as far as throwing a quilt over her bare mattress and was lying on her bed, looking at her phone. In the next room, Oliver, with some assistance from Kim, was busily arranging toys on his shelves and adjusting the angle of his bedside Spider-Man lamp until it was just so.

"We could replace these old curtains," Kim was saying as Renee poked her head in. "Do you want that? You could get some new honeycomb blinds?"

Oliver paused in his creation of a LEGO-figure tableau on his dresser and gave her a confused stare. "No," he said. "This is how it was before."

Kim looked like she had been stabbed in the lung, but she turned to Renee. "I think we have things under control here. How about you see if Caz needs any help?"

"I don't!" the teenager called from the next room.

Kim grimaced over Oliver's head, and Renee retreated to look for something to do in the kitchen, where flame and sharp objects were the only hazards.

The next item on the day's whirlwind agenda was the press conference, a testament to the Weatherups' no-secrets policy, and as the hour drew near, the family began to flutter around in preparation.

"What should I be doing?" Renee asked.

"You can just relax!" Kim said. "Take a load off! There'll be more for you to do when things settle down."

So, she sat down in the formal parlor and watched through the leaded green and gold panes of the front window as the whole world arrived to hear this family's honesty. In the tree-lined street, news vans jockeyed for parking spots, camera operators shouldered their devices, and reporters smoothed their hair before making a few initial remarks to the camera. Pedestrians slowed their pace as they passed by, some lingering to see what was going on, some approaching with purposeful steps as if they already knew. A man and a woman nudged through the growing crowd. They were both dressed casually, their arms full of black equipment bags, and to her surprise, they marched right up the steps to the house and knocked on the door.

She watched them through the window, wondering if they could see her sitting there and whether she was supposed to answer the door, but Ed, with Willow on one arm, swept in from the kitchen before she could decide. "Hey, folks, so glad to see your faces," he said, ushering them in.

"We wouldn't miss this for the world," the woman said, putting down her bags to give Ed a big hug. She looked to be in her early twenties, with dark hair swinging around her shoulders. Her black tank top revealed firmly muscled arms.

"You look great, man," said her companion, shaking Ed's hand. "And this must be Willow! What a cutie!" He was a couple of years older than the woman, with a carefully curled pompadour and noteworthy cheekbones.

"Guys!" It was Kim, trotting down the stairs in the navy dress she had just changed into. Her hair was pulled back, her feet clad in glossy black shoes, and though she looked yet more polished than before, there were tears in her eyes as she threw her arms around the newcomers.

"We've waited a long time for this day. I just wish it didn't have to happen here at the house," she added, sobering a little. "I don't want to attract weirdos."

"The optics here just couldn't be better," said the woman, giving Kim a reassuring pat. "People will see that Ed is just like them, a decent man in the bosom of his family."

"Renee!" Ed cried, gesturing for her to join the emotional group. "Come meet my saviors. This is Mariah Cusmano. She created the podcast about me that got me released. And this is her producer, Danny Dudek.

"This is Renee," Ed said. "She's joining our household."

"As a housekeeper," she clarified, shaking their hands and receiving a white-toothed smile from each. She felt a little starstruck.

"We want to get set up on the porch," Mariah said, gesturing to their pile of equipment. "Is Harrington here yet? I don't want you making a statement without him."

"He'll be here soon," Ed said. "And I've already let him vet my prepared remarks. Don't worry." Then, in a wry aside to Renee, "Now that they've gotten me exonerated, they want to keep it that way."

"Not funny!" Mariah called as she lugged a long case out the door.

Jokes at the murder press conference! It wasn't the vibe Renee had expected, but it did make sense. Nothing could bring Julie back, but Ed and the podcasters had worked hard to undo an injustice that had brought manifold hardships upon the bereaved Weatherups. They were entitled to celebrate. Maybe even she was allowed to feel the festive spirit a little.

Conrad Harrington turned out to be Ed's defense attorney, an imposing man in height and breadth who wore a gray pin-striped suit and whose arrival brought a businesslike energy to the house. Even the grandparents emerged from upstairs, straightening clothes and clearing throats.

"It's go time," Ed said. He had changed into a navy suit, which paired with Kim's dress, and though he submitted to final inspections by his wife and lawyer, every stitch was in place. He stood tall, surrounded by his entourage, reminding Renee of a politician about to take the stage for a historic speech.

"I'll go first," Harrington said. "And if you take any questions, I'll personally throttle you."

"Do you mind?" Kim said, tentatively offering Willow to Renee. "I promise childcare won't normally be one of your duties, but I don't want any of the kids' faces photographed out there."

"Of course." Renee took the baby, who seemed unperturbed, and retreated to the parlor, where she could watch obliquely through the stained glass.

The podcasters had set up a microphone stand at the head of the porch steps, and the family gathered there, backs to the house.

The assembled spectators and news teams now filled the sidewalk, spilling off the curb and forcing passing cars to crawl by. People jostled each other, some holding up signs that read **Welcome Home, Ed!** or **Justice at Last**. Some held up recorders and shouted questions Renee couldn't parse. There were a few uniformed police officers present, off to the side, hands on hips, either watching for unruly audience members or waiting to nab Ed if he said the wrong thing, she wasn't sure. Some of them made terse comments to a youngish man with a fresh haircut whose plain clothes did little to disguise his identity as law enforcement. He stood separate from the crowd on the other side of the street, his posture relaxed but attentive. Watching, not participating.

"Good afternoon," Harrington said, sternly bringing the crowd to silence. "We are gathered here to make a statement to the press marking the total exoneration of my client Edward Weatherup, who stands before you today, a free man."

The crowd cheered.

Renee looked down at the round face of baby Willow, who methodically plucked at a buttonhole on Renee's shirt collar. "It was smart of your parents to make me sign the contract before this happened," she murmured, bouncing Willow slightly. "Because this is totally bonkers." Maybe throwing yourself a press conference was a normal move in some people's lives, but she'd certainly never seen anything like this.

Still, the child felt solid and real in her arms, at once a stranger and, like any baby, completely natural cradled against her heart. It was such an intimate thing to hold another person's child, to watch from backstage at this climactic family moment. She wondered with a slight thrill if any of the snapping cameras out there would capture her shadow behind the stained glass window where she sat, almost part of the story.

After a shuffle, Ed took the microphone. "Thank you for being here. I'll be brief. I am overjoyed to be standing here on the steps of my own home once again, and I owe an eternal debt of gratitude to those who stuck with me through the past five years. I want to thank Conrad Harrington, Esquire, and the other members of his team for their unflagging legal expertise. And I want to thank the Richmond office of the commonwealth's attorney."

The crowd undulated, and some objecting voices filtered through the window.

"I know, I know. Some terrible mistakes were made in that office, but I want to thank the current commonwealth's attorney, Jared Deverell, for recognizing those mistakes and rectifying them. I want to thank Mariah Cusmano for her brilliant and tireless efforts on the podcast *Innocent Blood*, which did so much to bring my story to light."

Here, the crowd cheered.

"I know, she's the best. And I owe everything to my wonderful wife Kim, who has never let me give up hope and never let the home fires go out. I love her and my family more than anything, and all I want now is a fresh start and a new chance to be a father and a husband and to devote myself to caring for the family that has stood by me while I was wrongfully incarcerated."

Clapping.

Ed paused, glancing at Harrington. The lawyer nodded.

"But we can't forget—there is one person who isn't with us today, and that is Julie Anne Weatherup, who was our shining star. She was a talented legal mind, a loving mother and wife, and a cherished daughter to her parents, who stand beside me today. Julie has never gotten justice. Her killer is still at large, and while I am glad to be able to return to my family, I will never be at peace until that killer is found and brought to justice. I, along with the rest of Julie's family, deserve answers, and I call on the office of the Richmond commonwealth's attorney to work as tirelessly to find those answers as they previously worked to keep this innocent man in jail. Thank you for your time."

The assembled people erupted in a hubbub of questions and some scattered chanting—in some cases, "Justice for Ed!" and in others, "Find the real killer!"—but Harrington took the microphone back and said, "Thank you for your attention, folks. We will not be taking any questions, and I politely request that all parties respect the privacy of the Weatherup and Lauderbach families. They have been through a lot, and they deserve to lead normal lives moving forward."

"Don't we all," Renee whispered to the baby.

Or if not normal, at least new.

The crowd dispersed quickly after the conference concluded, though the last stragglers required some urging from the police officers to pack up their signs and move on. When they were gone, Linden Avenue was suddenly a residential street again, the news vans replaced with commuters returning home after the workday, the spectators replaced by parents walking small children to the playground.

When the way was clear, Debra and Dale Lauderbach prepared to depart back to Virginia Beach. She watched from a distance as the well-groomed couple bid a polite but emotionless goodbye to Kim and shook Ed's hand.

"It's good to see you home again, son," Dale said, giving Ed a single pat on the back, and Renee thought he meant it. After all, no one had forced the two Lauderbachs to stand up beside their murdered daughter's husband.

But the first flicker of discernible feeling appeared when Debra bent to hug her grandson, whose brown head nestled against her dyed-blond one. "Goodbye sweet boy. Grandma loves you."

"I love you, too, Grandma," he said with a sniffle.

Even Caz, the brusque teenager, hugged her grandparents with a tenderness that surprised Renee. "Come see us soon," she said. "We'll miss you."

"We'll miss you, too, honey." Dale wrapped her in a squeeze.

Renee inched herself down onto one of the mustard-colored velvet chairs in the parlor, hoping no one remembered she was there. The Lauderbachs seemed like deeply reserved people, but she couldn't imagine how hard it must be for them to leave the two children behind, and it felt rude to even witness their pain.

"You're welcome here anytime," Ed said as the grandparents waved from the sidewalk. When they were gone, he turned to his children. "You guys hungry? Should we make some spaghetti?"

Kim, who had already told Renee to plan for fajita wraps that evening, gave a small frown, but it was a moot point, because instead of answering, Caz pulled her little brother to her and gave him a rough hug. "You fix your room up yet?" she asked. "You want some help?"

"Yeah," Oliver said, and he darted for the stairs, pulling Caz behind him.

Kim opened her mouth to call after them, but Ed held up a hand. "They need time to adjust. It'll be okay."

"But they shouldn't be rude to you just because they're angry," she said. "You didn't do anything wrong by bringing them back."

"I don't think they're angry at me," he replied. "They'll come around."

The children might very well be angry, Renee thought, at being summoned from their established lives and reinstalled in the house where their mother died. And if they were, they had every right to be. They'd been through more than any of the adults in the room, and she didn't know if they should be expected to "come around" by themselves.

But she wasn't the parent here. Nor was she a media consultant, a lawyer, or a therapist. Really, she was the ultimate amateur, something she'd assumed would be detrimental to her job prospects. But later that evening, as she emptied the dishwasher in the darkening kitchen, hunting through cupboards for the proper place to put away each container and utensil, she wondered if, in fact, her naivety had been an asset. How many other, more experienced housekeepers had turned the job down before she'd come along? Maybe those people had been smart to steer clear of the true crime drama that had been playing out in this household for the past five years. Or maybe they just hadn't seen the good in the Weatherups the way she did: Ed's pride in having his children back, Kim's anxiety about being a good mother. Or, she thought with a touch of bitterness, maybe those other housekeepers had just had more options than Renee had.

Her phone vibrated in her pocket, and she pulled it out to see an incoming text from a contact she'd never expected to speak to again: Andrea.

Renee, we need to talk ASAP. It's important. You owe me.

Renee deleted the message. She hadn't expected a new life of clamoring press conferences, but she had gotten one thing she'd been hoping for ever since she started the Enid Salinas training course: to be behind the scenes in someone else's life, consumed by someone else's story for a change, able to leave her own behind.

CHAPTER 3

After the chaos of her first two days of employment, Renee was relieved to get into some real housekeeping. While Ed took the older kids to get enrolled at their new schools and Kim took Willow to a doctor's appointment, Renee cleaned up the breakfast things and then timed herself vacuuming the house, all three floors of it. "There's a lot to love!" Kim had said during the interview, and that much was certainly true.

Aside from the sumptuous foyer, which was a finely detailed hardwood affair with a sweeping staircase that led upward past a glowing stained glass chandelier, the downstairs contained the kitchen, dining room, the formal parlor where Renee had surreptitiously watched the press conference, and the less formal family room, with its exposed brick walls and leather couches. On the second floor were the children's bedrooms (sunny and bow windowed), Renee's bedroom (regular windowed), a study for Ed, a laundry room, and a couple of bathrooms. The third floor contained the main bedroom suite, with its king-size bed, Jacuzzi tub, annexed nursery, and exit onto a rooftop deck, which was unfurnished and apparently unused, despite being clearly designed for casual entertaining with a view of the city.

Altogether, it was more house than Renee had ever seen in one place, a sharp contrast to the compact single-story houses she was used to, houses where work boots lined up by the door, children shared bedrooms, and no one hired a housekeeper. And yet, the house and everything inside it was now her business. It seemed unfair that all those strangers who had gathered in the street the day before knew more about the Weatherups than she did.

She paused on the stairs, dustrag in hand, and produced her phone from her pocket. She was acting on professional interest, she told herself, not voyeurism, as she scrolled through the list of available podcast offerings. There, at number four on the popularity charts, was *Innocent Blood*, with its sepia-tone cover photo of Ed and Julie ducking under a shower of petals at their wedding. With a prickle of excitement that she didn't dare examine, she hit the download button.

Innocent Blood, Episode One: "Introduction"

MARIAH: [in studio] The more I learn about them, the more I see Julie and Ed Weatherup as people we all aspire to be, hard workers who invested in their community but still had time for romance and family. That's part of what makes the events I'm about to describe so tragic—that the world repaid them the way it did. In 2018, their home became the site of a gruesome murder, and that's just the beginning of a story that has rocked the city of Richmond ever since. My name is Mariah Cusmano, and last year I began an in-depth investigation into the Weatherup saga, which had more twists and turns than I ever imagined. Now, from the Radio Lab at Richmond University, I'm going to tell you what I know. Here is *Innocent Blood*. Listener discretion advised.

DALE: Julie was a ray of sunshine to everyone who knew her. I can't think of any other way to say it. People loved her, and she loved people.

MARIAH: This is Dale Lauderbach, Julie's father.

DALE: When she was in high school, all she talked about was wanting to become a lawyer, and we knew she would do it because she could do anything she set her mind to. Her mother and I offered to pay for law school, but she wanted to do it herself, and she did. I think her interest in law was twofold. She liked the thrill of being in high-stakes negotiations, of getting the best deal for her clients, but she also cared about helping people. And she got results. She really was born to be a lawyer.

MARIAH: Everyone I interviewed agreed that Julie had a sparkling personality and tremendous legal mind, and that she was beautiful too. It's no wonder that Ed was drawn to her when they met in law school. Here's Alan Cabot, a classmate at William & Mary Law School, where Julie and Ed both attended.

ALAN: Julie and the rest of us were all there for undergrad, and then Ed came along in 2001 when we were first-year law students. He had just moved to Williamsburg for law school, and Julie kind of enjoyed showing him around town. I think, you know, the attraction was immediate. They were both good-looking people, but I think they were also drawn to the aspiration they saw in each other. They both wanted to achieve things, to make a name for themselves, and to live well while they did it.

We were all ambitious back then, but Ed's ambitions had an edge to them. There was a story about him bribing a TA to get a sneak peek at an exam, and while I don't know for sure that it was true, I kind of believe it. He was determined to be the best at all costs. Julie didn't condone that kind of behavior per se, but I think in some ways, it was part of what drew her to him. He was a hard worker but a bit of a bad boy too.

Now that we're all older and have kids and stuff, it's kind of hard to imagine, but we would study twenty hours a day, take our exams, and then head straight to those college bars. I don't know how any of us survived, honestly. Ed was quiet at first. I think he felt a little out of place in Julie's social set, but soon he was enjoying life like the rest of us.

MARIAH: Everyone agrees that Julie had an intensity to everything she did. Like Ed, she always wanted to be the best and never wanted to miss out on anything. According to her parents, some of this was just her, the personality she was born with, but I have to assume that some of her drive came from the need to constantly prove herself in a traditionally male-dominated field. She must have felt pressure to get the best grades and to party like the boys did, and all her hard work launched her into a busy, successful life.

Just days after graduating law school, she and Ed married in a private ceremony at her parents' house in Virginia Beach. The family has given me permission to share a couple photos from their wedding, which you can find on our social media, but to me, all I see is how happy they both seem.

The newlyweds skipped the honeymoon and moved to Richmond, where Julie took a job at Cygnet and Obermeyer, a prestigious full-service law firm, and shortly after, Ed took a job at a small real estate law firm. They purchased a home in the historic Fan neighborhood, which they restored and decorated with an eye toward hosting charity fundraisers and black-tie cocktail parties for their friends.

Their first child, a daughter named Catherine, was born, and Ed and Julie celebrated their one-year anniversary with so much to be proud of. A few years later, another baby arrived, this time a son, and the family was complete.

Meanwhile, at work, Julie continued to shine. She specialized in trial law and worked tirelessly to serve the region's political and social elite. But the rich weren't the only people she cared about. Here's Micheline Cygnet, a senior partner at her firm.

MICHELINE: Julie was just this ball of energy. She packed more into her workday than anyone I've ever seen, and she had all these little tricks to be more efficient. She used to use abbreviations and acronyms, like *MP* was "mid-paperwork" and *FAB* was "file a brief." [chuckling] If anything, it slowed us all down until we learned what her codes meant.

She logged four times as many pro bono hours as anyone else at the firm. She gravitated to the really sad cases involving disadvantaged young people accused of terrible things, and she worked as hard for them as for our big-name clients. I asked her one time why she was doing it, and she said, "Micheline, everybody deserves a good lawyer, but also, one day, you're going to want to take a step back from work, and when that day comes, I want you to know that I'm capable of doing my job and two other people's jobs." At the time, it was a joke, but I know she could do all that and more. Now that

I'm starting to think about retirement, I really wish I had the chance to tell her she was right.

MARIAH: Julie told coworkers that she thought it was important to talk about career and money topics with friends and family.

MICHELINE: Julie said she wanted her kids to know where money came from and what to do with it, so she was pretty open about finances. She came from money, and her parents helped her and Ed pay off that beautiful house, but Julie was the main breadwinner, and she was proud of that. In September of 2017, she made partner with us and was doing really well for herself.

MARIAH: As good as Julie's life seemed to be, we know this story doesn't have a happy ending, and in some ways, it doesn't have an ending at all.

There's a lot of versions to the account of Julie's death, but everyone agrees on how the day started. April 6, 2018, was a chilly Friday. The Weatherup family's routine revolved around school, work, and home, but they had an unusual weekend planned. That day Ed would be traveling from their home in Richmond to attend a conference in Baltimore, so he got up early, helped the two children—twelve-year-old Catherine and five-year-old Oliver—get ready for school, and then he hit the road.

At 7:30 a.m., Julie drove the kids to school and waved goodbye to them as they headed for class. From there, she went straight to work.

MICHELINE: I worked closely with Julie that day. Our firm was handling a big case for a local company, and it was all hands on deck. Julie thrived in that energy. When you lose someone suddenly like that, you think back and try to figure out if there were warning signs, or if there was any clue to explain it, but there really wasn't. If anything, she seemed excited about her weekend.

MARIAH: As a working mom of two, alone time was at a premium for Julie, and on this particular night, she was scheduled to have the house to herself for the first time in a very long time. Ed would be at the conference all weekend. Catherine was going to spend the night at a classmate's house. Young Oliver would be having his first sleepover for a friend's birthday. Julie told coworkers that she was a little nervous about Oliver's first night away from home, but she trusted his friend's parents and was looking forward to an evening of peace and quiet.

Parking garage surveillance clocked her leaving work at 6:30 p.m. Her credit card statements show that she stopped for a bottle of wine and Vietnamese takeout on the way home. From the car, she called to check in on her kids and tell them she loved them.

Investigators believe Julie made it home around 7:30, and then there's this window of time, Julie's last hours, when no one knows exactly what happened. We'll get into theories in a future episode, but for now, let's stick to the undisputed facts.

That night, Julie's cell phone continued to ping towers from the area near her house, so it's plausible to assume that she stayed home, eating dinner and enjoying a quiet evening. Of course, we can't rule out the possibility that she left the house again at some point without taking her phone, but no one reported seeing her out that night.

The next morning dawned. She had previously arranged to pick up her daughter from the house of Stephanie Kowalski, where Catherine had spent the night with Stephanie's daughter Hadley. Julie never arrived, however, and the other mother became concerned. Around 10:00 a.m., Stephanie called Julie on her home phone and cell phone but got no answer. Increasingly concerned, she loaded the two girls into the car and drove over to the Weatherup residence, where they saw Julie's car parked on the street as usual. Here's her account of what happened next.

STEPHANIE: We knocked on the door because I didn't want to surprise Julie. I still thought she had overslept, but she wasn't the kind of parent to just not come get her kid like that. Catherine put her key in the door and said, "That's weird. It's already unlocked," and I had this really bad feeling. We live in a city, you know, there's part of you that's always on alert. I said, "Get back in the car, girls," and I told them to lock the car doors and wait for me while I went in to check.

Looking back, I shouldn't have gone in myself. I teach my kids that if you come home and find the door open, you don't go in, and you call the cops. Better safe than sorry, you know? I guess I didn't think anything that bad had happened, but there was this little part of me that knew Catherine shouldn't go in, and I'm grateful every day that I was able to spare her that little bit of suffering.

MARIAH: Stephanie says that she initially thought the house was deserted. She stood in the entryway, calling for Julie, but when she didn't hear anything, she went upstairs.

STEPHANIE: I felt this weird chilly breeze on my face, and the house had that fresh smell like a window had been left open all night. I went up to the third floor and saw that the door onto the rooftop patio was open, and my heart just sank.

MARIAH: What Stephanie saw was one of the grimmest crime scenes I've ever heard of. Julie lay dead on the rooftop patio. She had been stabbed multiple times. Blood saturated her white silk pajamas and pooled under her body.

The scene still haunts Stephanie Kowalski.

STEPHANIE: I still have nightmares that I'm back on that rooftop with all that blood just everywhere. I've been in therapy for years and I've tried hypnosis, everything you can think of, really, and I still wake up in a cold sweat. I have to get out of bed and lie flat on the carpet to make myself believe that I'm in my own home and not on that roof. But some nights it isn't enough, because I can't forget that Julie was alone in her own home, too, when someone attacked her.

MARIAH: Stephanie still bears the scars of what she saw that night, but at the time, she did everything right. She ran back downstairs, touching as little as possible, and called 911.

Police arrived in force. After all, it was an obvious murder in a wealthy part of the city. Right from the start, the Richmond Police Department wanted to show that it, too, was doing everything right. They took Stephanie's statement and immediately began canvassing neighbors and collecting security footage.

Around 11:30 a.m., the head investigator on the case, Detective Marshall Evans, called Ed Weatherup to tell him that his wife had been murdered. He broke the news over the phone because, and the importance of this cannot be overstated, Ed was still at that conference in Baltimore. In fact, five of his coworkers went on the record to say that they saw him leave a panel discussion to take the call from Detective Evans.

Ed got in his car and drove home, where he gave a statement to the police and then had the horrifying job of picking up his two children and telling them that their mother was gone. The family checked in to a hotel, where they were joined by Julie's parents, and together, they tried to make sense of the senseless thing that had occurred.

As we, too, try to make sense of this story, we have to back up to that Friday morning again and make a timeline of Ed's movements. The following is his account of his day, the last day of Julie's life. This is what he told me, but it's also what he told the police in his official statement, and it's the story he's stuck to in the years since. It's also worth noting that many aspects of his account are backed up by hard evidence.

Here's Ed.

ED: It was a good morning, you know? I made breakfast for the kids. Everybody was energized for the day, maybe rushing a little, but in a good mood. I drove to the conference center in Baltimore, which took about three hours, and checked in to the hotel. The firm paid for us to have rooms at the Hamilton Pier, right in the downtown harbor area, and there were a whole bunch of us coworkers there. We pretty much stayed together the whole day going to panels, and then we had dinner at a burger place a couple blocks away.

MARIAH: Everyone agrees on this part of the story. Ed's coworkers back him up; there are tollbooth cameras, hotel check-in logs, and receipts that verify his account of things.

ED: Julie texted me while I was at dinner to say the kids were all good and she was headed home for some me-time, and I just had that feeling you get as a parent where you know everyone is settled for the night, and you breathe a little sigh of relief. I hated myself for a long time that I went out of town and that I even had that feeling of "Okay, everyone's safe for the night."

We got back to the hotel around eight and went to the bar for a couple hours. It sounds dumb to go out of town just to have drinks with work people, but we had a good group dynamic, and a lot of us had young kids at the time, so a couple drinks at a hotel bar felt like a big deal to us. I'm an early-to-bed, early-to-rise kind of guy, so it felt pretty late to me, but we were all back in our rooms before midnight, and I just went to bed. I got up early the next morning, hit the fitness center, took a shower, got breakfast, and was back at the conference for the first panel session at 9:00 a.m. I was just going about my day, feeling pretty good about things, until I got that call from Detective Evans, and everything just fell apart from there.

MARIAH: Again, there's just so much evidence to support Ed's story. He was putting drinks on a company tab that was paid at 11:23 p.m. that night. In her official statement, one of his coworkers, a paralegal named Megan Duvall, reports that she shared an elevator with Ed at 11:30 p.m. Ed got off on the fourth floor, where his room was, and Megan kept riding up to the sixth floor.

Of course, there's no way to verify exactly what time Ed went to bed or that he stayed asleep (everything would have been so much different if there were), but security cameras in the hotel's fitness center show Ed entering the gym at the rather incredible hour of 4:15 a.m. You can see him walk in wearing workout clothes and begin using an elliptical machine.

Meanwhile, all night, on the second floor of the parking garage of the Hamilton Pier Hotel, a twenty-four-hour security camera was aimed at the back of Ed's car. We see him park it there late on Friday morning, remove his suitcase, and walk toward the hotel. The car doesn't move for a full twenty-four hours, at which point we see a distraught Ed running back to it. This is a man who has just been informed of his wife's horrific murder, but knows he has a three-hour drive ahead of him before he can see his children.

You might wonder why I'm going into so much detail here, but I have two points. As with many public places, the security footage at the Hamilton Pier is erased regularly to make room for new footage, so the fact that we're able to watch these clips of Ed's activities is a testament to how quickly Detective Evans and his team moved on this case. They were right there, collecting footage within a week of Julie's death.

But the second, and more important reason to tell you all of this is to show just how surprised and confused everyone was when, on April 25, less than three weeks after Julie's death, Ed was arrested and charged with her murder.

The outro music faded, and Renee found herself on the third-floor landing, her dustrag stalled on a bit of white wainscoting. It was all so horrible. She now fully understood why the beautiful rooftop deck was unused. It was creepy as hell.

And Ed's experience, as recounted by Mariah, was truly a nightmare—to be arrested despite having a solid alibi: The one thing that could always prove someone's innocence in the mystery shows.

And yet, something was bugging her. Not something from the episode so much as something she'd half noticed as she'd been dusting her way around the upstairs in a podcast-listening fugue state.

She retraced her steps to the little hallway between the primary bathroom and Kim's plush walk-in closet, an intimate little spot where a sentimental-minded decorator would hang a wedding photo or five. Except Kim's wedding had probably occurred in a prison visitation room, and her groom had worn a jumpsuit, not the kind of thing a woman like Kim would want to display. In lieu of photos, she'd hung a tastefully framed rectangle of official-looking paper with embossed letters and the state seal.

Certificate of Marriage: Commonwealth of Virginia
This is to certify that on *July 19, 2021*, **the officiant** *Rev. Herman Boothe* **joined** *Edward Christopher Weatherup* **and** *Megan Kimberly Duvall* **in matrimony.**

It was a keepsake of a wedding that had occurred after Ed had already been in prison for almost three years, and it was proof that Kim had been Ed's alibi before she was his wife.

CHAPTER 4

That night, Renee lay in the dark, finding it difficult to sleep.

Even after a few days, her new accommodations still felt strange and unhomey. The room wasn't huge, and still her belongings barely made an impression, just two books on the shelf, a phone charger here, a jar of moisturizer there. Her clothes filled only a quarter of the closet. On her first night, she'd made a video message for Aaron that he would see eventually, maybe a week or a month from now. "Check out this blank wall behind me," she had said, holding up her phone to take in the spartan room. "This is my grand new life." She'd played it as a joke, but she still felt uneasy at night here.

There were creaks and quivers in the walls around her, surely just an old house settling or a parent walking a sleepless baby above her, but she couldn't stop thinking about Julie, maimed and dead in her silk pajamas. And sure, Ed was eventually found innocent, but she felt a lot less comfortable with that now that she knew the woman who had vouched for him had turned around and married him. A fact champion of the exposé podcast, Mariah Cusmano, either didn't know or had failed to mention.

She got out of bed, crept to the door of her room, and turned the lock. She'd never locked her bedroom door at night, but then again, she'd never slept in a houseful of strangers before.

Back under the covers, she sought something warm and comforting to think about, urging her brain away from the image of Julie, bloody and lifeless on the roof above her very head, and toward something good.

Once, in eleventh grade, she and Brandon had gone to the river on a Saturday. He knew of an outcropping where they could sit by the water, warming their butts on the sun-soaked rock, cooling their feet and ankles in the rushing water. Something so simple between kids who had grown up together almost couldn't be called a date, but it had felt like one. When she made a joke, he turned to smile at her, his dark hair flopping heavily on the left side of his head in the way his mother reviled but Renee loved, and the sunlight caught the flecks of gold in his green eyes.

"You're a wiseass," he'd said admiringly.

Renee had gone in for a kiss so quickly that she'd overbalanced, and they'd toppled, half purposefully, into the water.

Something deep inside her smiled at the memory.

It seemed that someone else had their doubts about the official narrative of Ed Weatherup, and sometime in the middle of the night, that person shared their viewpoint.

The piercing beep of an alarm roused Renee, and she sat up in bed with the panicked idea that she'd negligently caused a fire somehow. As she became more awake, however, she figured out that it wasn't the shriek of a smoke alarm but an ominous, medium-tone throbbing. Heavy footsteps pounded down the stairs, and Kim's voice said, "Be careful, Ed," in a tense whisper from the landing.

Renee peeked out her door to find Kim just outside, peering over the railing. Caz and Oliver emerged from their rooms too. "What's going on?" the teenager asked, motioning for her brother to come stand beside her.

"I don't know," Kim said tensely. "It's the security alarm."

It might be a real emergency, Renee realized, and a thought, not one she was proud of but a rational one nonetheless, occurred to her. She could retreat to her room, lock the door, and let the family deal with whatever it was on their own.

The alarm stopped, and Ed came upstairs.

"Someone threw a brick through the front window," he said, out of breath. "But I think that's it. The security company has already dispatched the police. We should wait for them together." He looked around at the wide-eyed faces of his family. "Don't worry, gang. I'm sure it's just some harmless vandalism."

A choked sob erupted from Oliver, and everyone turned to look at him. "What if it's him?" he said, his small face contorted with the effort to keep his voice quiet and his terror inside. "What if it's the man who killed Mom? What if he's back?"

"Oh, son, don't worry about that," Ed said, reaching to rub the boy's back. "He wouldn't dare come back now that I'm here."

Now Renee felt annoyed in addition to anxious. What an unhelpful thing for Ed to say in this moment, as if he actually wanted Oliver to imagine his mother's murderer lurking outside, deterred only by Ed's own masculine presence.

Surely, she told herself, it was just a sign of his rusty parenting, but he seemed unaware that the boy needed better comfort, and it was Caz who wrapped her brother in a bear hug and held him that way.

Then again, Renee thought, as the minutes dragged on and the family stood clustered on the dark staircase, listening for any other sounds of danger, maybe Ed really did think Julie's murderer was prowling the property that night. If that was true, she'd misjudged everything. Mama had said, *It's so dangerous in the city.* At Renee's funeral, Mama would say, *My daughter never listened to me.*

The police arrived after what was probably only ten minutes. A pair of uniformed officers, one with a beard and one without, marched through the house and yard, confirming that whoever threw the brick was long gone. Only then did the family venture downstairs, and Renee got a glimpse of the scene.

Every lamp and overhead light had been turned on, and their sharp illumination drenched the front parlor with all its plush gold upholstery. As Ed had reported, a brick had flown through the stained glass front window, splintering the antique leading and scattering shards of sparkling glass across the carpet.

"Don't look," Kim said, moving to cover Oliver's eyes.

But Renee looked. The brick still lay where it had fallen, the word *Killer* scrawled on it in scarlet paint. Was it accusation or calling card? Either way, the letters still looked glossy, a drip from the final *r* creeping down toward the carpet. Whoever had written them had meant them to be cruel, had wanted to scare everyone in the house, and as far as Renee was concerned, it was working. She hated whoever believed Ed's children (and domestic staff) should spend the night in fear.

An hour later, there were no answers. Anyone could have thrown the brick, and there was no way for the police to guess who might have done it.

"The brick could have even come from your own property," the bearded officer said. "Do you have a patio or walkway with any loose bricks?"

Kim's eyes grew to the size of moons, and she clutched at Ed's arm. "There's a spare key under a brick on the back patio. You have to go check it."

The key was still in place, as it turned out, and the officers warned that there was unlikely to be much investigation of the incident.

"Could it have been a prank?" the bearded officer asked, directing his glance at Caz. "Maybe one of your friends?"

"What friends would those be?" Caz asked flatly, prompting Kim to rush in apologetically.

"The kids just moved here."

Seemingly out of ideas, the bearded officer began to help Ed nail a piece of wood over the broken window. Meanwhile, his barefaced partner gestured for Renee to follow him into the kitchen.

"So, you're the housekeeper," he said, referring to his notes. "How long have you been with the family?"

"Three days," Renee said.

"Everybody's a newcomer," the officer said, making a mark with a ballpoint. "And do you know anything about the brick that you didn't feel comfortable saying in front of your employers?"

"You mean did I throw it? Of course not!"

"Not necessarily," he said, as though innocently unaware that she might have taken offense. "Do you have any reason to believe that a member of the household threw it themselves? Perhaps to get attention?"

"Oh, I get it now." After all this, they still had Ed in their sights, still wanted to prove that they had been right about him the first time. "The entire family was asleep in their beds when the alarm went off," she said firmly. "And I think they've already had more attention than they want."

The officer made another note in his book. "Thank you for your time," he said. He went back to the front of the house to collect his partner.

"We get ne'er-do-wells in these better neighborhoods sometimes," he said to Kim and Ed on his way out the door. "They just want to damage property. If you're worried about further incidents, get a security camera or two, and move that spare key."

When the police were gone, Kim eyed the boarded-up window skeptically. "Do you think it's safe enough?" she asked Ed quietly.

"Sure!" He gave the plywood a thump that made Renee jump. "Safer than glass, right?"

"I just wonder if we would all sleep better tonight if we went to a hotel," Kim suggested softly. She drifted closer to her husband as if to shield their conversation, but Renee could still make out her whisper. "Because—do you think it's you-know-who?"

Ed put an arm over Kim's shoulders and pulled her close to him. "You're right," he murmured into her hair. "Let's be safe."

Renee, watching it all from the edge of the room, felt very cold, inside and out. When she'd gone to bed that evening, she'd assumed that the deadly events of 1125 Linden Avenue were in the past now, dwelling in the territory of press conferences and difficult memories, not the realm of intruders and late-night 911 calls. She'd been so, so wrong.

Would it be safe, she wondered, to run out to her car right now and drive away into the darkness?

Kim turned to her. "Renee, do you think you could help the kids pack an overnight bag while I get the baby's things together?"

In the foyer, under the blazing light of every available fixture, Oliver and Caz sat on the stairs, their pajamas rumpled, dark half moons under their eyes. At Kim's suggestion, Oliver glanced up at Renee expectantly, and she forgot her escape plan.

Being needed was a hell of a drug.

When the bags were packed, everyone relocated to the Howard Johnson a couple of miles away, where Ed paid for two rooms, one for Renee and one for the rest of them.

"It's like we're camping!" he said, giving Oliver a playful nudge as they got into the elevator. "We can sleep in and go for pancakes in the morning."

Oliver gave a pale smile, but Caz said, "Weren't we supposed to start school tomorrow?"

"I think we can play hooky for one day," Ed said with a wink.

It was around 3:00 a.m. when Renee locked her room door behind her, grateful for a few hours to herself. Sliding between the slightly caustic-smelling hotel sheets, she realized she was also feeling territorial. Everybody and their uncle seemed to feel entitled to an opinion about Ed because they'd read a few online stories or listened to a podcast, but she was the one who had already been there for the Weatherups during a crisis. She was the one who had eased the sleeping Willow into her car seat while Kim pulled on clothes. She was the one who had double-checked that the back door was locked before they left the house, the one who had heard Kim and Ed whisper about "you-know-who." She was the one who would come to know them as real people, to know the secrets no one else did.

Enid Salinas would agree: It was her job to know.

Innocent Blood, Episode Two: "The Conviction"

MARIAH: My name is Mariah Cusmano, and this is *Innocent Blood*. Listener discretion advised.

The city of Richmond was riveted by the daily press coverage of Julie's murder. It was full of everything that intrigues us about true crime: the scandal, the danger, and the mysteries that keep us up at night. But the question that plagued many people after Ed Weatherup's arrest was how he could possibly be charged for murdering his wife when he seemed to be in another state at the time.

To better understand this, we have to talk about the man who was the driving force behind Ed's prosecution: the commonwealth's attorney for Richmond, Raymond Randolph Prescott III.

When Raymond Prescott was elected in 2016, his campaign platform emphasized a clean-up-the-streets approach with a punitive stance on drug crime and a willingness to prosecute teenagers as adults. It had been a go-to campaign narrative for generations of conservative commonwealth's attorneys, but by 2018, the community had begun looking for something more nuanced. Just two years into his term, more progressive candidates were already lining up to unseat him in the next election, and Prescott was feeling the pressure.

Here's Ally Chung, a longtime crime reporter at the *Richmond Tribune*.

ALLY: Obviously 2018 was a tumultuous political time everywhere in the country, but I think Prescott was feeling personally betrayed. He got elected on the same proincarceration promises that his Republican forebearers did, but it wasn't working out for him the way it had for them. He wasn't popular, and he knew it.

MARIAH: Here's the audio from a press conference Prescott gave just two days after Julie's death.

PRESCOTT: [voice on tape] I want to confirm that my office is working closely with the Richmond Police Department to investigate the tragic death of Julie Anne Weatherup that occurred on April 6, 2018. This act of senseless violence has robbed a family of their mother, wife, and daughter, and it has caused fear and uncertainty in the entire community. I and my office will be working around the clock until the murderer is identified and brought to justice. This crime will not go unpunished. My thoughts and prayers are with the Weatherup family.

ALLY: I think Julie's death struck a chord with people in a special way because she was what TV producers have unfortunately been known to refer to as "a good victim." She was rich, white, beautiful, and successful. She had a life people aspire to, and none of that could protect her from being murdered in her own home. It was all particularly striking for me at the time, because just the week before, I wrote a small item about a woman named Tasha Morgan, who was murdered while engaged in sex work down on Richmond Highway—it was Jefferson Davis Highway then, of course, which is just, you know, a whole other part of it. I guess you can stop naming the road after a slave owner, but that doesn't automatically undo the economic legacy. Anyhoo, that article about Tasha got under a hundred views total, but my piece about Julie went viral. Everyone was sharing her story on social media, tweeting about it, the works. Our website crashed. [laughter] We started selling subscriptions again. [laughter] People were scandalized; they were frightened. It's the kind of story that sells papers, and it's the kind of case that can win an election for a commonwealth's attorney.

Prescott knew he had a chance to prove that he was the solution to the city's fear. And as soon as there was a hint that Ed might be guilty, I think he jumped at it because if he could nail one rich white man for a high-profile murder, he could point to that for the rest of his career whenever people criticized his record of prosecuting Black fifteen-year-olds in adult court.

MARIAH: Whatever Prescott's motive, he set his sights on Ed and built a case based primarily on one fact: that the week before her death, Julie Weatherup had contacted a divorce lawyer.

On March 28, nine days before her death, Julie visited divorce attorney James Mullins, and during that meeting, she retained his services. He was subpoenaed for Ed's trial, but all he could do was confirm that Julie had indicated her desire to initiate a divorce.

Mullins was somewhat limited in what he could say due to attorney-client privilege, but his answers also suggested that Julie simply hadn't given him much detail about her situation, and no one else seemed to have any insight into what might have prompted her to think about divorce. Everybody I talked to insisted that the Weatherups' marriage was outwardly normal. Here again is Stephanie Kowalski, who discovered Julie's body.

STEPHANIE: I wouldn't have called myself a close friend, certainly, but we saw a lot of each other in the normal course of life. My daughter slept over there; their daughter slept over here. We were always chit-chatting in the pickup line or at school events. It was a lot of mundane moments spread out over the years, and what I saw was a totally normal marriage. Julie and Ed were busy parents who wanted the best for their children. Maybe the romantic spark had died down some—you know, you wouldn't see them hugging and kissing, but who does that at a kid's soccer game anyway? I never saw them fight or get snippy with each other. Everything seemed fine.

MARIAH: Everything seemed fine, and that's the best answer I can get.

Regardless, this appointment with Mullins was the cornerstone of the prosecution's case against Ed. They said that if Julie divorced him, she would take much of the family's income with her, along with a substantial inheritance that would come to her when her parents eventually passed away. Custody of the children would likely be a point of contention, as would possession of the beautiful home on Linden Avenue. This, according to the prosecutor and his team, was motive enough for murder.

Here's an excerpt from a trial tape. Again, this is Prescott speaking.

PRESCOTT: [voice on tape] The fact is that Julie Weatherup visited a divorce attorney for a reason. Wives don't do that unless they're unhappy, and we must ask ourselves how likely it is that Ed, a smart man, could have been oblivious to the fact that his marriage was ending.

MARIAH: Reporter Ally Chung was in the courtroom that day.

ALLY: I was just sitting there like, "Well, it's not very likely, but it is possible." We don't always know what our spouses are up to, and Julie was a savvy businesswoman, after all. I certainly see a world where she wouldn't tell Ed anything until she had papers ready to serve. But the jury was nodding along. I think public opinion had turned against him already. Obviously, everything we published in the *Tribune* was just objective statements about the court proceedings, but the public sees a murder that bloody, and they see the husband arrested just a couple weeks later—they're going to assume he's guilty. And some media outlets really fed into that. I remember there was this one photo of him going into court, and he's wearing a suit and standing between his lawyers, and he has this smirk on his face and one eyebrow up like, "I'm going to get away with this." And who knows what was going through his head in that moment. Maybe he was about to sneeze, for all we know, but that was the photo that appeared on the cover of every tabloid. As a community, I think people really want the husband to be the guilty party because it's too horrible to think that something like that could happen randomly. If Ed was guilty, it meant the rest of us could sleep safely in our beds.

MARIAH: The media frenzy meant that getting an impartial jury was going to be difficult, and Ed's defense attorney took the first opportunity to appeal for a change of venue. The judge, the Honorable William Bowling, denied the appeal, maintaining, without much explanation, that he believed a local jury capable of objectivity.

Here's Conrad Harrington, Ed's lawyer.

CONRAD: The question of venue is up to the full discretion of the judge, and he doesn't have to explain his decision.

MARIAH: Were you disappointed that Ed's trial wasn't moved?

CONRAD: I will say that the decision was a blow to our case.

MARIAH: From there, things just got worse for Ed. The key to his defense was that he said he was asleep a hundred and fifty miles away, but the prosecution did what they could to poke holes in this alibi. Surveillance footage confirmed that Ed's car didn't move all night, but prosecutor Prescott argued that Ed could have found another means of transportation back to Richmond during the night of April 6.

PRESCOTT: [voice on tape] Ed is a resourceful man of means. He's intelligent, well traveled, and has the disposable finances to pay for whatever mode of transport he desires.

MARIAH: I want to pause here to talk about what Ed's transit options really were on the night of Julie's murder. We know that whatever he did that night had to have occurred between 11:30 p.m., when his coworker confirmed riding up in an elevator with him, and 4:15 a.m., when he was recorded on surveillance cameras at the hotel gym. That leaves a window of just under five hours.

We also know that Ed didn't use his own car and he didn't pay for any kind of transportation using his credit card. In fact, detectives pored over Ed and Julie's bank statements from that night and found no charges at all after Ed paid for his dinner and Julie, back in Richmond, paid for her takeout and wine.

The prosecution might have been suggesting that Ed used cash to buy bus or train tickets, but I spent an hour trying to book various combinations of tickets, and it's simply not possible to use public transportation to make a round trip between Baltimore and Richmond in the middle of the night.

In commenting on Ed's wealth, Prescott seems to insinuate that Ed might have used cash to hire a car service to drive him back to Richmond. While, of course, it's possible that he could afford that expense, Ed's bank account shows no large cash withdrawals either that night or in the preceding months. Ed had withdrawn about two thousand dollars five months before, but his defense team explained that.

CONRAD: We simply pointed out that a man like Ed would need cash for a thousand things in his daily life: He has to tip a barista, pay a babysitter, handle the kids' soccer dues, play fantasy football at work. Two grand is walking-around money to a man like Ed. It's certainly not enough money to hire a private plane, if that's what they were implying.

MARIAH: At trial, Ed's defense urged the jury to question the likelihood of a man being able to make a hundred-and-fifty-mile round trip, commit a gruesome murder, and clean himself up, all in under five hours, and the prosecution didn't deny that it was unlikely. Unlikely, but possible. That was Prescott's refrain for much of the trial. According to Prescott, Ed had motive, means, and the merest sliver of opportunity.

And then Prescott trotted out his star forensic witness, an expert voice that sealed Ed's guilt.

To help us understand what we're about to hear, I talked to cold case detective Mason Torian, who became a household name in true crime circles last year, when he successfully identified all seven of the Jane and John Doe victims of serial killer Randy Allen James, the Syracuse Ripper. When we spoke, I asked him why forensic analysis is so much more subjective than it looks on TV.

MASON: Well, you know, we're learning and reevaluating every year. Unfortunately, laws about what a prosecutor or defense attorney can present in court don't always keep up with advancements in technology, so a good investigator has to know the limits of each forensic tool, and a good expert witness won't overstate the evidence gained by any one technique.

MARIAH: The question of which forensic techniques to use on evidence is predicated, however, on the existence of the evidence in the first place, and in Julie's case, there just wasn't much in the way of tangible forensic clues.

Investigators collected thousands of fingerprints from the entire house, but all of them were found to belong to members of the family and their close contacts, all people with legitimate reasons for being inside the home in the preceding weeks. Forensic teams found no unidentified DNA in the home and no suspicious hairs or fibers. There were no unusual shoe prints or trash left by the perpetrator, and no murder weapon was ever located. Julie had been stabbed with a sharp knife, but all the knives in the household were stored safely in the kitchen knife block, and all tested negative for blood. It seemed that whoever killed Julie had brought the weapon with them and taken it away again.

Of course, when the case went to trial, prosecutor Prescott pointed to this dearth of evidence as a sure sign of Ed's guilt. "If no one but the family members left a mark on the house, doesn't it mean that a family member must have committed the crime?" he asked. But we can't be so sure. A stranger entering the house might simply have worn gloves and clean, full-coverage clothing. Because the murder occurred on the rooftop patio, which was exposed to the fresh air for up to twelve hours before discovery, it's also possible that any incriminating hairs or fibers might have blown away before investigators arrived. It's possible that Julie opened the door to let the perpetrator in and that unknown person just didn't touch anything before exiting onto the roof.

But even though Prescott was working hard to make an absence of evidence support his theory, he knew that he would need something more concrete for a jury to hold on to, and this is when he introduced his expert witness Dr. Henri Beaufort, a licensed blood-spatter analyst. And if you're asking,

"Do you mean like the TV character Dexter?" the answer is yes, sort of.

On the trial's third day, Dr. Beaufort described the crime scene. His words painted a picture of the horrific rooftop tableau for the jury and spectating public. You're about to hear some of his testimony on the court recording. Sensitive listeners may want to skip ahead.

BEAUFORT: [voice on courtroom tape] Mrs. Weatherup lay on her back with several stab wounds to the chest and front of her body. Her throat also bore knife marks. Her hands showed what we sometimes call "defensive wounds," lacerations received when she attempted to fend off the violent attack. She lost a great deal of blood, and that blood loss was her ultimate cause of death.

PRESCOTT: [voice on courtroom tape] What type of weapon was used to commit this crime?

BEAUFORT: According to the city's medical examiner, and I concur on this, the weapon was a sharp knife with a narrow blade about four inches long. It could have been a kitchen knife or small hunting knife.

PRESCOTT: Dr. Beaufort, what can you determine about the crime based on the blood at the scene?

BEAUFORT: Oh, a great deal. I am a certified blood analyst, and as such, I'm trained to look for patterns in the blood spatter. Because of the way the blood pooled under and around Mrs. Weatherup, we can be quite confident that, at some point during her struggle with the assailant, she fell or was pushed to the ground. Then, the most serious and ultimately mortal of her wounds were dealt to her as she lay there on the roof with the assailant standing over her. That was how the struggle ended, but that was not how it began.

PRESCOTT: What is your theory of the attack?

BEAUFORT: Well, the crime scene technicians did not find any blood in Mrs. Weatherup's bedroom, and no sign of disturbance there. It seems that Mrs. Weatherup was already on the rooftop patio before her assailant arrived, or they went out there together with little to no struggle. At some point, assailant and victim stood face-to-face, and he delivered the first blows with the murder weapon, drawing back the blade between each blow and causing blood to spatter against the wall behind him, that being the external wall of the house's third floor, which you can see here in the crime scene photos. Here is the door from the bedroom to the patio through which Mrs. Weatherup emerged. Here is the brick wall with the blood patterns upon it.

PRESCOTT: In your expert experience, what do those blood patterns on the wall tell you?

BEAUFORT: A great deal. We know from the angle and the dispersion of the blood particles that the assailant was right handed, that he was a relatively athletic individual with a strong arm, and that he was between five feet, ten inches and six feet, two inches tall.

PRESCOTT: Would you say that description matches Mr. Weatherup, who is here in the courtroom today?

BEAUFORT: Yes, most definitely. The quantity and vigor of the blows indicate a very depraved mind indeed.

CONRAD: [voice on courtroom tape] Objection!

MARIAH: I asked Mason Torian to listen to Dr. Beaufort's testimony and offer whatever commentary he could.
MARIAH: [voice on interview tape] What's your initial reaction to Beaufort's claims here?
MASON: Honestly, I'm a little speechless. I don't want to impugn anyone's reputation here, but I honestly don't see how anyone could make such confident claims based on the crime scene photos I have seen. If there's no blood in the bedroom, that's an indicator that the stabbing probably didn't begin there, but I can't say that for sure. I would agree with the theory that the victim fell once and bled to death. I agree based on autopsy reports that the murder weapon was a slender knife about four inches long, but I can't determine more than that.
MARIAH: What about the blood spatter on the wall?
MASON: Blood spatter is an evolving science, but the research says there are still too many factors in play to draw firm conclusions from blood spatter alone, especially in an outdoor setting. The blood droplets on that wall may have been flung there by the murder weapon or by Julie herself as she struggled. Their trajectory may have been impacted by the height and physicality of the assailant, but also by the speed of the attack and any wind that might have been present.
MARIAH: So, if I could press you on this, do you think it's fair to testify to the height of the assailant within just a few inches based on these blood droplets?
MASON: Not at all.
MARIAH: [voice in studio] But Beaufort spoke with an authority that appealed to the jury, and his credentials seemed trustworthy. He earned a medical doc-

torate in 1975 from Yale and served for twenty years as a medical examiner in western North Carolina. It's worth noting here that medical examiners are mostly volunteers in that state, though I'm not suggesting any impropriety in Dr. Beaufort's years of service. After retirement, he began to tour the country as a medical expert for hire, and it was at this point that he began to gather certifications that would help him speak to various aspects of crime scenes. He gained a certificate in toxicology and another in blood-spatter analysis, which he earned by completing a forty-hour course held at a Hyatt in Shreveport. This one-week course occurred less than a year before Julie's death, and it was the sum total of his experience in the field of blood-spatter analysis. Ed's defense team was not aware of this detail at the time of the trial, so they weren't able to press Beaufort on his credentials, and the jury became enamored of him.

ALLY: Beaufort was just everything you could want in an expert witness. He was comfortable on the stand like he'd been up there a thousand times. He had this tweed suit with the vest, and he seemed to bring so much clarity to the situation. I think the public and the jury were just so hungry for that clarity.

MARIAH: After twelve days of testimony, the jury deliberated for just seven hours before delivering their verdict of guilty. The judge sentenced Ed to twenty-five years in prison.

ALLY: It was just chaos outside the courthouse that day. No one could agree on what to think. There were people chanting, "Fry him!" and women shouting, "Marry me!" Prescott gave a statement patting himself and his team on the back for rapidly getting a killer off the streets, but some people definitely thought it was too quick. It just seemed to go against common sense that Ed could have committed the murder, and a lot of people worried that a mistake had been made.

MARIAH: Dale Lauderbach, Julie's father, gave a brief statement on behalf of the family.

DALE: [voice at press conference] Julie's children, my grandchildren, have suffered a great deal. They have lost their mother to a brutal crime, and now they must watch their father go to prison. Now, as we take time to grieve and try to put together the pieces of our lives, we ask for prayers and privacy.

MARIAH: As tragic and confusing as the whole saga had been, it seemed to be over. The Lauderbachs took custody of Julie and Ed's children and moved them home to Virginia Beach. The city of Richmond tried, uneasily, to move on. Those who trusted the conviction were reassured that they could sleep easily in their beds, but many wondered if Julie's killer might still be free and unidentified. Here's family friend Stephanie Kowalski.

STEPHANIE: I hated Ed. Absolutely hated him because I believed what they said in court, and I was glad he went to prison. It was a relief. But it was a strange story, you know, that he had found a way to hurry home from Baltimore and then hurry back again after committing the crime. I didn't want to have any doubt, but I would still wake up some nights in a panic, listening for any sound, and wondering if Julie's killer was still out there.

MARIAH: That's next time, on *Innocent Blood*.

CHAPTER 5

Workers came to replace the window the next morning, fitting clear panes in place of the original green and gold stained glass, which was too bad from an architectural standpoint, Renee thought as she stood by, listening to *Innocent Blood* and waiting to sweep up the inevitable bits of putty and sawdust.

The new window shed a brighter, sharper light on the interior of the house, but by contrast, the story of Ed's case just seemed to get muddier. The testimony of Dr. Henri Beaufort, the blowhard in tweed, made her itchy with indignation. Ed had not gotten a fair trial, that much was sure, but she was nagged by the fact that Mariah still hadn't mentioned Kim was Ed's alibi witness. It wasn't a great look.

"So, that was pretty weird last night," she said to Kim later in the day as they inventoried sheets and towels for the children in the second-floor linen closet. "Has that kind of thing happened before?"

"Absolutely not," Kim said, her eyes wide, rejecting the idea. "And I sure hope it doesn't happen again. This is exactly why I didn't want to have the press conference here."

"It sounded like you and Ed thought it might be someone specific."

"Oh." Kim looked startled, but she waved the question away. "No, that was silly. We're perfectly safe here." She gave a pillowcase a sharp flap and refolded it. "Everything will feel better when we get into a normal routine. The kids will start school tomorrow for real, and Ed will start job hunting full-time."

"Oh," said Renee this time, as she thought about the paychecks she was about to start receiving—maybe not a lot in the grand scheme of things, but more than she'd ever made before. "I guess I assumed he already had a job."

Kim gave an annoyed grimace. "He was exonerated, but people aren't very compassionate when they hear the p-word."

Pivoting to a lighter approach, Renee said, "What about you? What are your plans for yourself?"

Kim shared more easily on this topic. She had worked as a paralegal for years, both before and after meeting and marrying Ed. When baby Willow came along, she had taken a few weeks of maternity leave before going back to work, but she found increasingly that her day job didn't fulfill her.

"I honestly didn't think I'd ever have a chance to do anything different," she said. "Not with a husband in prison, a baby to support, and taxes to pay on this place." She gestured generally at the ceiling. "Julie never wanted Ed to be strapped for money like that. She had a huge life insurance policy, which of course they wouldn't pay out after he got convicted." She went on to explain that when Ed's conviction was overturned, the insurance company had to pay, and new options materialized. Kim had quit her job and taken Willow out of day care. She had always loved photography and wanted to create a lifestyle brand for herself on social media. "I'm going to do home decorating tips and lifestyle posts about blended families. And being a full-time mom," she added, with a flourish. "I want to do it all, basically, which is why I need you!"

Renee smiled and made some encouraging sounds, but deep down, she thought this plan was stupid. For her own sake, she hoped that life insurance payout was very large, because it didn't sound like Kim or Ed could count on a paycheck anytime soon. But how many murders, whether of the *Dateline* or Lifetime variety, had hinged on the existence of a large life insurance policy? She filed that detail away as another thing that the podcast hadn't bothered to mention.

The next morning, as Ed prepared to take the children to their first day at their new school, Oliver teared up over his cereal.

"What's wrong, bud?" Ed asked when he glanced up from reading the news on his phone.

"I just . . ." the boy muttered. "I just don't know what it's going to be like."

"Aw, it's okay, buddy!" Ed said, patting his son on the shoulder. "You used to go to this school. Don't you remember?"

Oliver sniffed. "Not really," he rasped.

Just then, Caz descended the stairs, having waited until the last possible minute, grabbed a granola bar from the kitchen, and exited the front door without a word to anyone.

"Let's get this show on the road!" Ed said, with a cheerful clap. "Party bus leaving the station!"

Renee watched the whole thing from the sink, where she was washing baby bottles. She wanted to shout, "Give your son a hug!" after the departing family, but she didn't. Enid Salinas had been adamant about that. "Don't intervene in family conflicts," she had said, wagging a pink-nailed finger at the camera. "And never give advice!"

But even Mrs. Salinas would admit that the Weatherups needed help, and Renee thought she could offer a little of that. Secretly, she loved the idea of swooping into this chaotic household full of deferred dreams, like Mary Poppins with a vacuum, and turning it into a place where everyone could learn to trust one another again. She could keep their clothes clean, their rooms smelling fresh, and their fridge full of healthy snacks. She could be a homemaker, the opposite of what someone had once whispered behind her in church. It might just take a little overstepping on her part, and that was fine. She wasn't one to butt out. At least not anymore.

That afternoon, she made her first foray into the basement. It was a dingy, unfinished space with lumpy stone walls and bare bulbs. The family had used it as catch-all storage for years, and it contained the usual hodgepodge of musty holiday decorations, dusty tools, and dented, empty luggage. It was a mess, frankly, and though there ought to be ample space for the tubs of the children's unseasonable clothing, the tubs that had brought her down there in the first place, she didn't see any obvious floor space to accommodate them. With a sigh and a glance at her watch, she began gingerly shifting some of the more obvious space hogs, a mildewy artificial Christmas tree that shouldn't have been stored on its side anyway, some mostly empty cans of paint, a stack of old magazines that could have been on top of another stack of old magazines.

She was making some headway when, like an archaeologist breaking through to a new stratum in the rock, she discovered something else. Beyond the anarchy was a layer of order, neat file boxes and moving cartons, stacked like with like, high and square, every box labeled with large block letters that were so unlike Kim's looping script or Ed's scratchy penmanship.

Schedules, Expenses, Taxes, Clothes to Donate, Soccer Equipment, Pool Toys, Halloween decor, Mementos.

This, she thought, was Julie.

Her hands felt damp, and she let a laundry hamper full of grungy garden hoses slip slowly to the ground.

Rummaging through storage containers just because she was curious was an obvious no-no in the Enid Salinas handbook. But oh, how badly she wanted to. It would be different, she told herself, if Kim or Ed had packed these boxes with the intention of going back to them. But these were a dead woman's boxes, relegated to the back of the basement where they could molder, completely obscured by the detritus of a household that had moved on without her.

Upstairs, the front door creaked and closed with the sound of the Weatherups leaving for the gym and its free childcare service. She glanced at her watch. Just one box couldn't hurt.

The **Mementos** box was the obvious choice. It was dusty on top, but inside, the contents were carefully packed in bubble wrap and tissue paper: homemade Christmas tree ornaments decorated in lumpy paint and sparkles, a handmade baby quilt, a Mother's Day card with Caz's tiny handprint in pink paint. They were the little trophies of motherhood, tucked away carefully—not for everyday viewing but for keeping always. Toward the bottom was a colorful child's tape deck with large buttons and a red handle for easy carrying. There was a tape inside, and, miraculously, functional batteries. She pressed play. There was a light whir of tape starting to spool and then a woman's voice—Julie's.

> JULIE: [voice on tape] Hi, Cat-cat! It's Mommy. I'm on a work trip right now. We talked about how I was gonna have to be away for a few nights, and it won't be long before I'm back. Meanwhile, I made this tape for you so you and Daddy can play it at bedtime, and it'll be just like I'm there, just like normal. I love you, baby, and I hope you have wonderful sweet dreams of all your favorite things.
> Tonight, we're going to read one of your favorites, *The Monster at the End of This Book: Starring Lovable, Furry Old Grover*. I bet you saw Grover when you watched *Sesame Street* today. Okay, here we go . . .

Renee hunched on the basement floor, tears streaming down her face as she listened to Julie's soft voice reading each page of the short book, pausing for dramatic effect along the way. Julie had a thousand responsibilities, and she never wanted a solitary one to go forgotten, never a holiday uncelebrated or a bedtime missed. She had certainly never planned for it to end up this way: her husband married to another woman, her children sad and angry, and a stranger sweeping her kitchen floor and theorizing, however guiltily, over the mystery of her death.

But Renee was also crying for herself and for the two children people said she had no right to cry over—not Caz and Oliver but Brandon's children, Emma and Wyatt: strawberry blond, smelling of summer and sunscreen. Last year at this time, she had been with them, soaking up the last warm weekends, frolicking with them at the playground, standing by to wrap them in towels when they emerged from the lake.

The tears felt selfish. Unlike Julie, she wasn't dead, and the children she was missing weren't even hers. But the fact was the same: She wouldn't be there to watch them grow up.

The day she and Brandon broke up had been the day before their high school graduation. They had just gone to the mall to pick up a few last critical accessories for their party outfits, and he'd been dropping her off at home. The whole conversation had taken place in his car in her parents' driveway, one of the few places where a couple of teenagers could be assured complete privacy.

The trip to the mall had been awkward, not because there was conflict between them, but because they had run into a group of friends, also out on a pregraduation mission, and it had been painfully obvious that both Renee and Brandon had more fun in that fifteen-minute chat with other people than they had in their whole afternoon together. Their conversations had become stale, and the ride home was almost wordless.

When they pulled into the driveway, Renee said, "Do you think we'll stay together?"

"What do you mean," Brandon said. "Like, forever?"

"Yeah, or even like, after tomorrow. We're high school boyfriend and girlfriend. Are we ever going to be something more?"

Brandon turned off the engine, and they sat, seat belts still fastened, as the car slowly warmed in the June sun. "I don't really know what I'm going to be like after high school," he said. "There's just so much I haven't tried, you know. Different jobs, having my own place, that sort of thing."

"Dating other people?"

"I guess, maybe? It just feels like there's a whole life out there and I don't know what we're going to want."

Through the windshield, they could see across the yard and down the hill to where the acres of Christmas trees began, sculpted, green cones of festivities future. As laughable as it now seemed, knowing what she knew, Renee understood what those two young people had felt in that moment. They really had believed that they were on the cusp of adulthood, that the next afternoon, they would be pronounced grown and all of life's adventures would be theirs for the taking.

"It's been good," she said.

"Totally good," he agreed.

They might have shaken hands as she'd gotten out of the car, or maybe that was a detail she'd put in after the fact.

After that, she and Brandon had given each other plenty of space. They'd seen each other, of course, at pool parties, keg parties, and bonfires. They didn't bear each other any ill will. In fact, she would have liked to talk to him more than she had, would have liked to sit beside him at someone's barbecue and really find out how his life was going, but she hadn't had the nerve. Maybe she'd been afraid to tell him that despite all the youthful adventurousness she had claimed, she hadn't gone anywhere after all. Leaving town required money, which required a job that paid more than minimum wage. It required a car that would start reliably, even in winter, and it required some sense of how to begin fresh in a new place, which was something neither she nor her parents, nor her grandparents before them, had ever done.

And then one day her mother had come home from the grocery store to announce that Deirdre Johnson said the Gaines girl, Andrea, was pregnant with Brandon's baby and they were getting married in a month.

Back then, she'd shut away her disappointment, feeling she had no right to it. She had made the decision to lead a life separate from him, and she couldn't be upset when he moved on. In the ensuing years, she'd gone about her own life, observing him from a distance through occasional bits of gossip or sporadic social media posts. Brandon and Andrea had bought a small house near the highway, and he'd gotten a construction job. Their first baby was a girl, Emma, who was born with much fanfare.

Sometimes Renee had had the impulse to get in touch, to send her congratulations, but she had been too afraid. What if he was blissfully happy and it just became that much more obvious that she wasn't? What if he sensed that she still had feelings for him, and they would both be embarrassed?

More time had passed. Brandon and Andrea had another child, a son christened Wyatt, according to the Baptist church's newsletter. After seeing his birth announcement, Renee had tried to get serious about dating. She signed up for an app and drove as far as Farmville to go to the movies with one or two prospects. The dates hadn't been terrible, but she couldn't imagine inviting any of those people into her life, introducing them to her parents, letting them see her room.

Finally, it was one of those dead-end jobs that had brought Renee and Brandon back together. She'd been working as a cashier at the grocery mart—not her favorite job, but they were always hiring in the fall after the teenagers quit to go back to school. One Friday afternoon, she'd looked up, and he was at her register. She hadn't seen him approaching, but he must have chosen her line specifically, because he was beaming at her.

"Renee, hi! It's good to see you!"

"Oh, wow!" was all she could think of. She'd been so absorbed in the repetition of scanning items that she didn't have any dialogue prepared, but soon, they were talking as she rang him up. He did have a lot of groceries, suitable for a growing family, and ten pounds of oranges to slice up for Emma's soccer team.

"I can't believe she's old enough to play soccer!" Renee said. "You and Andrea must be so proud of her."

"I am," Brandon said. "Well, we both are, but the soccer is more my thing. We're separated," he added, as if in a rush to get the words out, and discomfort colored his cheeks. "Andrea and me. I think that's it for us."

"Oh." Her fingers stumbled over the code for bananas. "I'm sorry."

"Thanks."

"Hey," she said, handing over his receipt. "Do you want to get coffee sometime and talk about it? I mean, we don't have to talk about *it*, we can just talk." It might have been an innocent question, but it wasn't.

His eyes brightened. "I'd really like that. Your number still the same?"

She nodded, her breath catching in her chest.

Everything fell into place after that. They did meet for coffee, a visit that lasted all afternoon and into the evening. They were the same Brandon and Renee they had been in high school, still laughed at the same jokes, still liked to walk down the state park trails and shoot the breeze. But they were also older now, less naive, better able to appreciate each other. They were officially a couple again before the week was out.

Of course, there were complications. After separating from Andrea, Brandon had moved in to his brother's basement, and there were still custody arrangements to be negotiated. Bringing him back to the Christmas tree farm was an absolute impossibility. The idea of explaining to her parents that she was sleeping with a technically married man was as preposterous as the idea of sneaking him into her room through the back window.

So, they spent their first night together (their first night ever) on a metal-frame futon in his little basement abode. The room smelled of mustiness and fabric softener from the laundry room next door, but still, she woke in the middle of the night and lay awake listening to the unfamiliar sound of his sleeping breath, and she felt like her luck had finally turned.

They had been destined for each other all along but had lessons to learn and hardship to endure before they were ready to be together. She saw this moment as her reward for keeping her distance from him this whole time. She hadn't interfered in his marriage, hadn't lurked on the sidelines of his life, annoying his wife or distracting him from his children, and in good time, he had returned to her.

Now, as she closed Julie's box of mementos and climbed the closet stairs, she understood why she had plunged so quickly into the Weatherups' boxes and their business. When it came to Brandon, she had successfully minded her own business for years because she thought it was the right thing to do. *Don't presume. Don't intrude.* But the ultimate result was that she wondered every day whether she had just wasted time they might have had together.

Losing Brandon had turned her into someone who itched at inaction, who distrusted the feeling of caution itself. There was love on the table years ago, and she should have taken it. Now, maybe there were answers on the table about what had happened to Julie, and she was going to look for them.

"You know," she said to Kim that Wednesday afternoon. "I'm trained to assist with formal entertaining as well. Do you plan to host guests?"

Kim paused over peeling an orange. "What a lovely idea," she said. "Are you sure that's something you're up for?"

"Of course," Renee said optimistically. "Maybe you could invite Mariah Cusmano."

"Ed used to host fancy parties and galas here all the time," Kim said. "This house is made for it, and I used to think I'd never get to do anything like that with my husband." Her voice shook. "Now, I can't think of anything I'd rather do."

Kim mentioned the idea of the dinner party to Ed when he returned home from his meeting with the career adviser.

"I just think it would be a beautiful way to celebrate being a family again," she said.

Renee, who was chopping vegetables for dinner, prickled with pride.

Ed dropped a folder of papers on the counter and sighed. "The alarm wasn't on just now. I'm serious about everyone keeping it on, even during the day."

"I forgot," Kim said. "It's not that big a deal."

Ed gave her a stern look. "Renee, has the security system been explained to you? I want it in use at all times. And if you don't enter the code within fifteen seconds, it'll wail loud enough to wake the baby."

"Yes, of course, Mr. Weatherup. Security is important."

Kim threw her hands up. "Okay, yes, I'll remember to use it. But about this party! I could make hors d'oeuvres, and we could do everything up nice. We could invite Mariah and Danny as a way to thank them."

Ed took in his wife's excitement, and his earlier agitation faded. "Yes," he said, moving to kiss her. "That sounds amazing. I love a good party."

Kim fluttered into the family room with her computer to look at "recipe inspo." It seemed she had already forgotten that the party had been Renee's idea, but Renee didn't mind. The party would be legitimately nice, and if it gave her the chance to learn more about the podcasters and why they seemed to have left details out of Ed's story, so much the better.

As Renee's second week began, the household settled into a routine built around the children's school and extracurriculars. Caz kept long hours at band practice and calculus tutoring, often arriving home late, only to take a plate of leftovers up to her room to eat while she did homework. Kim rankled at Caz's lack of interest in family time, but Ed discouraged her from bringing it up with the teenager. "It's her senior year," he said. "She should be focused on academics."

Oliver, by contrast, was eager to sit at the kitchen island for dinner with his father, stepmother, and baby sister. He was a talkative child who turned the recounting of his day into an elaborate performance designed to make them laugh. Nothing delighted him more than to tease out a smile from Willow, and he would turn himself inside out making comical noises or silly dances if he thought he had her attention.

Only occasionally did Oliver's good attitude slip, but when it did, the results were sudden, tearful, and difficult to soothe. Some nights, he would wake from nightmares, screaming, half conscious and inconsolable. Once, when Kim replaced his dinosaur toothbrush without warning, the boy emerged from the second-floor bathroom shaking and despondent. "My toothbrush!" he wailed. "I don't know what happened. Someone took it."

Kim hustled up the stairs and held out her hands, hoping to forestall the thing that had already begun. "No one took it, honey!" she said. "I just saw yours was getting worn out, so I got you a new one. Look, it's Batman!"

"Come on, buddy!" Ed remonstrated impatiently. "It's just a stupid toothbrush. Don't be like this!"

Renee watched these heartbreaking interludes from the sidelines, wishing she could step in and solve it. As a compromise, she often volunteered to hold Willow during particularly hectic moments, enjoying the warmth of the baby's soft body against her chest, the sweet-smelling hair, the heavy head on her shoulder.

During the day, she mainly had her run of the house, interrupted intermittently by Kim or Ed, who would go to the gym or run errands but who mostly hung out doing Renee wasn't sure what, Kim in the third-floor suite, and Ed in his study. Initially, they would stop and talk as they encountered her, but these conversations diminished quickly into an absent-minded greeting here and there, which she preferred. In unit three, Enid Salinas had charged her to keep small talk to a minimum, and besides, there were only so many times you could chitchat with someone while holding a laundry basket of their unmentionables.

In the evenings, she looked for ways to fade into the background. She laid the groundwork for the family's dinner, made something for herself, and then drifted away to eat in her room. At 5:00 p.m., she was off the clock, but she found her free time difficult to fill. She was physically tired from the workday but was too aware of occupying someone else's space to fully relax anywhere. It was an odd combination of being perpetually alone, separate from the family conversations, and yet never alone enough to have her own private thoughts.

Sometimes, on nice evenings, she would sit on the tiny back patio, enjoying the wedge of summer sunset she could find between the high neighborhood fences. But even then, she couldn't help scanning the aging, gappy masonry around her and wondering if the brick that had smashed the window had come from there, or if one of the other loose bricks would find its way into the house one night.

She also couldn't stop thinking about the stash of Julie's boxes in the basement, and every now and then, when she had spare time and people were out of the house, she would go down, pull the chain to turn on the bare bulb, and rummage around in the space only a housekeeper would dare to touch. She didn't know exactly what she was hoping to find, but she wanted to put her hands on things that Julie had touched. Maybe there was something here investigators had missed, a detail in a diary or an appointment with an unfamiliar name that might lead Renee somewhere. Silly, maybe, but she could hope.

One box, marked CALENDARS, was full of leather-bound planners, each embossed with a year, and each full of appointments and reminders in blue pen.

C, soccer—4PM

O, pediatrician—10:15

Lunch with M

Yoga B4 plumber comes—11:30

VMA fundraiser BLK TIE

The books were a meticulous record of the family's life. Celebrations, medical events, work commitments, house repairs—Julie had corralled it all, defining the family's world in her small handwriting. She had led a busy life in which she had kept her children active and invested a lot of time in maintaining the physical appearance of herself and her home. Hair appointments and manicures had been booked like clockwork, always with her same trusted professionals. She'd called in someone to power wash the front of the house every season, and she'd often experimented with trendy exercise programs like barre classes and hot yoga.

As far as her social life, there had been occasional lunches or drinks with someone called M, whom Renee had eventually figured out was Micheline Cygnet, Julie's senior partner at her law firm. Julie had also attended a surprising number of gala events, but they were all listed as fundraisers or charity events of some kind, and Julie had always gone to the salon ahead of time.

As the months and years went by under Renee's flipping fingers, it really did look like Julie had had no casual friends. She hadn't socialized with people outside of work or society functions, and while she might have liked it that way, Renee felt sad thinking about it. She imagined Julie being desperate to spend time with someone she didn't work for, someone she didn't have to impress with a new formal gown.

Of course, Renee reminded herself, maybe Julie had turned to Ed for those casual, private moments where she could literally let her hair down from its updo, but she doubted that. All Ed's activities had been logged in the calendar, from his golf lessons to his physical therapy appointments, and while it could have been a sign of Julie's need to keep tabs on everything, it had the effect of making it look like Ed had just been another of her children, someone to be reminded of appointments and shuttled from event to event. It was easy, perhaps too easy, Renee acknowledged, to see what might have prompted Julie to make that supposed appointment with James Mullins, the divorce attorney—though, of course, that meeting hadn't made it into her diary.

On another occasion, when Ed and Kim were at the gym and Willow, whom Renee had volunteered to babysit, was asleep, she took the baby monitor down to the basement and dove into the **Expenses** box, which reflected the same meticulous mind that the calendars had. It contained folders of sorted receipts: household, entertainment, dining, apparel, clipped together in order. Some receipts bore additional notes in Julie's signature blue. *Gown for C&O Holiday Gala 2017. Gym Dues Jan. 2018.*

Household receipts were separate: regrouting the kitchen in 2016 and a new washing machine in 2017, along with smaller items—a blender, a grill set—all cataloged in reverse chronological order.

Renee thought of what Ed's defense lawyer had said about how a man like Ed has expenses. *Pay a babysitter, handle the kids' soccer dues . . .* Ed may very well have enjoyed a couple grand in "walking-around money," but she found it hard to believe that he had been responsible for any of the routine household bills.

There, on the top of the stack of receipts, was the most recent, a short credit card slip from Anchor Kitchen Supplies dated March 29, 2018. The charge was $16.46, and Julie had commented, *Steak knife to replace chipped one in set.* It was the last thing she had filed in this box, the last time anyone had kept up with her system of diligent recordkeeping.

Renee ran a fingertip down the three-inch slip of paper, which was brittle with age. She thought about how Julie was the last person to have touched it, to have smoothed it and clipped it to its fellows with the satisfaction of a bothersome task complete. It seemed unfair that such a small thing should hold any significance at all, and yet, she wondered if it might.

That night, after everyone had gone to bed, Renee slipped quietly out of her room and tiptoed downstairs to the kitchen. She wasn't sneaking, exactly; she had every right to go to the kitchen at night for any number of reasons. But her current mission didn't feel particularly innocent, and she didn't want anyone to see her do it any more than she wanted to wait for the morning.

The forensic showman, Dr. Henri Beaufort, and the painstakingly precise detective, Mason Torian, had given two very different interpretations of the physical evidence at Julie's murder scene, but they had agreed on one thing: The missing murder weapon was a sharp knife with a narrow blade about four inches long.

She turned on the light, poured herself a glass of water, and stood by the sink, drinking and listening. When the house remained quiet, she turned to the knife block on the counter and began removing steak knives from their wooden slots. The knives were slender with blades about the length of her palm, and she laid them one at a time in front of her. One, two, three sharp, straight blades, and a fourth one, chipped.

***Innocent Blood*, Episode Three: "The Ride"**

MARIAH: I want to pause the story of Ed and Julie Weatherup for a moment and skip ahead to something that happened a few months before and six blocks away from their Fan District home.

On the night of January 14, 2018, a thirty-four-year-old Richmond University graduate student named Elizabeth Barnet left her on-campus apartment at about 10:00 p.m. Elizabeth was a well-beloved member of the RU community, a part of student government and the a cappella group, and a PhD candidate in biology. Her friends and professors knew her to be friendly, studious, happy, and reliable to a fault. That night, she told her roommate that she was going for a walk.

In a haunting interview with a local news station, her roommate, Daisy Richards, tearfully described Elizabeth's mood that night as excited.

DAISY: [voice on archival tape] She seemed wound up, kind of. I said, "Are you going to meet someone?" And she was like, "You never know!"

MARIAH: Elizabeth left the apartment and never came back.

The next day, when she seemed to be missing, campus security launched a search of the university grounds and questioned her many contacts, none of whom had seen or heard from her since before that late-night walk. It was so out of character for Elizabeth to skip out on her responsibilities, and her closest friends insisted that if she were struggling with anything personal, she would have told someone. News of her disappearance spread, and soon volunteers were searching every inch of the shaded walking paths, opening every utility closet, and looking inside every dorm room and office.

Around nightfall on January 16, Elizabeth's body was discovered near a drainage ditch behind the rec building, dead from several vicious blows to the head. The campus and the wider community was outraged and devastated. How could someone kill a young woman on a safe, well-lit college campus without anyone hearing anything? How could any parent of an RU student sleep again?

This last question was especially critical to my family because I had just become an RU student myself. My parents were torn between pride and fear, but I was eighteen, excited for this independent new chapter and already in love with the brick-and-glass campus. What's more, I was obsessed with the story of Elizabeth and her murder. I read the news daily with the mingled fear and fascination that many of us feel when we are exposed to the worst of human behavior.

Today, we know that Elizabeth's murder remains officially unsolved, though several sources have speculated that her ex-boyfriend was the prime suspect. She had recently broken up with him, and while there is no direct evidence linking him to the crime, there were rumors of domestic violence, and we know that, statistically speaking, the most dangerous day in a woman's life is the day she leaves a dangerous man.

That's what we know now, but at the time, with the help of the press, we all examined questions about Elizabeth's life and conduct. Was she chaste or promiscuous? Did she go out dancing or stay home studying? Did she smoke, drink, or do drugs? Her bank records showed an unusual cash deposit about a month before. Where did that money come from? Did she do anything that might have invited her horrifying fate? In a nutshell, when she went out for a walk that night, did she stray from the appropriate path, either metaphorically or literally?

I'm fully aware how problematic this whole line of thought was, but looking back, I can understand my fixation better than I did at the time. In many ways, Elizabeth was an older version of me—an eager student, excited for the opportunities that college had to offer—and by reading the coverage of her case, I was learning how society scrutinized and judged her and, by extension, how I would be judged as a woman entering the world. As an idealistic teenager, it seemed to me that the way the media viewed her was creepily similar to the way her killer might have viewed her on that January night when he encountered her on that tree-lined path and calculated whether or not she was a quote, unquote *good victim*.

It was with this fire in my belly that I enrolled in self-defense classes and joined hundreds of my female classmates in learning how to escape a would-be attacker who grabbed us from behind. I also declared a major in journalism.

When I joined the staff of the RU Radio Lab, I partnered with my producer, Danny Dudek, on plans to make a podcast of our own. We were on the hunt for a true crime story that would allow us to talk about some of the tricky topics that had brought us to journalism in the first place. Ed Weatherup's case was one of the first ones we considered, but I was skeptical. I didn't think there was anything meaningful we could add. I, like most people, believed Ed must have been guilty.

Still, we decided to at least go talk to him. So, one day in the early spring of 2021, Danny and I went to the Dinwiddie Correctional Facility, south of Richmond. Here's a recording from that visit. If our voices sound muffled at all, it's because we're wearing masks.

MARIAH: [voice on interview tape] Talk to me about the day you were arrested for Julie's murder. What was that like?

ED: [voice on interview tape] Honestly, I was surprised and annoyed more than anything.

MARIAH: Annoyed? Not scared?

ED: Not really. I thought the police would realize their mistake as soon as they had time to vet my story. I was just upset that the detectives were wasting their time on me when they could have been finding the real killer.

MARIAH: How was your marriage doing in the weeks and months leading up to Julie's murder?

ED: We were doing great. I mean, we'd been married for fifteen years at that point and had jobs and kids to worry about, but Julie and I were always on the same team. Always.

MARIAH: Did she tell you she was thinking about divorce?

ED: Never. We never went to bed angry. When the police told me she'd spoken to a divorce attorney, I thought they were lying. I still don't really believe that part, honestly.

MARIAH: What can you tell me about your case that hasn't already been reported on?

ED: Well, the police incompetence, for one thing. That Detective Evans didn't waste any shoe leather, if you know what I mean. Once they got me in their sights, they stopped following other leads. The prosecutor was worse. He weaponized the media and whipped people into such a lather, you would have thought I was Jack the Ripper. It would be laughable if it hadn't actually happened to me. [laughter] I swear the jury was giggling and passing notes during the trial. They were so excited to nail me.

MARIAH: So where does your case stand now?

ED: We appealed on the basis of jury misconduct because of the prejudicial press coverage. That appeal went to the same trial judge, William Bowling, and he ruled right away that the news coverage colored just inside the legal lines. We're working on another appeal on the grounds of insufficient evidence, but I don't have high hopes. I think the world has made up its mind about old Ed.

MARIAH: You mentioned other leads?

ED: People at her job, for one thing. A lawyer makes enemies. Some of her clients resented her for not being able to do the impossible, and some people she beat in court held grudges. There was also the guy from her high school, and the voicemail.

MARIAH: Voicemail?

ED: Julie left someone a very strange voicemail before she died. No one's been able to explain what it meant. And no one's ever been able to explain why she went out on that roof that night. Well, there was the one girl who claimed to know what happened, but that was incredibly dark.

MARIAH: [voice in studio] Danny and I left the Dinwiddie Correctional Facility not really knowing what to think. Ed seemed surprisingly balanced and personable for someone serving a prison sentence for murder, and we found ourselves wanting to like him a little. He had talked to us openly, without grandiosity or blustering, and he even seemed to have a businesslike rapport with the guards, as if they were all colleagues at the same workplace.

Still, we didn't know if Ed's story had what we needed. Sure, he said that law enforcement and the prosecutor's office had used him as a convenient scapegoat, but that's an easy claim to make and a hard one to prove. Besides, he had a well-respected legal team representing him. He didn't seem to need the kind of advocacy or public attention a podcast like ours could provide.

We decided to set Ed's story aside for a time and keep looking at other cases, including one that the FBI had been involved in a decade before, but I did make a post on the Radio Lab's Twitter account to update our followers on how hard we were working to bring our new podcast together. "Traveling statewide to learn about VA's most interesting cases," the tweet said. "This week: Dinwiddie Correctional Facility & meeting with agents at Langley!"

To this day, I don't fully understand why this single post was enough to get the reaction that it did. The day that I wrote it, I didn't think there was anything particularly noteworthy, or even informative, but someone did.

The next morning, I woke up to more than a dozen DMs. They were from a handful of different accounts, all of which looked like they had been created for the sole purpose of contacting me. They had usernames like justiceserved and judgmentday666, and while the wording of their messages varied a little, they all had the same idea.

"Leave Ed Weatherup where he is," said one message. "If you interfere, you'll be sorry."

Another message from an account called angelofretribution said, "Ed belongs in prison, we all know it. If you undo what's been done, you'll ruin lives, including yours."

At around 3:00 a.m., angelofretribution sent me another message. "If you want to go on living your nice little life, leave the Ed Weatherup case alone. Trust me. I have friends who will make your life a living hell if you poke your nose where it doesn't belong."

I showed the messages to my producer.

MARIAH: [voice on tape] How did these people figure out we went to see Ed? I didn't even mention his name.
DANNY: [voice on tape] Maybe they just assumed? He's got to be the most famous inmate at the Dinwiddie facility. Maybe they thought we went to talk to the feds about his case.
MARIAH: [voice in studio] We didn't know what to make of the messages, but the fact that someone was so serious about warning us away from Ed's case got me thinking. Maybe the story of the Weatherup family wasn't over yet, after all. Maybe someone still had something to hide.
Bottom line, I wanted to know for sure whether it was possible for Ed to have killed Julie the way the prosecution said he did, and so, I went on a late-night road trip.
The prosecution's theory of the crime involved the most mundane of details: the length of time it takes a car to travel from one place to another. That's what I set out to discover.
[car door slamming]
MARIAH: [voice in car] It's Friday, April 2, 2021, 11:30 p.m., and I'm here with Danny Dudek in the drop-off circle at the Hamilton Pier Hotel in downtown Baltimore. We are all gassed up and ready to make a round-trip drive between this spot and the Weatherup house. It's a nice night, a little cool, but we've got a good moon. How are you feeling, Danny?
DANNY: [voice in car] A little nervous, honestly. I think tonight's going to tell us a lot about Ed's story.
MARIAH: I think so too. [car engine, turn signal] Danny is taking the first shift driving, and we're going the

fastest route, according to the internet. We chose a Friday night in April so, as much as possible, we can experience the same traffic conditions Ed would have had if he did make this same trip. We're also going to do this as quickly as possible. Nothing reckless, of course, but we are going to try our best to get there and back in the window of time allowed. That means no stops along the way. We know that Ed's car was parked in the garage under the security camera all night, but we're going to set that issue aside for now.

MARIAH: [voice in studio] On the night my producer and I made our trip, there was a little light traffic getting out of Baltimore, but once we were on the freeway, we made good time past DC, all the way to Richmond. We drove straight to the Weatherup house in the Fan District. Because all the neighborhood residents were home for the night, there was no parking near the house, but we decided to pretend that, for the sake of argument, Ed might have immediately found convenient parking.

MARIAH: [voice in car] We made a pit stop at the convenience store closest to the Weatherup house, and now we're back in the car. How long did we end up being stopped for?

DANNY: [voice in car] Nine minutes.

MARIAH: Nine minutes. All right. Obviously, that's not very long, but the clock is ticking. We have to make it back to the hotel by 4:15, which is when Ed was seen at the on-site gym. In the interests of safety, we changed drivers, but it's becoming really obvious that this is a long trip for one person to make in the middle of the night. I think we're both starting to feel the strain of it.

DANNY: Agreed. The road never really gets empty along this route. Someone could speed a little here and there, but you couldn't go ninety all the way.

MARIAH: Let's assume Ed hired a driver with cash. It's an odd request to make, like, take me all the way to a different city, let me go into this house for a few minutes, and then take me back to where we started. I suspect a driver would remember a ride like that.

DANNY: Sure, but if they were a Baltimore-based driver, they might have missed some of the press coverage of the murder. They might not have ever had a reason to think about Ed again.

MARIAH: Or they are an undocumented immigrant or a parolee, someone who might have known there was something going on but didn't feel comfortable coming forward.

DANNY: Also possible.

MARIAH: [voice in studio] When we arrived back at the hotel, the sky was just starting to lighten up.

MARIAH: [voice in car] Time check?

DANNY: 4:58 a.m.

MARIAH: [sighing] Well. Okay. We're thirty-eight minutes late. Is there any way we could have done that faster?

DANNY: We could have done more speeding, I guess? You okay?

MARIAH: I'm exhausted, honestly. I can't imagine wanting to go do a workout in a hotel gym right now. [car door slamming]

MARIAH: [voice in studio] Thirty-eight minutes might not seem like a lot. Commonwealth's Attorney Prescott might say that it's a small margin of error, and it's possible that Ed made the trip faster than Danny and I did. But keep in mind: Our trip didn't account for the time Ed would have needed to exit the hotel and connect with his driver or the time he would have needed to change into his workout gear.

Finally, there's one other big thing we didn't account for: My producer and I didn't murder anyone on our trip.

Whoever entered the house that night would have needed time to locate Julie and have some kind of confrontation with her. Their fight might have been brief—after all, the intruder was armed, and Julie was surprised in her bed—but there was at least enough time for her to get up, run out onto the roof deck, and fight for her life, as evidenced by defensive wounds on her hands and arms.

After Julie was dead, evidence showed the perpetrator went back downstairs and washed their hands, as proven by trace amounts of Julie's blood found in the drain of the kitchen sink. While I don't know for sure how long the intruder was inside the Weatherup house, I can't imagine achieving all of that in less than nine minutes.

After our road trip, it was time to make a choice about whether to proceed with Ed's case. Obviously, the prosecution's theory of the crime had a lot of problems, but what helped me make up my mind were the threats that continued to trickle in over social media. "Leave Ed where he belongs," one message read. Another said, "Don't cross the people who put Ed Weatherup in prison."

Someone, or several someones, were very unhappy that I was asking questions about Ed's conviction. It smacked of a cover-up, and, like any reporter, I saw that as a challenge.

And then, of course, there was the voicemail that Ed mentioned, the biggest question mark in the Julie Weatherup case.

Around 1:00 a.m. on the morning of April 6, just hours or maybe minutes before her death, Julie placed a call to one of her contacts. The call went to voicemail, and Julie left this message, the last known recording of her voice.

JULIE: [voice on tape] What are you doing here? We already talked about this, and there's nothing more to say. [slightly muffled] It's over and I'm empty. [sound of another muffled voice] What are you talking about? What have you done? [muffled noises] This is cab! Stop! [sharper] Just stop! *No!* [swishing noise, thud]

MARIAH: I listen to the voicemail every day, trying to understand what Julie's last known words mean. Her voice is clear, and she speaks with confidence, even partway through the message when she seems to have angled her face away from the phone. Sometimes I think she sounds like a woman who is angry, frustrated, and done playing games. Sometimes, I think she's scared for her life.

I still have so many questions about this message, but there is one thing we know for sure: The man Julie left the voicemail for is named Arlo Ardell, and she had been having an affair with him for years. That's next time, on *Innocent Blood*.

CHAPTER 6

Renee felt obsessed. As she moved around the house, she found herself constantly thinking about Julie, replaying the other woman's frightened voice in her mind, wondering where she was when she made that call, wondering what had happened to that new steak knife Julie had bought and why the chipped one never got thrown away. It wasn't necessarily a clue, but it felt like one. On the night of the murder, there had been a knife in the house that investigators didn't seem to know about. In fact, maybe no one but Julie knew the replacement knife existed until the murderer seized it, raised it against her, and then carried it away into the night.

But there were plenty of other explanations, she determined, as she lugged a hamper full of pillowcases and towels to the laundry room. Maybe the new knife was stuffed in a closet somewhere, forgotten in the horror that followed its purchase. Maybe Julie had thrown away the chipped knife, replaced it with the new one, and then sometime in the ensuing five years, another knife had become chipped.

It wasn't healthy, she thought, as she rocked Willow in the nursery while Kim went to take a shower. It wasn't right to have those thoughts in her head when she was supposed to be making the home a good place for the children. But the thoughts were already there, and she couldn't shake the feeling that the house itself held more clues that only she was looking for. Each day, as she tidied and washed her way through 1125, she kept her eyes open, just in case.

Her tiny, surreptitious investigations turned up plenty of Weatherup family secrets, though not all were of equal evidentiary value. For example, Oliver, who never complained about the healthy salads and grain bowls Kim favored, had squirreled away a large bag of sour gummy worms on a shelf in his closet, a private indulgence Renee found so charming that she wanted to cry.

Caz's room, meanwhile, was the picture of overt teenage rebellion, with her all-black wardrobe and horror-movie posters. She, too, had a stash of gummy candy hidden in the back of her underwear drawer, but hers was laced with cannabis. More surprising was a stack of vintage pinup photos Renee discovered under Caz's bed, in which buxom women, mostly clad in cinch-waisted dresses and buckled pumps, flashed their garters and pouted coyly at the camera. The colorful images of hypertraditional femininity seemed so at odds with Caz's otherwise norm-busting attitude that Renee stopped and stared at them for a long moment. Was Caz exploring her sexuality or considering a massive aesthetic shift? After vacuuming, she put the pinups back where she found them, and when she returned to the teenager's bedroom later in the week, they were gone or better hidden.

Then there were the unexpected intimacies that came with the housekeeper territory. Most of it was totally fine. While she occasionally had to pick up Oliver's underwear, which he had almost managed to throw into the hamper, or sweep tissues marked with Caz's mahogany lipstick into the trash, she didn't mind. It did feel uncomfortable, however, to go into the top-floor bathroom when the scent of Ed's shampoo was still damp in the air and pick up Kim's birth control pills so she could wipe down the vanity. One morning, she happened to notice Kim hadn't taken that day's pill, and she stood, frozen, the foil card in her hand, wrestling with what to do.

To go downstairs and remind Kim would be a gross breach of professionalism. To keep silent might mean letting her employer bumble into unplanned pregnancy. Unfreezing herself with effort, she put the pills back in their place and moved forward with her sponge, but on the following day's circuit, she did note, with relief, that Kim had gotten herself back on track. The whole thing made her wonder about baby Willow's origin story. She didn't think prison conjugal visits were a real thing anymore, a fact confirmed by a quick web search.

She had so many inappropriate questions.

While Renee was wondering about her personal life, Kim seemed to be enjoying her first efforts to build her social media lifestyle brand. She would create small, artistic tableaux around the house by clearing everything from an end table or shelf, polishing the surface vigorously, and then styling it to capture whatever effect she had in mind: a lamp next to a wooden bowl of apples, a trailing houseplant next to three hardcover books. Renee didn't know what kind of reaction the tableaux received on social media, but she did know that each tightly controlled visual moment stood in contrast to the disorder just out of frame, an unruly pile of newborn clothes that awaited sorting on the floor, a shelf overflowing with books and trinkets that had failed the beauty contest, a tangle of shoes Kim herself had discarded. It fell to Renee to deal with these unsightly realities, as Kim wandered off to find another corner of the house to "style." While she didn't begrudge Kim her little postable fantasies, Renee took a smug pleasure in knowing that they could only exist because of her own labor.

As for Ed, the rest of the world seemed to be holding its breath, waiting to see how he would handle the transition back to normal life in its new form, but to Renee, Ed's default status was chaos. He seemed able to maintain grown-up decorum in the shared rooms of the house, picking up dishes and reminding the children to put their jackets away, but the pretense of order vanished in his study on the second floor. Documents, receipts, business cards, and mail appeared out of nowhere and covered the desk in an interlayered blanket that was one dab of paste away from a papier-mâché sculpture. Small wads of cash, mostly ones and fives, dotted the desk, shelves, and even floor, as if Ed emptied his pockets each day but couldn't agree with himself on where to put his spare change. Here was a pair of gloves, here a coffee cup balanced on the seat of an armchair, there a phone charger coiled like a snake among some socks.

Still, Ed was actually working in the study. At least, he seemed to be filling notebook pages with general thoughts about his time in prison. The notebooks would fall off the desk sometimes, and he would let them lie. One morning when she came into the study to gingerly dust, Renee picked up one such notebook and saw what appeared to be the opening of his life's story.

> BEGINNINGS
> I was born into a hardscrabble life, the youngest son of the late Angus and Gert. They were working-class people, if such a title can be attributed to people who never work, and their lack of ambition was only matched by their lack of interest in educating their children. Before their death in a reckless driving accident, their idea of broadening our minds was a strong dose of the opium of the masses, something they had overdosed on long ago. Every Sunday and Wednesday found my brothers and me at the local Baptist church, where the minister preached about salvation in the next life, while I sat there thinking about how I could build a better life for myself in the here and now. The church was called Good Hope, but I had something better than hope: a plan.

"Oh, brother," Renee muttered. She knew writing had therapeutic value, but she hoped that was all this was. Baptist churches were a dime a dozen in Virginia. Everybody probably had a couple of Good Hope Baptists in their hometown, and no one was going to want to read about Ed feeling sorry for himself. She slapped the notebook on the desk and went to ask Kim what she should do about the study. Kim made a face. "Just clean around it all, I guess?"

It was only later that Renee returned to the thought of Ed's parents. Maybe not *everybody* had a Good Hope Baptist.

That afternoon, she collected the trash from around the house into one main bag. With her rattly plastic excuse in hand, she headed outside to the trash bins and then through the gate in the high wooden privacy fence into the alley, where she was confident she wouldn't be overheard. She took out her cell.

The phone rang, and Mama's voice, cracking slightly, labored through the decade-old voicemail greeting. They would be outside, Renee thought, tending the trees in the last light of the fragrant fall day, repairing the tractor, or organizing the barn so it would look fresh come Christmas season.

"Hi, Mama," she said, when the machine beeped. It was her first time calling home since she left, and she suddenly felt sad, regretful, and annoyed all at once. Her parents probably thought she should have called sooner, should have *wanted* to call sooner. How disappointed they would be when they realized they'd missed her long-awaited contact. And that she was only calling about this.

"Everything's good here," she said. "Hope you're doing well. Listen, I was calling because I wanted to know if you ever heard of a couple called Gert and Angus Weatherup. They're dead now, but they might have gone to that Good Hope Baptist that's down on Hubbard Road. You know the one I mean? Anyway, I'll call again later."

She hung up and took a deep breath, both guilty and relieved that she hadn't gotten through.

CHAPTER 7

The celebratory dinner party was coming up fast, and Kim could not have been more heavily invested. It was a chance to highlight the culinary and food-design skills she had been building in recent months and to show off the beautiful house that was suddenly full of life and family again. She planned an extensive menu for the occasion and purchased fat glazed pine cones and tiny orange pumpkins to decorate the dining room table with a trailing arrangement that, in Renee's book, was more art installation than centerpiece. Ed, too, seemed excited. He didn't have any creative opinions, but he was happy to hear Kim's ideas and run the requisite errands to craft stores and flower shops.

The embarrassing truth behind the festive spirit was that the guest list was only two names long. Understandably, Ed had lost touch with his social contacts during his prison stint, and after listening to the first few minutes of *Innocent Blood*, Renee suspected that any former friends had been Julie's more than his anyway. She understood why they might quietly purge any convicted murderers from their holiday-card lists.

Kim also seemed to have lost more friends than she'd made lately. When she and Ed were discussing who to invite, she racked her brain to come up with a few acquaintances from the mommy-and-me activity group she had just joined, but the names didn't inspire much enthusiasm.

"I just want everyone who comes to be happy to be here, you know?" she said.

That left the Lauderbach grandparents, who were too far away to drive up just for dinner; Conrad Harrington, who politely declined via his secretary; and the podcasters, Mariah and Danny, who RSVP'd yes with the hunger of young people eager to revel in their success and get a free fancy meal, though Renee couldn't blame them for that. After all, she had planted the party seeds with them in mind.

The day before the event, another adjustment had to be made when Caz announced, on her way out the door for school, that she would be spending the night at her new friend Natasha's house.

"Okay," Ed said. "Just be back in time to help set up for the party."

"Oh, no," Caz said, looking blank, almost startled at the request. "I'm not going to that thing."

Kim, at the counter beside Willow's high chair, froze, a spoonful of fruit puree halfway to the baby's mouth. Ed set his coffee cup down and turned toward Caz with measured self-control that made Renee's spine tingle. She was about to find out how this family handled conflict, and she dearly wished she wasn't trapped in the corner by the sink with no easy escape.

"What are you talking about?" he asked. "Of course you'll be there."

"No," Caz said. "I won't. I don't want to celebrate with those people. Look," she added, holding up her hands, not to mollify but at least to acknowledge that this news might be upsetting. "Obviously I'm happy you're not in prison anymore, Dad, but I don't enjoy the company of those media whores."

"Catherine!" Ed's voice was sharp enough that both Renee and the baby jumped. "Mariah and Danny deserve your respect, and so do I. Give me one good reason why you shouldn't spend time with them."

A shadow passed across the teenager's face, and she turned to leave. "Think about it," she said over her shoulder. "Maybe you'll figure it out."

The front door closed, and there was silence.

"It's okay," Ed said, turning to Kim, but she dropped the spoon on the baby's tray and ran out of the room, tears in her eyes.

Ed's gaze met Renee's suddenly across the kitchen. "House full of women, am I right?"

"Oh, no worries," she said limply and snapped her eyes back to the soapy sponge in her hand. She didn't like the casual misogyny, but Kim's reaction did confuse her. Was this the first party Kim had ever hosted?

Ed sighed. "I need a little fresh air. You've got the baby, right?"

Without waiting for an answer, he left the room, and Renee heard him letting himself out the front door.

From her high chair, Willow looked around with mournful eyes. It occurred to Renee that the baby still barely knew Ed. Did she even see him as a parent? Maybe all she knew was that these relative strangers had made her mother cry and run out of the room.

"Of course I've got you, Baby," Renee said, taking Kim's place on the stool by the high chair and picking up the spoon. "You never have to worry about that."

Later, when Ed returned from his walk and the kitchen was cleaned up, Renee steeled herself to go up and talk to Kim. She was afraid of what kind of mood she might be interrupting, but if party preparations were to proceed, she required Kim's final approval on the shopping list.

So, with a dry mouth, she went upstairs and knocked on Kim's bedroom door. "It's Renee about the groceries."

"Come in."

Kim was in bed, covered in a mountain of duvets and throw blankets, but she sat up and wiped her eyes when Renee entered. "I'm sorry about all this," she said. "I know things are tough and whatever, but I don't know why Catherine has to be so difficult."

Surely, Enid Salinas would have a graceful technique for redirecting the conversation to business matters, but Renee hadn't paid for the advanced course, nor could she forget that the woman in front of her didn't have a single personal friend to invite to her husband's home-from-prison party. So, instead of saying anything, she moved into the room and took a seat on the wicker bench at the foot of the bed.

"All I wanted was a family, you know?" Kim said, the words spilling out of her. "I don't have any close family of my own, and when I married Ed, I wanted him and everything that came with him." She gestured vaguely at the ceiling. "It was nontraditional, but I didn't mind. That's why I had Willow. It was IVF," she added, "in case you were wondering."

Renee perked up at this. She had been wondering, of course.

"Ed had some of his material frozen after Oliver was born because of some cancer scare that turned out to be nothing. So, a couple years ago, I realized that was the only way we'd have a child together, so I went for it. How was I supposed to know he would be out so soon and we'd have this chance to start again and do everything the normal way? And now Catherine . . ." Kim threw up her hands in a supplicating gesture to the ceiling. "I've tried so hard with that girl, and she still just creeps me out."

Renee didn't think two weeks of general caretaking counted as trying particularly hard, nor did she think Caz's light goth aesthetic was enough to creep out an adult, but none of that was hers to speak on, so she merely made an inquisitive face.

"Oh, I know I shouldn't say things like that," Kim said. "I just don't always feel comfortable around her. Not that you need to worry about it," she added in a hurry. "Let me see that list so you can get on with your day."

Renee handed over the sheet of paper, hoping she would never have to hear about Ed's "material" again. But on the plus side, she was learning new things constantly, and she was hoping that she would get a chance the following day to learn more about why Caz disliked the podcasters so much.

CHAPTER 8

The next evening, Renee was polishing fingerprints off the banister when the doorbell rang. She jumped. Surely, there was a dusty surface or an untidy throw blanket somewhere on the main floor, but it was too late to do anything about it. The drinks were chilling, the house glittered in low golden light, and the curtain was rising on the first formal event of her professional career.

She stowed her rag in a cupboard and opened the door to welcome the guests of honor—the only guests.

Mariah and Danny had arrived together, and they stood on the porch in the hippest of all-black evening wear: she in a spaghetti strap dress and he in a slim-fitting black button-down and black jeans that created a long, lean line and made him seem even taller than she remembered.

Renee, who wore her only good sweater, a frumpy brown turtleneck, was momentarily in awe of them, their glossy hair, and the enigmatic nature of their relationship. As she closed the door after them, she caught herself checking to see if they were glamorous from behind as well. They were.

"How are you settling in, Renee?" Mariah asked.

"Quite well, thank you," she said with every bit of Salinas-brand grace she could muster.

And yet, as she took the guests' coats and hung them in the closet under the grand stairs, she caught a whiff of Mariah's musky perfume and thought about her smooth, self-assured voice on *Innocent Blood*, and felt a thrill that the other woman had remembered her name.

The Weatherups descended then, ushering the party into the kitchen, where Ed poured wine and Kim somewhat nervously directed the guests to the trays of bacon-wrapped somethings. Renee poured cran-grape juice in a wineglass for Oliver, who was pumped to be partying with the adults. She felt a spark of pride when she looked at the boy in the button-down shirt she had ironed for him. He looked happy. It was good to see.

"To three million downloads," Ed said, raising his wine. There were laughter and the requisite clinking of glasses.

"What are you working on next?" Kim asked as the group settled at the dining table and Renee served dinner. Kim had given careful instructions about how to plate the food, but it was Renee who had arranged the stuffed pork loins and scalloped potatoes on each plate and had dotted the pomegranate seeds carefully across the salad greens. She moved around the table in a silent dance of plates and glasses.

"I'm tossing some ideas around," Mariah said. "I think Danny and I are both looking for another chance to work together. We've also been invited to speak on a panel at Pod-A-Thon in November." She turned to Ed. "Actually, that's something we should talk about, when you get a sec. It's for journalists and investigators, mainly, but there are often some . . . I don't know what you want to call them. True crime celebrities, maybe. I bet they'd want you to speak if you're interested."

"Of course," Ed said. "Sounds like a great idea."

Renee retreated to the kitchen, sliding the pocket doors almost closed, leaving enough of a gap for her to see Mariah, silver rings on most of her fingers, holding court under the crystal chandelier. They were all hanging on her words: Kim with the eager face of a hostess worried about the success of her party, and Ed with something that looked to Renee like stars in his eyes. Was it gratitude and admiration for the woman who had given him his life back? Or was it a different kind of interest with which he poured wine in her glass and gave her his most charming smile? If Kim noticed, it didn't seem to bother her.

It struck Renee that Mariah was actually younger than she'd first guessed. With all her apparent confidence, she seemed like a woman in her rising career, but that wasn't quite right. Renee fixed her own plate and ate leaning on the counter, recalling autobiographical details Mariah dropped in the third episode of *Innocent Blood.* If her math was correct, Mariah was only twenty-two now and had been a college junior when she'd started work on the podcast. She was barely a grown-up.

An ugly mixture of feelings twisted in Renee. There was jealousy that such a young woman could have already found so much success just because she made the right choice to not grow up on a Christmas tree farm, but there was also the glamour-by-proxy, a desire to sidle up to Mariah and see if any of that popularity and grace could rub off on her. And, when she saw through the crack in the doors that Ed's fingers grazed Mariah's back as the group moved into the parlor to finish their wine, there was protectiveness. Mariah was young, but she had found herself in a very adult space.

They both had.

Neither Mariah nor Renee had known Julie, but their paths to this house had been set when she died. The question now was whether either of them was ready to handle everything they had signed themselves up for.

She found herself gazing at the dark window above the sink, the reflection of the lighted kitchen obscuring anything or anyone that might have been outside. She didn't feel completely safe in the house, but the causes were complicated. Back home, safety came from the knowledge that no one else was around. Here, there was never a moment without traffic noises or voices outside. Shouting, laughter, beeps of car horns, and sirens filled the day and the night, and while none of it was threatening exactly, it was a constant reminder that her world was full of strangers now.

"You having an okay evening?"

She whirled to find that Danny had pushed open the pocket doors and slipped into the kitchen without her hearing him. Now, he stood by the counter, an empty wineglass in hand.

"Sorry," he said. "I wasn't trying to startle you."

"No, no," Renee said, recovering. "Did you all run out of wine out there?"

"Actually, I just came in to say hi. Kim went up to check on the baby, and Ed and Mariah are talking shop. It felt weird that you're just in here by yourself, but I don't know what the etiquette is. I can leave if this is, like, improper or something."

"It's not weird." She wiped her hands on a kitchen towel. "Or, I don't know, maybe it is. I'm still getting used to being staff in someone's house. But it's still a party," she added. "I still like human conversation."

Danny smiled, his teeth white under his neat brown mustache. "How's the new gig going?"

"Good, I think. I don't have a lot to go on. It's my first job like this, and where I'm from, people don't really hire household help."

He laughed. "Me neither. I'm from here, but I was a latchkey kid with a single mom. We fended for ourselves."

There was a half-full bottle of wine in the fridge, and she poured them each a glass. Enid Salinas would not approve, but she wanted him to feel chatty, comfortable enough to give her any behind-the-scenes gossip he might have on his mind. "The podcast is very compelling," she said. "But you already know that."

Danny chuckled. "Thanks. We're proud of it. The public reaction is great, of course, but it's mainly nice to see our work pay off in such a meaningful way, you know? I can only take a little credit, though. Mariah's the real investigative genius behind it all. She got so many people to open up."

Together, they glanced through to where the investigative genius was telling a story in the glow of the candles Kim had lit everywhere. She was making Ed laugh.

"So, are you two together? It's hard to tell."

Again, he chuckled. "No. Strictly professional, though I guess we know each other well enough to be a couple. It's been a long few years with a lot of traveling, but we never got involved. It's emotionally draining work, you know, the prison visits, the uncertainty, the sitting outside people's offices, waiting for them to come out and say 'No comment.' And don't get me started on the endless social media side of things. Doesn't leave a lot left over." He took a sip of wine. "Besides," he added with a touch of archness, "she's a little young for me."

It was flirtation, and it made her blush instantly, not just because it was happening but because she recognized it.

"Let me ask you a question," she said, leaning forward, and spinning her wineglass between her fingertips.

"Shoot."

"Did you all know that Kim was Megan Duvall, who gave Ed an alibi that night at the hotel?"

"Oh, my," said Danny. "You have been paying attention, haven't you? Yes, we knew. But it shouldn't affect your perception of his innocence. They were work acquaintances at most when she originally made that statement and testified and everything else. It was only much later that they started getting close."

"And people just accepted that she was a reliable alibi?"

"What's to accept?" Danny said with a toss of his head. "Other people saw him in that hotel bar, too, and by the time the appeal rolled around, everybody knew the prosecution's case was shot anyway. For the purposes of the podcast, Kim wanted us to call her by her middle name, which she never goes by. She thought it would be more private, and Mariah didn't want to make a big deal about it because she thought it would ruin the lines of the story, so to speak."

Yes, Renee thought. *You wouldn't want to mess up the story.*

"What's your honest opinion?" she asked. "Who do you think killed Julie?"

"You haven't finished the podcast?" He gave her a playful scowl.

"I'm working on it."

He chuckled. "I don't want to spoil anything, but we did come up with a pretty good suspect in episode four, someone local, someone with a good motive. We couldn't prove it, of course, but Ed's pretty sure that's who did it."

He said it with pride, but the words struck ice into Renee's stomach. She thought about Kim and Ed muttering about "you-know-who" on the night of the brick incident. "And do you think this person would be likely to come back?"

He waved a hand. "No, no, definitely not. It's not that kind of thing. Sorry," he added. "I'm used to just talking about crime like it's normal. Hazard of the job."

"Maybe you can help me understand something," she said. "How did Ed get that second trial? I know it had something to do with the prosecutor's office, but what exactly happened?"

"To be honest, none of us expected it, but while we were in the middle of airing the episodes and Ed was filing his last appeal, a bunch of dirt came to light on Raymond Prescott, the commonwealth's attorney. It turned out he had an alleged history of bribing or threatening witnesses. He had a little army of jailhouse informants who would say whatever he wanted in exchange for making charges go away. He allegedly threatened people's immigration status to influence eyewitness testimony. People even said he used his status to get favors from business owners. Like, literally one restaurant said he would flex on them to get free spring rolls. It was wild."

"Wow." She wasn't shocked. She'd known slimeballs before, and Prescott had seemed to fit the mold.

"It's still being litigated," he said, "but there was enough to get him arrested and charged, and it was a come-to-Jesus moment for the rest of the city officials. People wanted to distance themselves from him, even as they might have been scrambling behind the scenes to clean themselves up. But the main thing that happened was that defense attorneys and judges started looking hard at Prescott's previous convictions, and obviously Ed's case was at the top of the list because, as all this was happening, Judge Bowling was considering Ed's appeal, and I think it's no coincidence that just a few days after Prescott's arrest, Bowling granted Ed a new trial on the basis of insufficient evidence."

"But he didn't automatically get off at that point?"

"Oh, it's okay," Danny said, misinterpreting the concern behind the question. "The second trial was fast and perfunctory. Deverell, the new prosecutor, knew they didn't have much to work with, and I think he just went through the motions to get it off his plate. He argued that Ed stood to lose so much if Julie divorced him—social status, public embarrassment, this house." He waved a hand at the marble countertops. "But he still didn't have any means or opportunity to point to, though, and when the jury announced a unanimous verdict of not guilty, pretty much everyone in the room cheered. It was a great moment."

"What do you think of that motive?" she asked, sidestepping her opportunity to comment on the greatness of the moment. "Divorce, embarrassment—is that really a reason someone would murder?"

He shrugged. "Sure, I mean, people kill for less. It's not really about the objective value of a thing that motivates murder—it's the symbolic value to the murderer. The prosecutor was telling this story that Julie represented 'making it' to Ed, and if he lost her, he would be a failure. But that's not really the action of a sane man. Ed's ambitious, sure. He's a social climber and likes the finer things in life, but he isn't irrational. Julie wasn't just some kind of abstract achievement to him."

Kim's footsteps creaked on the stairs above them, and Danny leaned forward to rest his elbows on the counter beside Renee. "Look," he said. "We don't have to just talk about murder. Let me show you around the city sometime. We can go to Maymont park and see the river, or if you like nightlife, Charro's and the Millennium Taproom are really hot right now. But my favorite is to stroll down to a coffee shop called the Postman a couple blocks from here. They make a great latte, and they have couches in the window. Let me give you a local boy's tour."

It was a ridiculous proposition. She wasn't going to make life weirder than it already was by dating one of her employers' only two friends. Simultaneously, however, she enjoyed, for a moment, the idea that while she'd never sat in a coffee shop window, never danced in a nightclub, never kissed anyone but Brandon, Danny seemed to see her as the kind of person who might do any of those things.

She was wondering how to shunt him aside in a friendly way when Kim swept in.

"I've gotten a reprieve," she said, gesturing upward toward where Willow must have gone back to sleep. She took in the kitchen scene with dissatisfaction, as though it were one of her multilayered tablescapes that needed tweaking. "Shall we have dessert? Renee?"

"Yes, of course." Renee set down her glass.

"I think those two will talk podcasts all night if we let them," Kim said, linking her arm through Danny's and leading him back to the others in the parlor. "Surely, it's time to talk about something more fun. We could argue about politics or climate change." She let go of Danny to drape an arm across Ed's shoulders and give him a kiss.

The party wrapped by ten. Ed and Kim went upstairs to put an overtired Oliver to bed and then disappeared to the third floor. Renee moved through the downstairs, turning off lights until only a little glow lingered in the kitchen, where she stayed to finish loading the dishwasher and put away the last of the food. Technically, she should have been off the clock, but if she didn't clean up now, the next morning's breakfast rush would be that much more of a hassle. Besides, there was a satisfying sense of completeness in the peaceful kitchen, a sense of a party well executed. Maybe this job wasn't just the compromise of an inexperienced woman with few options. Maybe she was actually good at it.

She turned off the kitchen light and was about to head upstairs when she heard a woman's voice speaking softly from somewhere. Instinctively, she drifted into the dining room to listen more closely.

"Well, I didn't really call to talk about that."

It was Kim's voice, coming from the family room on the other side of the grand stairs, her soft words bouncing off the exposed brick back to Renee, who made a mental note never to hold any private conversations in that stylish echo chamber.

"I just needed to know we're on the same page. Everything between us has to be completely over. You get that, right?"

There was a pause, and Renee found herself moving closer to the wall, where she was less likely to be spotted if Kim emerged suddenly. She wasn't hiding, exactly, though a more accurate term for what she was doing eluded her.

"Of course not!" Kim hissed. "Why, have *you* been trying to make *me* jealous? Look," she went on, seemingly in response to a mollifying comment from the person on the other end of the call. "I don't regret it either. Neither of us expected him to get out, but the miraculous has happened, and I don't want anything to stand in the way of this second chance we have—first chance, really."

A pause for comment.

"I don't care what I said before. This is what I'm saying now. I have a marriage and a family, and I need to do everything I can to make it work. And don't even tell me that you haven't been seeing other people in the meantime. You'll be fine."

Another pause.

"Whatever. You said you wanted to be casual. This is what casual means. We have to pretend nothing happened. Can you agree to that?"

Another pause and a sigh. "Okay, good. Yep. Bye."

Renee took two giant tiptoe steps back to the kitchen so she could be innocently wiping something in the dark if Kim happened to come this direction, but she didn't. The staircase creaked, followed by a fainter creak from the flight going up to the third floor, and the house was silent.

She stood frozen for a long time. The phone call and its implications made her skin quiver with interest. As she lay in bed an hour later, swaddled in her comforter, eager questions kept her brain from relaxing. If Kim had carried on an affair with someone while Ed was in prison, Renee could see why. Kim had signed on to marry a man who, regardless of his innocence, would probably stay incarcerated for the rest of his life. It was a lonely existence, and sometimes love has to make the best of a bad situation. She really wished she knew more, though: who the person on the other end of the phone was, how long the affair had gone on, why Kim had chosen this moment to reiterate the breakup, and how the dumpee had reacted. She batted these questions away, begging something else to take their place until, finally, the only thing that could replace them did.

Renee and Brandon had kept their relationship a secret for a couple of months after they got back together, partly to avoid gossip and partly because they wanted a chance to enjoy one another's company wholeheartedly for the first time since high school. They reclaimed some of that youthful romance, going on long walks in the nearby state park and having picnics by the river, saving their expressions of affection for remote places where only the squirrels and birds could witness. They loved each other like they had before, but even more wonderfully, they appreciated each other now in a way they hadn't as teenagers. She enjoyed having serious conversations with him, seeing him as an adult, a father, and he made her want to be more grown up and responsible herself.

When it became clear that things were serious between them again, he introduced her to the children as a friend, and the four of them went on short hikes and fishing trips together. Emma and Wyatt were cute, round faced, and a little extra eager for adult attention now that their parents were apart. They soaked up whatever love Renee offered them, and soon, she found herself with more to offer.

Before long, she and Brandon realized they had actually chosen each other, not because of simple proximity but because they really wanted to be together. It was time to tell her parents, time to emerge into the world as a couple.

"What will everyone think?" she asked one evening when they had driven out to the river to eat popcorn and sour candy under the moon.

"Who knows," Brandon said. "But we know we aren't doing anything wrong."

"What about Andrea?"

"She won't care. She's got her own life."

That much was certainly true. Renee knew from general gossip that Andrea had been dating here and there for months. Whether she was actively looking for a partner or simply enjoying her new single status, Renee didn't know or care, but either way, it seemed Andrea really was moving forward with life postmarriage. The way was clear for them.

The news of their rekindled relationship received a lukewarm reception. In fact, the only person who seemed truly happy for her was her brother, Aaron, who sent her a video message from his base at some unknown location.

"I knew it!" he crowed, jiggling the camera with glee. "I knew you two would get back together eventually. You can't hurry love, and you can't stop it!"

Renee's parents, who still thought of Brandon as the flop-haired seventeen-year-old who had slouched around the house a decade before, felt differently.

"Oh, Renee, haven't you had enough time to get over him?" Mama asked.

"He's married to Marvin Gaines's daughter," Daddy said. "Didn't he tell you that?"

"They're only married on paper," Renee said. "They've been separated for more than a year now."

"Married is married," Mama said.

"Why is he still married on paper, then, if it's so over?" Daddy asked.

"Divorce is expensive," Renee said defensively, wishing she hadn't even told them.

The rest of the world, or at least the small portion who cared about Renee's life, seemed to have a similar opinion. Her friend Sarah May said, "I'm happy for you, honey, but married ladies like me just don't like to hear about someone else's marriage falling apart."

When they attended church together for the first, and only, time with Mama and Daddy, a woman in the pew behind them whispered "Homewrecker!" in Renee's ear.

On Valentine's Day, they went to a fundraiser brunch at the volunteer fire department, and one of the church deacons, who had already enjoyed a few beers, launched into a tirade about the sacred bonds of matrimony.

"Maybe we just shouldn't leave the house ever again," Renee said when they were back in the car. "It would be easier."

"Or we could get married," Brandon said, buckling his seat belt.

"What? Because that drunk jerk made a big deal about it?"

"No. Because I want to marry you."

Her first impulse was to laugh. Surely, he wasn't serious, talking about marriage here in the parking lot after the least romantic Valentine's brunch in history, but the way he was grinning at her, expectation sparkling in his green eyes, made her pause.

"What do you think about that?"

"I think . . ." she said, the idea growing possible for the first time, even as she said the words. "I think I want to marry you too."

They considered themselves engaged after that. For a week or so, they basked in the idea of really being together, getting a place of their own, setting up rooms for Brandon's kids to stay with them part-time, and building a happy home. Renee felt lightheaded all day every day. She was about to go from living in her childhood bedroom and being a somewhat directionless social pariah to being a real adult with her own family to care for and her own life to lead.

But of course, the biggest obstacle to their wedding was Brandon's existing marriage. In late February, he went online and drew up divorce papers with the help of some free websites. He and Renee decided that after work on one Thursday night, he would go to Andrea's and serve her the papers. They would talk, negotiating how to move forward with custody and anything else that needed to be done.

Then he would get in his car and drive the seventeen miles west to Farmville, the closest large town, where Renee would have booked a hotel room. They would have a late dinner out at a real restaurant, where no one knew them to yell at them, and spend the night alone together, a real couple at last.

When Renee left the house that afternoon, she gave her parents a rough outline of what was happening. They seemed to vaguely disapprove, of which part she wasn't sure. Nor did she care. She felt elated as she drove toward Farmville, as if she were reaching out and taking a piece of happiness the world had told her she wasn't allowed to have. She didn't even care that the weather was crummy, cold rain causing the temperature to drop and the sky to grow prematurely dark.

She checked in to the hotel room and made a reservation at the restaurant. Then she kicked off her shoes and watched TV in bed until around 7:00 p.m., when she received a text from Brandon.

> Had the talk. Could have gone better, but it's fine. Main thing is it's over now. I love you! Headed your way.

I love you, Renee texted back. See you soon!

But an hour went by, and Brandon didn't arrive. He didn't respond to texts or calls. She pushed the dinner reservation back twice and then finally canceled it, not knowing what else to do.

She lay in bed with the light on, unable to get warm, bargaining with herself that she would surely hear from Brandon by midnight. Or by 2:00 a.m. Or at least by morning.

But she didn't.

When it was daylight, she checked out of the hotel and drove home, exhausted and terrified. It was later that day when she finally found out what happened. Brandon's car had hit a patch of ice on the road that night and he'd skidded off into a tree. He died before paramedics arrived. His emergency contact was Andrea, so she was the one who got the call from the hospital. It was also Andrea who called Renee the afternoon after his death.

They'd never spoken on the phone before, and Andrea conveyed the news in curt, perfunctory terms, either too traumatized or too angry at how her last conversation with Brandon had gone to offer anything in the way of sympathy to Renee.

She went to bed and lay in the dark for days.

Brandon's family handled the funeral arrangements, and Renee attended with her parents, sitting somewhere in the middle of the church. She kept her head down for most of the service, partly to avoid making eye contact with anyone, and partly because she just didn't have the energy to raise her head.

Andrea was among those who spoke. "Brandon was the most kind and loving person I have ever met," she said. "He loved our family and our two beautiful children more than anything. Marriage is always hard. Anybody who says otherwise hasn't tried it." Here she mustered a tearful smile for the assembled mourners, who chuckled back. "But Brandon and I would do anything for each other, and we were looking forward to strengthening our marriage bond in the years ahead. I just can't believe we won't get to do that."

As soon as the next hymn started, Renee slipped out of the pew and hurried outside to sob in the car. She knew why Andrea had done it. The other woman had lost the father of her children in a shocking turn of events, and she wanted people to remember a narrative about a committed, loyal couple, not one where Brandon's last act had been to serve her divorce papers. But to be written out of his story altogether—Renee couldn't bear that.

She went into seclusion for several months, barely stepping off the Christmas tree farm. Sarah May checked in on her a few times, but Renee didn't give her much positive reinforcement for doing so, and that was a good enough excuse for Sarah May to stop trying, to stop associating herself with the sinner in this town's parable. Mama and

Daddy did what they could to take care of her. As uncomfortable as Mama clearly was with the situation, she seemed to understand that the magnitude of Renee's grief left no room for judgmental comments, so she provided food, clean laundry, and silence. Daddy gave her a few commiserating pats before pulling on his work boots. "Best to get back to it," he said.

Which was all fine and well except she had no *it* to get back to.

Finally, it was Aaron who gave her something new to think about. "If there's one thing you think would help," he said one day when they had managed to coordinate a rare video call, "what would it be? Even if it doesn't seem possible."

"I need to get out of here," Renee said, looking around at the pink and purple accents of her bedroom. "I need to get out of this house and out of this town."

"I think that's doable," Aaron said. "You just need a plan."

With his help, she had made a plan, one that had brought her here, to the Weatherups' kitchen, where she washed endless dishes while her employers went about their lives. Yes, there were uncomfortable things about this house, the unsolved homicide being top of the list, obviously. But there were also the children's sadness and her nagging suspicions that the podcast didn't tell the whole story. No, it wasn't ideal, but it was better than lying in bed in the dark, ears filling up with her own tears.

CHAPTER 9

The next day, Saturday, a day off for Renee at the end of her third week on Linden Avenue, began on a sour note. Caz arrived home early, unrepentant and only intending to stay long enough to grab breakfast before her calculus tutoring.

"You don't want to see your brother and sister?" Kim asked as Caz wolfed down some toaster waffles while standing at the kitchen island.

"Do you want me to do that instead of going to tutoring?" Caz asked. "You already complained about how much it was costing."

"I just think it would be nice for you to act like part of the family sometimes," Kim said, her tone dropping as though she was already aware she'd started a battle she wouldn't win.

Renee, who had only come down to get herself some toast, hustled back upstairs before she could witness the end of the scene. She felt annoyed on Caz's behalf. If Kim really did intend to make her new family work, as she had claimed to her former paramour on the phone the night before, she was going to need a new, more thoughtful tactic with the teenager.

In her room, Renee opened her laptop and was queuing up something soapy to relax with when her phone pinged with another message from Andrea.

I'm serious. Call me. This can't wait.

After Brandon had been so much on her mind lately, she somehow felt guilty ignoring Andrea, so she left the message sitting in her inbox, as if that were more respectful than deleting it. She snapped her laptop shut with a sigh. She needed a walk, a change of scene.

Outside, it was a bright fall day, just cool enough to require a sweatshirt, with a breeze that rustled through the craggy-barked trees and along the painted brick facades of the imposing Victorians. She ought to clear her head, to be alone with herself for a while, Renee thought. Instead, she put in her earbuds.

Innocent Blood, Episode Four: "Not as Perfect"

MARIAH: I'm Mariah Cusmano, and this is *Innocent Blood*. Listener discretion advised.

When you're trying to understand a murder, the first place to start is with the victim's life. We want to know as much as possible about who the victim was, how she spent her time, and who she associated with so we can know what bad actors she might have encountered. It's just one of many ways a victim loses her privacy after a murder. The crime scene technicians sift through her home and belongings; the medical examiner pries into the very secrets of her body; and investigators, detectives, and journalists alike explore her decisions and relationships. All these intrusions are necessary if we want to know the truth, to punish a perpetrator, or give answers to a grieving family, but it's an intrusion, nonetheless.

Simultaneously, there's value in seeing Julie as a whole person. She was an active inhabitant of her own life and a charismatic participant in the lives of her family, coworkers, friends, and clients.

I went to the law firm of Cygnet and Obermeyer to ask Micheline Cygnet whether Julie might have made any enemies at work.

MICHELINE: [voice on tape] The world of law is all about adversaries, you know. Any lawyer has adversaries: opposing counsel, judges they don't get along with, clients who didn't get the result they wanted. From the outside, lots of these people might look like enemies, but I think lawyers don't really see it that way. You win some, you lose some, you know?

MARIAH: [voice on tape] So, was there anyone in Julie's life who might have graduated from adversary to actual enemy? Was there anyone she was afraid of?

MICHELINE: Well, there was one very unfortunate situation with a pro bono client Julie represented about six years before her death. He was a young man, probably seventeen years old when she first took him on, named Charles Perkins. He was accused of selling narcotics and a couple of weapons charges, fairly standard stuff for a young low-level gang member, which is what Charlie allegedly was. It was a sad story, of course. He had a truly terrible childhood and no meaningful support network, so when Julie took him on, he really clung to her. I think he saw her as a mother figure, as a savior, and she really put in the hours on that case. Unfortunately, he did get convicted and sentenced to five years in prison. Anyone familiar with this type of case knows that the sentence could have been much worse, es-

pecially in a court system that doesn't look sympathetically on young offenders of color, but Charlie didn't see it as a success in any way. He wrote to her from prison all the time, all kinds of letters. He blamed her, but he also wanted her to keep helping him. When she made it clear that she couldn't do anything else for him, the threats started.
MARIAH: What kind of threats?
MICHELINE: Standard stuff, really. "You're going to die," "I'll make you pay," that kind of thing. I think it hurt Julie's feelings more than it scared her. Charlie was a young man who the world had stepped on, and she really wished she could have done more for him, and, maybe selfishly, she wished he understood she'd done everything she could.
MARIAH: Was it ever more than just threats?
MICHELINE: Yes, unfortunately. Charlie was paroled in February of 2018. Almost immediately, Julie started getting hang-up calls from the phone at the halfway house where Charlie was staying. She strongly suspected it was him, but she didn't report it because she didn't want him to get into trouble. About a month later, one afternoon when she was home with the kids, Charlie showed up, banging on the door, very distraught. He was yelling at her, and he said he had a gun.
MARIAH: He *said* he had a gun?
MICHELINE: Yeah, Julie thought he was lying about that, actually. The children were scared, but Julie always had a cool head. She said she invited Charlie in and made a pot of coffee. They sat in the kitchen and had a long talk.
MARIAH: Do you know what they talked about?

MICHELINE: Not really. Julie just said later, "We had a good talk." And then Charlie went away, I guess. Ed was furious when he found out about it, though. He was so angry that she let a supposedly armed ex-con into the house with the children, someone who had sent death threats, no less. Julie said to me, "Ed was like, 'What if something happened to you?'" She said, "I get why he was angry, but it was just Charlie. I knew he didn't really want to hurt anyone." After that, Ed had a security system installed. That was all just a few weeks before she died. I remember Julie talking about this at the time, but they also covered it in depth at the trial.

MARIAH: Were there security cameras?

MICHELINE: No. Wouldn't that have been nice.

MARIAH: What did the security-system log look like on the night Julie died?

MICHELINE: Investigators said the system log indicated that the house remained locked after the family left for the day. Then it shows that Julie's code unlocked the front door around seven, seven thirty that evening and relocked right away. We assume that's her coming home. Then around 12:45 a.m., someone uses Julie's code to disable the system again, and it stays off for the rest of the night.

MARIAH: So, they think Ed arrived at the house barely more than an hour after he said good night to his coworkers at the hotel in Baltimore?

MICHELINE: That's the official theory.

MARIAH: What do you think?

MICHELINE: I don't have any official opinions. All I know is that after Ed lost his case, I wouldn't hire

Conrad Harrington to defend me if I got a parking ticket.

MARIAH: What do you mean?

MICHELINE: Look, I think Harrington did his best to point out that it's unreasonable to think Ed could have made that trip, but he was outshouted by the so-called expert witnesses and the public's bloodlust. Even so, he could have done more to present alternate theories of the crime. Ed wasn't the only obvious suspect for Julie's murder, you know.

MARIAH: Are you talking about Charles Perkins?

MICHELINE: Yes, for starters. I put one of our investigators on him after Julie died. He learned that Charlie went missing from his halfway house on the night of April 6 and didn't return until early the next morning. His fellow residents later reported that he'd been sneaking out after curfew several nights a week before that date. If gossip is to be believed, he was keeping appointments with members of his former gang. I've seen it before. Gangs try to get recent parolees back into the fold as quickly as they can. He'd served prison time for them, and that would make him a high-value pawn in their business. This is, of course, speculation on my part, but it does happen. They promise promotions and other incentives to work for them again, or take the fall for them again, more likely. The bottom line, though, is that no one knew where Charlie was on the night Julie died. He might have paid her another visit. I'm not saying he did, of course, but she'd let him into the house once before, and she might easily have done it again.

MARIAH: Was Charlie ever questioned?
MICHELINE: Briefly, I think. He went back to prison a few months later for some parole violation. Either way, though, police didn't seem to pursue him seriously.
MARIAH: [voice in studio] I showed Micheline the anonymous threatening messages I had received when I started investigating Ed's case.
MARIAH: [voice on tape] Do you have any idea who might be this upset about me investigating here?
MICHELINE: Oh, any number of people, I would imagine. The prosecutor's office and associated staff won't be happy about potentially being embarrassed, and same goes for Richmond PD. But let's face it, if you manage to make a case for Ed's innocence here, assuming that's what you intend, the people who have the most to lose are the other suspects in the case. You've heard about the voicemail, right? And then, of course, there's the witches angle.
MARIAH: [in studio] To understand what Micheline calls the "witches angle," we have to go back to some names we've heard before, specifically Stephanie Kowalski and her young daughter Hadley. You may remember that on the night Julie died, her daughter, Catherine, was having a sleepover at the Kowalski house. According to Stephanie's original statement, she got the two girls from school that Friday afternoon, and they picked up pizza for dinner on the way back to the Kowalski home, which was about a half mile from the Weatherup house.
STEPHANIE: Hadley and Catherine did what any other pair of girls would do at a sleepover. They watched a couple of movies, braided each other's hair. I think

they did pedicures and painted their nails. I put Hadley's younger brothers to bed at maybe 9:00 p.m. An hour later, I checked on the girls. They were in Hadley's room. She had this little trundle bed at the time, and Catherine was going to sleep there. They were in their pajamas, and I told them it was time for lights-out. I'm sure they stayed up talking for some time after that, but they were good girls. I figured they were just going to stay in bed until they fell asleep.

MARIAH: Was that the last time you saw them that night?

STEPHANIE: No. I got up around 3:30 a.m. to use the bathroom, and I checked in on all the kids at that point. The girls were sound asleep in their beds. The house was completely quiet all night.

MARIAH: [in studio] It was a straightforward enough story, and no one questioned it during the initial investigation. That all changed a couple months later, when Hadley Kowalski walked into the Richmond Police station and asked to make a statement. Hadley is one year older than Catherine, which made her thirteen at the time of Julie's murder and fourteen when she arrived, alone, at Richmond PD. Officers moved her into an interview room, where they offered to get her water or call a parent for her. She declined both. Official camera footage shows Hadley waiting alone in the interview room for a few minutes. She looks tall and poised for her age, with long brown hair and a pulled-together style. She seems at ease in the sterile surroundings of the interview room, crossing her legs and tapping one foot lightly as if simply waiting for her number to be called at a deli.

About seven minutes after she arrives in the room, something striking happens, something that has been analyzed countless times by psychologists, armchair detectives, and YouTube pundits. Hadley raises her eyes and looks directly at the camera. She stares for a moment without expression, and then breaks into a smile, as if recognizing someone, and speaks quietly to the camera. Here's an audio clip.

[light background static, rustling]

HADLEY: [voice on police interview tape] Glory to you, Lady of Darkness.

MARIAH: Detective Evans, the principal investigator on the Weatherup case, enters the room a few moments later and introduces himself. He sits down across the table from her.

EVANS: [voice on police interview tape] So you said you had information about a serious crime.

HADLEY: Yes, I know who killed Mrs. Weatherup.

EVANS: And who was that?

HADLEY: Catherine. Well, Catherine and me.

MARIAH: The story Hadley tells is as bizarre as her demeanor while telling it. She says that on the day she got her first period, she began worshipping a deity called the Lady of Darkness. In Hadley's telling, the Lady of Darkness seems to be an amalgam of several pagan ideals, part earth goddess, part evil witch, who can grant young women special powers if they make a sacrifice of innocent blood to her. Hadley says that she began grooming Catherine to help her make this sacrifice the year prior to Julie's death.

EVANS: Why Catherine? Why go after her and her mother?

HADLEY: Catherine seemed ready for it, you know? She wanted to know more about having powers and being a real woman in this world. I thought we could kill her mother together and then move on with our lives.

EVANS: How about you tell me how the night went down?

HADLEY: We pretended to go to bed, and then when everyone was asleep, we sneaked out of the house.

EVANS: How did you get out, door or window?

HADLEY: We just walked out of the front door. We walked down to their house, and Catherine let us in with her key.

EVANS: Did you have to disarm the security system?

HADLEY: Catherine took care of all that.

EVANS: And what time was that?

HADLEY: Around midnight. You know, the witching hour.

MARIAH: Hadley speaks in a calm tone. At times she smiles or laughs as if she and the detective are having a chat over coffee. She tells a story about how she and Catherine go upstairs and find Catherine's mother in her bed. They lure her out onto the rooftop deck under the pretext of seeing a beautiful moon. There, Hadley claims, the two girls work together to murder Julie, and used her blood to complete a ritual to the Lady of Darkness. They then go back to the Kowalski house and are back in bed by the time Stephanie checks in on them around 3:30 a.m.

Hadley gives a lurid account of the murder, but I'm skipping over most of that here because it's unnecessarily gruesome, and also because it probably didn't happen. While, of course, Catherine's fingerprints and

DNA were found in quantity at the Weatherup house, there was no physical evidence of Hadley's presence there. Hadley stuck to her ritual-sacrifice story through several rounds of questioning, but Catherine consistently denied being part of her mother's murder. No charges were ever filed against the two girls, and neither of them were asked to testify for either side during Ed's trial.

Now, obviously, Hadley's story is far fetched. The concept of the Lady of Darkness seems more like a teen fantasy than something that would motivate an otherwise normal young person to kill. It also seems unlikely that Hadley would have been able to convince Catherine to participate in the crime. Hadley's confession, true or otherwise, does remind us of two important things, however. The first is that there are several occasions when other people might have entered the Weatherup house that night, including people Julie knew and trusted. The other takeaway from this chapter in the saga is that there were several interesting stories that never made an appearance at Ed's trial, further evidence that Prescott and his team of prosecutors turned their attention single-mindedly to Ed, even when there were other suspects to pursue.

Chief among those suspects is a man named Arlo Ardell, for whom Julie left that chilling voicemail on the night of her death.

We'll hear that voicemail again now so what I'm about to describe makes sense.

JULIE: [voice on voicemail] What are you doing here?

Renee jabbed her finger at the fast-forward button. She'd already heard enough of that recording. It was a little gross, she thought, playing Julie's last words for shock value once, let alone twice. Maybe Mariah could be excused because of how inexperienced she was, but Danny or someone else should have taken a heavier hand with editing.

> MARIAH: To understand the mysterious voicemail Julie recorded on the night she died and the person she left it for, Arlo Ardell, we have to jump back in time to the mid-nineties and travel to the Virginia Beach community where she grew up. Only then can we begin to theorize what she meant with her cryptic words "It's over and I'm empty."
> Julie attended a small private school in a wealthy neighborhood. Here's Bethany Davis, a close friend from that time.
> BETHANY: [voice on interview tape] It was a tight community. Everybody knew everybody, that sort of thing. Look, here we are. That's me and Julie. I'd say we're about fourteen here. Look at that frizzy hair! We thought we were so in vogue. [laughter] We weren't, but we thought we were. [laughter]
> MARIAH: Bethany shows me some old photos of their high school years. Julie is a sunny looking teenager with a big smile and a wardrobe full of colorful T-shirts. In yearbook pictures she looks more formal, dressed in sweaters, her hair pulled back. In her senior photo, she's wearing a suit.
> BETHANY: Julie always had big plans for herself. She knew she wanted to go to law school when she was maybe just twelve years old, and she never deviated from that plan. She did all the extracurriculars, Model UN, debate team, all the stuff that would

help her get into a good college. She would go to the parties, hang out with people, but she never drank, and she never missed curfew. I used to tell her, "Julie, baby, you're a teenager, you gotta cut loose, like, once or twice," but she would just grin at me.

MARIAH: [voice on interview tape] Did she date?

BETHANY: Barely. I mean, she had a couple boyfriends, but I'm not sure how serious they were.

MARIAH: Was Arlo Ardell one of those boyfriends?

BETHANY: No, definitely not. We knew Arlo, of course, but we didn't exactly run in the same social circle. He wasn't the clean-cut, respectful type she dated. He was a moody, artsy kid who let his hair grow and wore metal necklaces. He was a little bit punk, you know? In our eyes, he seemed like a bad boy, I think, but what did we know? Probably the worst thing he ever did was smoke a joint once or twice. It would be kind of charming if it hadn't ended the way it did. Bottom line, though, Julie was completely smitten with Arlo. We'd show up to a party, and she'd be looking around for him on the sly, and when she saw him, she'd sort of make her way over until they happened to run into each other. She was like a moth to the flame. Arlo liked to play it cool. He didn't fawn over her, but I think that was just part of the mystique he cultivated about himself. I think their attraction was mutual. He would flirt with her for hours sometimes. They would stand closer and closer together.

MARIAH: Is that as far as it went? Flirting?

BETHANY: I think so. Arlo wasn't part of what I used to call her "thirty-five-step plan for success." I think she denied herself a real fling with him.

MARIAH: [voice in studio] As far as her friends know, Julie lost contact with Arlo after high school. She went on to college and law school, where she met and married Ed. But something brought her and Arlo back into contact before her death.

I tried getting in touch with Arlo. My producer and I left him voice messages, sent him emails, and tried to contact him through social media. It took a few months before we heard a response, at which point he left me a voicemail of his own.

ARLO: [voice on tape] You have to stop harassing me with these calls and Facebook messages. If I wanted to talk to you or anyone else about this, I would have, right? Okay? Don't call again.

MARIAH: My producer, Danny, left him one more message to clarify that we weren't trying to harass him, and then we respected his wishes. We didn't contact him again. A couple more months went by, and then everything changed for all of us here at *Innocent Blood*.

On August 4, 2021, the first episode of this podcast launched for the world to hear. We didn't know what to expect, and we tried to be prepared for any reaction. Ed and Julie's story is a controversial one, and something many people already had strong feelings about. But more than that, we hoped we had treated the story respectfully and with all due diligence. I'm not sure we were prepared for what happened. Within a week, *Innocent Blood* had surged to the top of the charts. Our show had come to the attention of Shelby and Sydney Myers, sisters and cohosts of the hit podcast *Shelby and Syd Do True Crime*, and they had given us a shout-out on their recent episode.

SHELBY: [voice on podcast] For today's "Props Minute," I want to give major props to this new podcast just coming out. It's called *Innocent Blood*, and the story is just bonkers!

MARIAH: Soon, *Innocent Blood* was getting attention in the mainstream media, on news programs and talk shows.

MAN, ANNOUNCER'S VOICE: The controversial case involving the murder of local Richmond woman Julie Weatherup is back in the public eye again thanks to the podcast *Innocent Blood*, which has begun asking questions about the conviction of Weatherup's husband. The popularity of this podcast has underscored once again the public appetite for true crime content, and here to talk about it with us is city correspondent . . .

WOMAN, TV PERSONALITY'S VOICE: Ladies, I have to tell you, I can't get enough of this new podcast *Innocent Blood*. Once again, we just have to ask the question—you know the one I'm talking about—did the husband do it?

MARIAH: In the middle of this media storm, I got a call from Arlo Ardell. He said he was ready to talk. He invited us to his condo in Southside, and Danny and I agreed to meet him there. We paused in the parking lot to gather our equipment.

DANNY: [voice on tape] Are you sure you feel good about this? We don't know a lot about this guy.

MARIAH: [voice on tape] Yeah, I mean, we have to get his statement, right? And he's willing to talk to us.

DANNY: I guess I just wonder why he wants to talk now.

MARIAH: [voice in studio] We picked up our recording equipment and went up to the apartment. Arlo seemed resigned to our presence as he ushered us into his sparsely furnished living room. Julie's high school friend Bethany had described teenage Arlo as being a "little bit punk," and though he was older now, that description still applied. His dark hair was carefully tousled, and he wore a slim-fitting black sweater and several rings on his fingers.

ARLO: [voice on tape] Just sit wherever. Yeah.

MARIAH: I wonder if you could just start by telling us how you and Julie knew each other.

ARLO: We went to high school together. I wouldn't say we were friends, exactly, but we would hang out, talk sometimes.

MARIAH: Were you romantically involved?

ARLO: No. Or yes, but not the way you mean. It was a chemical thing between us. We both felt it. I think people in proximity felt it, it was that strong. But we never acted on it back then. After high school we drifted apart the way most people do. We went to different colleges, and social media wasn't really a thing back then. I got married; she got married at some point, obviously. We went for more than a decade without talking.

MARIAH: How did you reconnect?

ARLO: It was around Christmas in 2015. Julie was back in Virginia Beach visiting her parents for the holiday. She had her kids and husband along. I was also back there to visit my folks, but my wife didn't come with me that time. I was just out at a coffee shop standing in line, and I heard her say my name. I just turned around, and she was standing there with this big smile on her face. We talked for a while, and it just felt like old times. We traded information and found out that we both lived in the Richmond area. After the holidays, she connected with me on social media, and we started exchanging messages.

At first it was just reminiscing about old times, but then we started having real conversations about big life stuff. She talked to me about being a parent and a lawyer. I talked to her about graphic design and my aspirations. Then we started talking about our marriages. Back when we were kids, we used to have these deep conversations about life. Other kids would be copping a feel in a closet somewhere, and we would just talk. I think that's why, after we reconnected, we were able to be honest with each other in a way we weren't with other people.

The truth is, we weren't happy in our marriages—not happy enough, anyway. My wife and I got married young. We had all these dreams of being artists and traveling the world and stuff, but life got on top of us. Julie, on the other hand, had achieved so much, but she didn't have the romance she wanted. She told me that she married Ed because she liked his ambition and she thought they would make a good team that could go places, but once they got settled in their life, he stopped trying. He stalled out at work, missing promotions, taking on as few responsibilities as he could, so he had time to play golf and putz around the house in his sweats. She wasn't ready to give up their life together yet, but he just didn't excite her anymore. But I did.

MARIAH: What do you mean?

ARLO: We still had that same chemistry between us. It was like part of us had been waiting for each other all this time. We had drinks one night when her husband had taken the kids to a movie. It was around Christmas, again, and we met at this restaurant that was all lit up with lights and candles. Two drinks in, we were [beep] in the bathroom like high school kids. We were each other's unfinished business, me and Julie.
MARIAH: How long did the affair last?
ARLO: I wouldn't even call it an affair.
MARIAH: What would you call it?
ARLO: It was an outlet, a celebration of a part of ourselves no one else could see. We used to meet up a few times a year, whenever we could find a couple hours where no one would miss us. We'd have drinks, maybe dinner, and slip away to find somewhere for sex. We'd [beep] in motel rooms, in our cars, in department store changing rooms. [laughter] It was fast, dirty, and exciting.
MARIAH: And how long did it last?
ARLO: It never really ended. I mean, it was still going when she died. She was making moves to leave Ed at that point. I'm not saying she was leaving him for me, but she was leaving him.
MARIAH: How do you know that?
ARLO: Well, the last time we saw each other was in February of 2018. It was right before Valentine's Day, actually, and we slipped away on a Friday night when my wife was visiting her parents. Julie told Ed she was hanging out with work friends. We got a room at this little historic bed-and-breakfast in Ashland, where no one would recognize us. They had a fireplace, and we sat there drinking scotch

and talking. It was different from our other dates. Don't get me wrong, we put the bed to good use, [laughter] but we talked a long time. Julie told me she couldn't go on with how things were.

MARIAH: Couldn't go on how?

ARLO: She just said, "I can't go on with everything the way it is now." And then at the trial, they said she talked to a divorce attorney, and I knew I was right.

MARIAH: That sounds kind of vague. Did you ever wonder if maybe she was thinking about breaking things off with you instead of Ed?

ARLO: No, that doesn't sound right to me. Maybe we only got to see each other every few months, but Julie and I were soulmates. She had a beautiful home and a rich life, but she would leave all of that to meet me. I possessed a part of her that her husband probably never even knew about.

MARIAH: What happened after the night at the bed-and-breakfast?

ARLO: Nothing abnormal. We parted ways late that night. I stayed in the room—it was paid for—and she went home after she knew Ed and the kids would be asleep. We didn't have any more contact until the night she died.

MARIAH: Was that normal, that you wouldn't be in touch?

ARLO: It wasn't abnormal. I'll be honest, my marriage was on the rocks at that point. My wife was getting suspicious, so Julie and I didn't exchange messages that often. We'd meet up, then go radio silent for a couple months. The day Julie died, my wife and I had a fight, one of many, and she decided to spend the weekend with her parents. I bought myself a bottle of scotch, turned off my phone, and passed out. When I woke up, there was that message from Julie. I tried to call her back. Some cop answered. That was how I found out she was dead.

MARIAH: So, you didn't go to Julie's house that night? Her husband was out of town. It seems like the perfect opportunity for you two to get together.

ARLO: No, like I said, I didn't go anywhere.

MARIAH: On that voicemail, Julie says the following. "What are you doing here? We already talked about this, and there's nothing more to say. It's over and I'm empty. What are you talking about? What have you done? This is cab!" And then she says the word *stop* twice and the word *no*. What did that message mean to you?

ARLO: I've always assumed that she pocket dialed my phone while she was breaking up with Ed. She was telling him it was over, obviously. Maybe she even called me on purpose to have a record of the conversation for her lawyer.

MARIAH: And what about "This is cab"? What do you think that means?

ARLO: I have no idea, but it's a recording made in the heat of the moment. Maybe she stumbled over her words or said something else, and we just think she said the word *cab*.

MARIAH: What about "Stop, stop"?

ARLO: Well, I assume that's when he attacked her. You know, the husband.

MARIAH: [voice in studio] Arlo, like the prosecutor's office, finds the voicemail to be a fluke event that supports the narrative of Ed's guilt. They believe that if a married woman is fighting with someone, it must be her husband, and they dismiss parts of the recording they cannot explain, but this seems quite narrow minded to me.

In the interests of pushing back on Commonwealth Attorney Prescott's theory of the crime, I want to propose my own hypothetical explanation of the voicemail. On the evening of April 6, Julie was about to enjoy a rare night at home with no children or husband. It seems like the ideal chance to see the man she'd been carrying on an affair with. Arlo, whose movements cannot be verified, may have come over to the Weatherup house. Arlo and Julie may have gotten into an argument about the future of their relationship. Julie may have been reconsidering what she wanted, and he, a person who seems proud to have, in his words, possessed a woman, admits that his marriage was rocky. Her phone may have placed a call to his phone that night, not because of a pocket dial, but because it may have misinterpreted Julie speaking Arlo's name out loud as a voice command. When she says "This is cab," she may, in fact, be indicating that she has called a taxi and wants the person she's arguing with to leave. All of this is complete conjecture, of course, and there is no clear evidence that Arlo Ardell was present at the Weatherup home at any point, but the idea that the phone call captures Julie arguing with Ed is complete conjecture as well. The truth is that only someone who was in the house that night could have understood the context for the phone call, someone who witnessed or even participated in Julie's death. Sadly, the search for that person continues, next time, on *Innocent Blood*.

CHAPTER 10

Renee looked up, startled to discover that she had no idea where she was. She had crossed through the university district, where pizza and bubble tea shops lined the streets and young people crossed at the intersections in herds. As she walked, she had drifted semiconsciously away from high-traffic areas toward quieter, more residential streets, where she could hear Mariah's voice more clearly through her earbuds. She had ended up in what felt like a completely different part of town than where she'd started. Instead of tall, narrow row houses and taller apartment buildings, she was surrounded by boxy one-story houses covered in white and yellow siding. Chain-link fences enclosed small yards, and trash cans lined up in front of each house. Nearby, the paved road gave way to a gravel track leading to a deserted-looking electrical substation the size of an elementary school. Beyond that were weeds and, beyond that, the echoing noise of an interstate she couldn't see. Only a couple of hours had passed since she left the house, but it felt as if she'd walked to the end of the earth.

The mental image of Hadley Kowalski looking up at the police surveillance camera creeped her out, and the idea that hardworking, virtuous Julie had a private affair with strange, disheveled Arlo unsettled her.

She wanted to get back on familiar footing, literally, but she had no idea how to begin retracing her steps. Each of these odd little streets looked the same. It didn't help that her phone, a late-model something paid for by her parents' budget phone plan, couldn't seem to connect to the satellite enough to access a map. She should have acted sooner to get her own phone plan. She should have paid better attention to where she was going. She should have done anything else besides end up here. But of course, she'd wandered away from the city given the first opportunity. She didn't belong there.

When she called Kim, her employer answered with a brusque "Hello?" In the background, Willow wailed.

Her cheeks hot with shame, she explained the situation.

"What cross street are you at?" Kim asked. "I'll send Ed. Sit tight," she added, a little more gently.

Renee sat down on the curb to wait, tugging her jacket around her. It was barely 3:00 p.m., but clouds had rolled in, and the day was cooling. Crows, large and glossy, landed on the fence surrounding the substation and cawed loudly to each other. If there had been any doubt before, there wasn't now: Summer was truly over.

The Weatherups' green SUV pulled around the corner and slowed to a halt in front of her. Ed leaned across to unlock the passenger door and gave her a wave.

"Sorry about this," she said, getting in. "I know this isn't how things should work."

"Don't worry about it," he said. "You're new to town, but I honestly don't know how you found this little place back here."

He navigated the curving streets of the neighborhood away from the highway and the substation, and Renee realized that this was the first time they had really been alone together. It felt too personal after listening to the podcast account of his wife's affair. The only way she could think of to ease the awkwardness was to continue apologizing. "I would have gotten back on my own, but my phone gets terrible signal sometimes. I'm going to upgrade it as soon as I can, so this won't happen again."

"It's okay, Renee," Ed said again. "When you get a better phone, we'll get you set up with some kind of rideshare app so you don't have to worry about getting stranded. And you won't be tempted to try hacking," he added, with a chuckle and a sideways glance at her.

"Hacking?"

They had pulled up to a red light now, and on the other side of the intersection was a barber shop and florist she thought she remembered seeing on her walk.

"It's getting an unlicensed cab. Basically, hitchhiking but in the city." He took one hand off the wheel of the car and made a gesture, his arm down, two fingers waggling, as if signaling a car, though there was an uncomfortable suggestiveness to the gesture, compounded by the smile and wink he gave her. "Just being silly," he added, in response to her startled expression. "Obviously it's not safe, especially for a nice young lady such as yourself. You don't want to just get in the car with a strange man."

Nothing made her feel less safe than a man coyly pointing out how dangerous men could be.

The light turned green, and they were moving again. She forced herself to look ahead and not stare at the firm-jawed man with the salt-and-pepper hair beside her: father, suspect, ex-con, podcast celebrity, near stranger. She actually really didn't like Ed. It was the first time she'd admitted that to herself. She didn't like the way he seemed entitled to the attention of everyone around him, and she really didn't like his insensitivity to the pain his children carried with them.

"How do you think things are going?" she blurted.

"What?" he said again.

"I mean with me. Is there anything I should be doing to help you out more?" It was the absolute opposite of what she thought—Ed didn't need other people doing more things for him—but as the words came out of her mouth, she realized she felt a pressing need to ingratiate herself in that moment. "I mean, besides not getting lost," she added with a forced laugh.

They were pulling onto Linden Avenue now, and Ed found a parking spot. "Don't worry about me, Renee." He turned, bracing his hand on the back of her headrest as he prepared to parallel park, a gesture that brought them unexpectedly face-to-face. She smelled a hint of cologne, something smoky and subtle she hadn't noticed before. He met her eyes and gave her a slow smile. "I can take care of myself."

Later, Renee lay in bed trying to enjoy a day-off nap, but she couldn't. Downstairs, she could hear Oliver's voice plaintively raised, and she bet Willow would be crying shortly as well. It felt sad to hear the oncoming meltdown and not do something to help.

But worse than that, she couldn't stop thinking about the conversation with Ed. It was the most bizarre thing, but she thought he might have told her exactly how he could have procured transport home on the night of Julie's death.

And he seemed to have told her on purpose, as if it didn't matter that she knew.

CHAPTER 11

The next day, Renee found herself monitoring Ed's movements around the house and feeling more comfortable when he was gone. As she packed school lunches and made beds, she felt fixated on how uneasy he had made her in the car. She didn't know if it was just the normal discomfort of a woman alone with a man she didn't know very well, or if there was something more. But in the meantime, there were other things to deal with.

She bought a new phone, a milestone on her journey of independence, and used it to search, alternately, for the names Edward Weatherup and Arlo Ardell. There were hundreds of hits on Ed's name, but articles about the murder case had eclipsed any web presence he might have had before Julie's death. Arlo, on the other hand, had a modest online trail revealing that the ensuing years had brought him physically much closer to the Weatherup orbit than Renee would have guessed, closer than she was comfortable with.

He was working now as an instructor in the graphic design department of Richmond University, just blocks away from the Weatherup house. She found a picture on his faculty profile. Mariah's description of him was accurate enough. His hair was still dark—carefully colored, perhaps—and he was signaling his artistic bent with a ring in one ear and a tattoo peeking out of his collar. Attractive? Sleezy? Renee couldn't quite tell. Either way, this was the man the podcasters seemed to think was the best suspect in Julie's death. She wondered how he felt about his portrayal in the podcast. Would he be angry enough about Ed's acquittal to saunter down the street in the middle of the night and throw a brick through the window?

As she looked at the picture and browsed Arlo's teaching schedule on the RU online course matrix, she thought maybe her experience with Brandon had given her some kind of kinship with Julie. She, too, knew what it was like to have unfinished business.

—

The next afternoon, Renee rushed through her errands as quickly as possible and then took a detour past RU, where she parked at a metered spot and walked across campus toward the building where Arlo would soon be finishing a class called Fundamentals of Graphic Design II. Her plan was simple: sit on a bench outside his classroom and watch him leave. She wasn't stalking him, and she wasn't going to approach him. She just wanted to get a look at him in person, to see if he gave her the same icky feeling she was starting to get from Ed. Maybe she would look at him and know in her heart that he was a killer, and things would be simpler for her after that.

Young people passed by her on the sweeping walkways, little toys and key chain decorations jingling from their backpacks as they went, jug-size water bottles in their hands. This, Renee thought as she circled Humphries Hall looking for the main entrance, was the college experience she'd never had. She tried to imagine herself there as a student, but this life of classes and competition seemed so inaccessible to her. And these students all looked so young, barely older than Caz, who seemed like a child to Renee.

"Excuse me, are you looking for something?"

She jumped, discovering that she had almost run into a man who was exiting a side door of Humphries with a laptop bag on one arm and a pile of folders in the other.

"Oh!" she said involuntarily. The man was dark haired, with tattoos visible below his rolled-up shirtsleeves. He was unmistakably Arlo Ardell.

Recognition had shown on her face, and it was too late to take it back.

"I'm sorry," Arlo said. "Tell me your name again?"

"Renee?" she said automatically. Instantly, she knew she should have given a fake name. Her heart was pounding. People thought this man had killed Julie.

"And which class do we know each other from?" He pivoted his body out of the pedestrian traffic in front of the building and held the door for a passing group of students. It was such a polite gesture. He was putting a good face on his confusion.

She really hadn't prepared for this, but this was probably the only chance she would ever have to talk to him.

"We don't know each other," she said. "I actually just wanted to ask you some questions."

"For the love of God." Arlo gave a dramatic slump of his shoulders and turned. "Every goddamn time," he said to himself as he walked away.

"Please wait," Renee said, hurrying after him. "I just—"

"There are a million podcasts!" Arlo called over his shoulder. "Go harass some of the other people."

He was hustling down the sidewalk now, and as she tried to keep up with him, she knew they were attracting attention. He seemed to be beelining to one of the blue security lights that dotted the area.

"I know the Weatherups," she said, breathlessly. "I'm the housekeeper. I take care of their children, Julie's children."

Arlo jolted to a halt and turned on her, his face grim. "Is this some kind of a threat? Are you threatening the children? What is your problem?"

Renee held out her hands. "It's not a threat. I love those children. I was in the house when someone threw a brick through the window in the middle of the night. I think Ed thinks it was you, but I don't know if I trust him."

Arlo sighed, and his eyes seemed to dim a little. In the podcast, he had been portrayed as an edgy man with a sexual fire inside him, but now he just seemed to want to put down what he was carrying. "You take care of Julie's kids?" he asked finally.

She nodded. She'd actually said she loved them, and she didn't know if she meant it or if it was just something that popped out. She'd have to come back to that thought later.

He gestured toward a bench a few yards off. "I have five minutes," he said. "Ask what you want to ask," he added, when they were sitting.

"Did you throw a brick through the window?"

"No." Arlo was calm but firm. "And I didn't kill Julie. I used her and our relationship to avoid dealing with my own problems, and I'm not proud of that. She deserved better, and my ex-wife deserved better, and there are a lot of things I did and said that I wish I could take back. But I never hurt her, and I never went to her house like Ms. Cusmano suggests I did. Before or since."

"What do you think happened?"

"Renee? Is that right?"

She nodded.

"Renee, losing Julie was a horrible thing for me during an already bad time in my life. But that podcast and all the wild accusations that came out of it made the whole thing infinitely worse. I've had to change jobs, move houses, fend off fans of Ed and people like you, frankly, who show up and try to interrogate me. And for what? Julie's killer is still out there. All this is to say that I would be a hypocrite if I made my own accusations based on very little." He turned to face her more closely and dropped his head to look into her eyes. "But you work in their household? Him and his new wife?"

She nodded again, too embarrassed to speak.

"Do you feel safe there?"

Her breath caught in her chest. "Safe enough," she said, thinking about Mama's warnings about the dangers of city life. "Are any of us really safe?"

"Well." Arlo gathered his things and stood. "Keep an eye out. Ed is not a good person."

"Can you tell me why?" she asked.

He paused, frowning. "I'm only telling you this so you can be on the lookout and protect the kids if you need to. Julie thought Ed was keeping a secret from her in the last few months of her life. She said he was acting strangely. That's all I know. Don't come back."

He walked away and disappeared into the next available building, probably so it would be hard for her to follow him to his car.

She sat on the bench for a while and then went back to her own car, glancing over her shoulder as she hurried along the unfamiliar campus paths. Why did she feel pursued, she wondered, when she'd been the one doing the stalking?

CHAPTER 12

"Let's have another party," Ed said, breezing into the kitchen the next morning. "The last one was so fun!"

Willow had a cold, and Kim had been up most of the night with the restless baby, who had only just gone down for a nap. "It was so much work," she said, pouring herself a double-size cup of coffee.

"I thought you liked that kind of thing," Ed said.

"I do, but I'm not a show pony who can do it on command," she retorted. "Besides, who would we invite? We already established that we don't have any friends."

"Mariah and Danny! Who else?"

Kim scrubbed her hands over her face. In a rare lapse of her beauty regimen, she hadn't put on makeup that day. "I think we could probably all use a break from each other, don't you?"

Ed seemed to soften, and he moved to put his arm around his wife. "We could all use a little more celebration in our lives, I can tell you that. But I've got some good news to share, and I think you'd all like to hear it."

"Good news?" Kim's irritation faded. "Job news?"

Ed winked at her. "You'll have to wait and find out."

The couple moved out of the kitchen together, discussing dates and times, leaving Renee where she stood at the sink. It was an odd thing, she thought, to be present but invisible. She was the one who had done most of the work for the last dinner party, something Kim seemed to have forgotten, but why not? Why not bring the child podcasting prodigy and her flirtatious producer back for another round? Maybe they would know what secret Ed might have been keeping from Julie just before she died.

The second dinner party was more dinner than party, with take-out Greek food and a few candles on the table. Still, Renee tried to make it feel festive, warming up the food in chafing dishes and aerating the wine before the guests arrived with a bustle of greetings.

"Good to see you again," Danny said, giving Renee a warm smile and a quick hug. He smelled good, and his beard felt soft as it brushed against her temple.

"Gather 'round, everybody," Ed said, after the party moved into the kitchen to acquire drinks. "Raise a glass. You, too, Renee! I have some exciting news to share."

Kim beamed and leaned in close to her husband so that he could put his arm around her.

"I should say that *we* have exciting news to share," Ed continued, tipping his head toward Mariah in her signature all-black. "Mariah and I talked it over, and I've decided to write a book! It'll be about my life and experience with the justice system."

Everyone raised their glasses, Renee following reflexively, but her eyes were on Kim as the woman processed this information, her smile growing tight. "A book?" she said, turning to Ed. "Wow! That's not what I was expecting."

"I think the market is really poised to be responsive," Mariah said. "We can write Ed's story quickly and get it out there."

"Sounds like a lot of work," Kim murmured.

That night, as she lay in bed, Renee could hear voices hissing in a hushed argument on the third floor. She assumed she knew Kim's position, that she'd been depending on her husband to get a job and start earning money to support their newly large family. It was harder to guess what Ed was saying and why his muttered retorts seemed to match hers in urgency and emotion. What could he possibly have to be angry about?

—

The next day, Ed came downstairs early with baby Willow. He put her in her high chair and offered a few brief words to Renee about how Kim was sleeping in, and then he left to go to the gym. Renee, who was in the middle of her morning routine of coffee and breakfast making, had to switch gears in record time to chop banana and find a new pack of rice puffs before Willow had a hunger meltdown.

Kim did not emerge to help the older children get ready for school, and for the first time, Renee noticed how much responsibility Caz took for Oliver. The absence of the actual parents almost didn't matter, because it was Caz who asked Oliver if he had his homework and double-checked that Renee would be available to pick him up after school. It was Renee who gave Willow a bottle, and Caz who took her upstairs to change her diaper before bringing her back down with an apologetic look. "I can't actually find Kim," she said, handing Willow back to Renee. "And we have to get out the door if we're going to be on time. Sorry."

"It's okay," Renee said. "Have a good day at school."

The front door shut behind the children, and the house fell deeply quiet. Renee bounced Willow reflexively, as if to soothe the dimple-chinned baby, but Renee was the one bothered by an ominous feeling that the two of them were alone in the house. "Let's go find your mom," she said.

The second floor was empty, as was the third. Kim wasn't in her own bedroom or the spacious primary bath. It was on her second pass that Renee realized the door to the rooftop deck was unlocked, and her chest tightened. She thought about Stephanie Kowalski stepping through that same door to find Julie's bloody body and had a sudden vision of Kim out there, crumpled and bleeding.

"Shit," she whispered. "Sorry," she added to Willow. She told herself not to be ridiculous. This was normal life, not a true crime podcast. Except that discovering Julie's dead body had been part of Stephanie Kowalski's real life too. Shifting the baby so she couldn't see whatever might be out there, Renee eased open the door and peeked outside.

There was Kim in her silky pink bathrobe. She stood in the middle of the deck with a tape measure in her hand. "Oh, hey," she said, fluttering over. "Hi, Baby! Sorry," she added, scooping Willow into her arms. "I got caught up in something."

"What are you up to out here?" Renee asked, urging her heartbeat to slow before it started echoing off the brick wall behind them.

"It's just this space out here," Kim said, gesturing around at the deck. "It could be so nice, but it just sits here."

Renee took in the weathered deck boards and white-painted railing. It was hard to imagine it being a nice place when she knew what had happened here. There was a reason, after all, that in her quick search for Kim, Caz hadn't even considered checking this spot.

"I know. I know why Ed's against it, of course," Kim said. "Bad memories and everything, but are we just supposed to ignore it? Wouldn't it be better to decorate it and make it a place of our own? Put out some furniture, a grill. We could entertain next to this amazing view."

She gestured to a park half a mile away, where the trees were beginning to turn from green to yellow and gold. "Make some new memories, you know? I got this at a yard sale for eight dollars." She picked up a large metal sunburst that had been leaning against the wall and displayed it for Renee's inspection. It was a bit rusty here and there, a little warped by weather, but otherwise cheerful and well made, the metal rays of the sun spiking out in every direction with an on-trend energy that gave Renee a glimpse of what Kim saw when she looked at the rooftop space: wicker chairs and tables, lighted tiki torches, and a photogenic purple sunset.

"I was trying to hang it on the wall, but it's really hard to mount things into brick," Kim said, pointing to one off-kilter nail. "Ideally, I could get another couple nails in there, but I don't know. Do you mind?"

Renee took the sunburst, trying not to poke herself with it, and boosted it up to the nail, which wobbled but held firm.

"It'll have to do for now," Kim said. "I don't even know whether Ed will freak out when he sees that I've made changes out here." Her voice quivered a little, but she went on. "I just want one thing in this house that is for me, you know? I got my name on the deed when he was in prison, so it's technically just as much mine, but it still feels like I'm living in someone else's life. I knew it wouldn't be easy." She sighed. "But it's just been so much more than I expected. I think I might have made such a big mistake."

Renee nodded, at a loss for what to say. If Kim had been naive to think she would know how to handle the ups and downs of family life at 1125 with the specter of Julie observing every move, Renee had been just as naive. She put an arm around the other woman, and Kim leaned her head against her in gratitude. "See, wouldn't it be nice to have some furniture out here?" she asked. "We could just sit and talk."

"Sure."

After a moment, she rallied. "I supposed the baby needs a change."

"Caz did it before she left for school."

"Oh." She seemed surprised. "You probably think I'm coldhearted about those kids."

Renee did wonder how much Hadley Kowalski's gruesome and imagined tale of Caz killing her mother colored Kim's vision every time she looked at the teenager.

"I just barely know them," Kim rushed on. "I tried to adopt them, you know, officially, when we got married, and I brought it up again last week. But Ed says there's no point. Maybe with Catherine, sure; she's going to be eighteen really soon. But why not Oliver? Why can't we at least pretend to be a normal family?" The tears were coming again, and this time Willow caught the vibes and began to whimper.

"Okay, okay," Renee said. She held out her arms for the baby, a somewhat desperate gesture, she realized, but she hoped that doing something practical would help tamp down the reciprocal feeling of loss that was rising like bile in her chest. "How about I get her dressed and take her for a walk in the stroller? Then you can finish your measurements."

"Really?" Kim gasped. "That's so awesome of you!"

She hadn't signed up to be the babysitter, but it seemed increasingly to be her role, both practically and in her own mind, if what she'd told Arlo Ardell the day before had been true. At least an infant's fears and wants were knowable and predictable in a way that the adults' certainly weren't.

She put her young charge down in the crib while she rummaged around the nursery for socks and something warm. Willow's laundry hamper was full, something to deal with today, if she ever got a chance to do any of her normal tasks, and she had to dig into a drawer of sized-up outfits to find a clean sweater. At the bottom of the stash of clothes, her fingers brushed against a poky corner of paper. She pushed aside a stack of twelve-month rompers and inspected the envelope under them.

It was a standard white thing addressed to Kimberly Weatherup, and the return address was for a company called DNAssure Testing Department. The envelope had been sliced open, but the contents, a single sheet of paper, were still neatly folded inside.

Renee didn't pull the page out—she would never do something so brazen. But she did, ever so gently, insert two fingers into the envelope and push apart the sides enough to read the official writing inside.

The paper contained a neat, short list of information.

> **Product:** Expedited Sibling Test
> **Requestee:** Kimberly Weatherup
> **Sample A:** infant buccal (cheek) swab
> **Sample B:** dinosaur toothbrush from potential minor sibling

> **Results:** Test results strongly suggest that the donors of the two samples are half siblings who share one parent. While a half-sibling relationship is likely, we cannot confirm definitively. Half siblings share, on average, only 25 percent of their DNA, sometimes less. This means that the two donors may be half siblings or first cousins.
> **Recommendations:** If the above results are satisfactory, no further action is needed. If the requestee requires more conclusive results, we recommend submitting a buccal swab for both potential siblings and/or a paternity test with a buccal swab from the potential shared parent, if available. Any samples from adults or children older than sixteen must be accompanied by a signed consent form.

"Well." Renee pushed the clothes back over the envelope and closed the drawer. "I guess we know what happened to Oliver's dino toothbrush." She returned to Willow, who kicked placidly in her crib as Renee slid her arms into sweater sleeves. "Even you have your secrets, don't you, Baby? But if you were made through IVF, why would there be any doubt who your siblings are? Or was your timing a little awkward for Mommy and her secret friend?"

It was a nice day for a walk. As September turned to October, the weather had cooled, but the sky was exceptionally blue, and the air was still. Renee took her time, walking Willow down several streets into the quieter and more expensive corners of the neighborhood.

Things were getting really weird. She couldn't deny that, now, but she couldn't tell if it was in reality or just in her own head. Going to see Arlo had been a pretty bold move in retrospect, but it was the move of someone who didn't really think the man was a killer. If so, what did that mean about her personal theory of the crime? Was she truly that suspicious of Ed? Had she really thought Kim was dead on the rooftop that morning? Either she was losing her grip or some part of her thought she was living in a house with a murderer. Neither scenario was great.

A reasonable person, she thought, would stop wondering what secrets Ed was keeping and start looking for a way out, a tactful severance, a new job. But that would mean driving home to Cumberland, moving back into her old bedroom, telling Mama that she'd been right. Going home would feel like going backward into grief and depression.

She paused under a maple tree with leaves that were starting to blush with fall color and checked on Willow in the stroller. The baby had fallen asleep, her head lolling, her cheek getting a little pink with the warmth of slumber. Even the idea of saying goodbye made her sad.

CHAPTER 13

At first it looked like an Americana scene from a greeting card: two children, a girl and a boy, dressed in chinos and T-shirts for school, standing beside each other on the sidewalk of Linden Avenue. They were both facing Renee as she approached, and when they saw her, the girl waved excitedly and the boy brandished a bouquet of stalky wildflowers.

It was Emma and Wyatt, Brandon's two children, alone on the street in front of 1125. Her pace quickened, and she hurried the stroller forward, hoping Willow wouldn't wake up.

"Renee!" Emma cried, rushing forward to hug her waist. Wyatt, three years younger than his sister but almost as tall, followed suit, and she released the stroller to hug them back.

"Well, hello," she said, trying to keep her voice pleasantly neutral. "How did you get here?" She couldn't think of any good answers to this question, and she felt alert to the fact that she seemed to be alone on the street with three children, none of whom were hers.

"We came to see you!" Wyatt said, proffering his flowers.

She accepted them, struggling to think of a follow-up question, when a car door beside her opened and Andrea stepped out. She wore white shorts and a drapey top, and she had the pleased look of someone whose plan was working better than expected. "We came out to surprise you and go to lunch," she said. "Isn't that right, kids?"

"We had a half day at school," Emma said. "Remember when you took us to ice cream when we had a half day?"

"How did you find me here?" Renee asked.

"Oh, you know how it is," Andrea said, with a careless toss of her ponytail. "Your mom told my aunt, who told my mom."

At that moment, the front door of 1125 opened, and Ed stepped out, home from the gym now and freshly showered. He appraised the situation, taking in Andrea's assertive stance, Renee's look of alarm, and the children hovering at her elbows. "What's up?" he asked, with something like amusement.

Andrea turned and gave him a slow up-and-down. "This must be your new boss," she said with her best girl-next-door smile. "Well, hello there!"

"Sorry," Renee said. "I've run into some"—she fumbled for the word—"friends from my hometown. I hate to disappoint, guys," she added to the children. "But I'm in the middle of a workday right now."

Ed descended from the porch. "Don't worry about it," he said. "Looks like you all have things to discuss. Take your time, Renee." He gave her a wink over the children's heads. "You can tell me all about it later." He took charge of the stroller and navigated it back toward the house with one more bemused look over his shoulder.

"Considerate *and* cute," Andrea murmured.

Renee didn't think he was either one. "All right," she said with a sigh. "What's this about lunch?"

They went to a retro diner a few blocks away and settled at a table in the window with BLTs and milkshakes Renee purchased without negotiation. The last time she'd seen the children had been at their father's funeral. They had been limp, red-eyed versions of themselves then, huddling next to their grandparents in the church pew. She hadn't spoken to them then or since, a thought that made her desperately sad, but it's not like she could have asked Andrea for a playdate. Until now, apparently.

They seemed to be in a chipper mood today, though, eager to tell about the beginning of their school year with new teachers and new friends.

Andrea watched them talk, only interrupting to remind them about an apple-picking field trip that was coming up later in the month.

"We're gonna get to pick our own apples!" Wyatt crowed. "Straight from the trees!"

Throughout the meal, Renee shaped her face carefully into a smile. She focused on the children, making sure to show her approval, her enjoyment of their jokes. Inside, she ached and raged. They looked like Brandon, his green eyes and unruly hair, but they were more beautiful than him in some ways, each of his features improved upon a little in their faces. She wanted to hold on to them and never let go. And Andrea had brought them here to torture her.

They walked back to the car, and Renee gave each child a long hug and an urging to work hard at school. When they were safe inside the car, she turned to Andrea.

"What do you want?"

"I'm going to lose the house," Andrea said matter-of-factly. "I can't work outside school hours because I can't afford childcare. Brandon's parents are doing everything they can to help, but they have jobs, too, and medical bills. My mom tries to watch the kids, but she can't walk anymore. We're struggling. I can't give them the lives they deserve."

"Of course." Renee felt herself hardening inside. "I should have known you wouldn't acknowledge my existence if it wasn't about money."

"Maybe. God knows I wouldn't have chosen any of this. But—" She held up a hand as Renee turned away toward the house. "But that apple-picking trip has a twenty-dollar fee per kid. That's basically my grocery budget for the week. They can't go unless you help us. I know you can afford it. I know your hot boss in there is, like, crime-famous or something."

"This might be the most manipulative thing you've ever done," she said in a low voice. "I'll never forgive you for this." Andrea was just like the brick thrower, she thought bitterly, someone who would jump at a chance to get something out of other people's pain.

Andrea shrugged. "Maybe," she said again. "But it was good for them too. This is the most excited they've been about anything in months. How do you think that makes me feel?"

Renee rubbed her hands across her face. She wished she could cry. The tears she'd been holding back felt like they were poisoning her. Maybe she was just as bad as all of them. After all, wasn't she trying to use the Weatherups' trials as a chance to redeem herself, in her own eyes if no one else's? "How much do you want?"

"Five hundred a month," Andrea said. "Not forever, just until I get back on track."

"That's absurd." She tried to keep her face neutral in case the children were watching. "I'm not part of your family. We don't have anything in common anymore."

"But you were going to be. Six months ago, you were ready to become a mother to them."

Renee aimed her face at the sky and closed her eyes for a long moment, feeling tears drain down the insides of her sinuses. Ever since Brandon had died, she had wished someone would say that very thing out loud, wished she could say it out loud. Andrea was the last person she'd expected to acknowledge it, but it was still true: With her whole heart, she'd been ready to become Emma and Wyatt's stepmother, to spend a lifetime loving them, supporting them. Now that Brandon was gone, they only needed her more. When she opened her eyes again, she said, "Okay."

They exchanged online-payment-app information, and when $500 had passed from one account to another, and Andrea had driven the children away with a last series of cheerful waves, Renee trudged inside feeling used but not ashamed. Ed, who was reading a newspaper in the parlor, watched her close the door behind her. For all she knew, he might have observed the entire interaction with Andrea through the glossy new front window.

"Seems like you've had a day," he said with a glint of amusement. "Is everything okay, there in Renee's world?" He had moved Willow's stroller into the parlor but hadn't taken her out of it. She was looking hot in her sweater and was twitching restlessly.

"Everything's fine," she said. "Sorry about people unexpectedly dropping by. It won't happen again."

"Not to worry," he said. "We all have secrets. I know you know a couple of mine." There was a smugness to his smile, as if the idea tickled him.

How was it possible, she wondered, that Ed knowing her secrets gave him power over her but Renee knowing his secrets also gave him power over her? She didn't like that arrangement, and she didn't like him.

Instinct told her to take a page from Mama's playbook of deflection and attack. "I've got to ask you something."

"Shoot."

"If you work on this book instead of getting a job, are you going to be able to keep paying me to do my job?"

"Of course," Ed said. "The world can't get enough of old Ed."

"Well," she said, picking up the baby, "you better get on that, then."

"Yes, ma'am," he said with a chuckle.

She settled the sleeping Willow more comfortably in her crib and then went downstairs to prep dinner and Oliver's after-school snack. Whatever Ed's game was, she wasn't impressed, but she'd already been forced to give up one family, and she wasn't going to run away from another one that needed her.

CHAPTER 14

"It's an online calendar all of us can access," Renee said, turning her laptop screen toward the assembled Weatherups as though presenting to the shareholders. It was a Saturday morning, the first time she had managed to catch everyone at home in days. "We can put your appointments in there. We can keep track of the kids' activities, who is picking up and dropping off. I think it might make things run a little more smoothly."

"I love it!" Kim said. "So modern. Obviously, we have Oliver's soccer today. I have a hair appointment this week, and Willow has a checkup on Tuesday."

Modern, perhaps, but that wasn't why Renee had set up the calendar. She hoped it would help her keep an eye on Ed's habits, let her know when she was safely alone in the house and when she might expect him to be lurking around. It also felt like the smallest homage to Julie, a digital twist on her rigorous basement organizational system.

"Don't forget to block off the whole day tomorrow for the *Innocent Blood* taping," Ed said. "It's the last episode," he added in response to Renee's inquisitive look. "Mariah and Danny are coming to record interviews to wrap up the series. I'm calling it the 'Happy Ending Episode.'" He pulled Kim toward him and gave her a kiss on the forehead.

"I'll always be grateful for what they did for us," Kim said. "But I'll be glad to put the podcast era behind us. It's too much attention. Too much drama."

"I won't be doing an interview," said Caz, who sat at the kitchen island drinking a cup of black coffee. She'd been experimenting with drawing over her eyebrows in heavy mascara, and they were looking particularly intense that morning.

"What do you mean?" Ed asked. "Don't you want to be able to tell all your friends that you were in a podcast?"

"I've already been in the podcast, unfortunately," Caz said. "Besides, it's not really a happy ending. Mom is still dead, in case you forgot."

"Of course that's not what your father meant," Kim said. "We're just all happy that we can be together again."

Caz drained her mug and put it in the sink. "Thank you for the coffee, Renee," she said, then stalked out of the room.

"See?" Kim said. "Endless drama."

Renee thought even Enid Salinas would waggle a finger at this insensitivity. Perception seemed to mean everything to Kim and Ed, but they didn't seem to care what secrets and pain went unaddressed while they were curating the public image.

Case in point, later that morning, while the family was out at Oliver's soccer game, her vacuum discovered a condom under the couch in Ed's study.

"Of course," she muttered as she extracted the thing from the vacuum's rollers. It was brand new, still in its wrapper, with an expiration date far in the future. "Who left this here?" she lamented to the empty house. "What is wrong with you people?"

Ed was undoubtedly the kind of person to thoughtlessly leave a condom somewhere, but Kim had been having her own fling while he was in prison, and Caz was a teenager, though Renee was increasingly sure Caz didn't prefer boys and wouldn't have had an opportunity to invite a romantic buddy into the house in any case. Regardless, whoever had failed to keep track of this particular prophylactic was only adding to the confusion.

The front door rattled downstairs with the family's return. Renee threw the condom back under the couch and jerked to her feet. She was starting to feel like she was being pranked.

The Weatherups were tired and sweaty from their time at the soccer field, and the baby was cranky. "Willow needs a nap," Ed was saying as he came through the door.

"You say that like I don't know," Kim retorted. "Why don't you put her down? I need a nap too."

The adults went straight upstairs, leaving the diaper bag and a snack cooler by the door. Oliver, still in his grass-stained soccer jersey, saw the chance to get some unregulated screen time and pulled out his Nintendo, seemingly from thin air, leaving Caz to pick up the food and water bottles and trudge toward the kitchen.

"I'll help with that," Renee said, and Caz nodded her thanks.

As she transferred a few dozen leftover orange slices to a smaller container, Renee watched Caz load bottles into the dishwasher. "How are you doing?" she asked, not really expecting an answer.

Caz shrugged. "People were all over Dad at the soccer game. Women, I mean. He was holding court and making jokes about prison food. All the soccer moms are like, 'You're so brave.' Though I guess it's better than throwing a brick through the window," she added, gesturing generally to the front of the house. "This is our life now, everyone hating us or loving us because of that podcast."

It was so much more than she expected that Renee paused, an orange slice dripping in her hand, afraid that any eye contact or sudden noise would spook the teenager. "What do *you* think about it?" she asked.

"I wish I could just avoid it, but it's always on social media. Even my actual friends are always sending me news stories or retweeting things. A couple of kids at school are already calling me the Lady of Darkness. Fucking Mariah." She gave Renee a narrow look. "You probably think I should be grateful, when she basically got my dad a new trial."

Renee shrugged. "I assume you aren't happy about how you were portrayed."

"Something like that. Hadley Kowalski—whatever, she was a stupid kid who wanted attention. Her parents were getting divorced. I thought she was a friend, but I guess not. I don't care. But I'll never forgive Mariah for giving that whole witch-girl story a national stage. It was nothing, and she made it into something."

"It wasn't fair to court sensationalism when it was a child's story."

"Right." Caz's brow lightened a bit, as though she hadn't expected support. She closed the dishwasher and drew a deep breath. "But it's not just that. I know my dad didn't kill my mom. I just know it. I know he wanted to get out of prison, and he was trying everything that would work. But—" There were tears in her eyes, and her voice quavered, shaping words that had never been spoken before. "But he was the one who told Mariah about Hadley's so-called confession. He suggested that she use it in her podcast, and he legitimately doesn't see the problem there. He's all means-to-an-end, and he thinks it's ultimately okay to suggest that when I was twelve years old, I stabbed my mother with a knife and did fucked-up things with her blood, as long as it's a good show and the public is watching."

Tears were flowing now, causing gray streaks of mascara to reach as far as her chin. "And he doesn't get why I'm mad about that."

Renee wanted to put her arms around the girl and pull her close, but instead, she sat on a kitchen stool and clasped her hands on the counter. "I'd be mad too," she said.

"We wanted to stay with our grandparents. We were happy there, and we had friends and stuff. Oliver is such a people pleaser, so he didn't make a fuss about it, but I argued for us to stay. My dad wanted us here, though. He wants to win every fight, you know. He thinks that having his kids back in his custody is the ultimate proof that he isn't a murderer."

"What did your grandparents think?"

"They would have kept us. I think they wanted to, but they believe he's innocent too. They've always said that, anyway. Maybe they regret it now because they didn't have an excuse not to sign us back over to him. And now we're just more trophies in his fight against the state, and I just have to wait until college or whatever so I can be independent." She reached for a paper napkin from the holder on the counter and blew her nose.

"You know," Renee said, "I learned a lesson about independence recently. Sometimes, you can't wait for it. You have to take it."

Caz nodded as she dabbed her eyes. The tears had stopped flowing already, and Renee knew this moment of vulnerability was not likely to be repeated. "I get that," the teenager said.

The conversation gave Renee a warm feeling that lingered through the evening. She knew one heart-to-heart didn't make her and Caz BFFs, but it did make her feel better about herself. It was proof she had something of value besides being the Weatherups' dishwasher and Andrea's piggy bank.

Nothing could top off a weird day like a phone call from her mother.

Renee was lying in bed watching TV on her laptop that evening when her phone rang. She had already turned off the emotional spigot for the day, exhausted from ignoring condoms and mentoring teenagers, and she didn't want to answer the phone. But years of being her parents' emergency contact, of having a brother on active duty, made her fingers respond on their own to the chiming of the call. There was always the chance something terrible had happened.

"Hi, Mama. How are you?"

"Doing just fine. I was calling to let you know that you're wrong about those people."

Renee grimaced. "I took the job, Mama. We can't keep having this conversation."

"No, I'm talking about the people you were asking about on the phone. I saw Dottie Prince at the farm supply yesterday. She's the church secretary at Good Hope Baptist now, and I asked her about them. She says she knows them, Gert and Angus Weather."

Renee's attention sharpened, and she dove under her comforter, wishing she could feel surer that no one could overhear the conversation. "Gert and Angus Weatherup?" she asked in a low voice.

"No, just Weather, and they aren't dead."

"What?"

"They both still attend services every week. They live on Old Forest Road."

"Well, that's very odd," said Renee.

But it was more than odd, she thought as she hung up the phone. Assuming Gert and Angus Weather were the same as Gert and Angus Weatherup, Ed's parents might be completely alive, despite what he'd told everyone. She knew well that a person might want to distance themselves from embarrassing or difficult family members, but more to the point, why would a man like Ed want to make it hard to connect him to his family of origin?

It was already late, but this question made her feel alert with curiosity. She closed the TV show she was watching on her laptop and opened a new browser.

Legal name changes were technically public information, but that didn't mean the records were easy to find. After an hour of scrolling shady legal advice forums and clunky government websites, she figured out that name change records were stored by individual county circuit courts. From there, she began the laborious task of checking counties one by one. Ed hadn't changed his name in Cumberland County or any of the neighboring ones, nor had he done it in the Richmond area. It wasn't until, on a whim, she checked the circuit court of Williamsburg, where Ed and Julie had attended law school, that she found what she needed.

Williamsburg District Court of the Commonwealth of Virginia

August 25, 1998

In re the Petition of: Everett John Weather

The petition of the above-named person for an order changing his/her current name came before the court on this date; the court, having reviewed the petition and any supporting information and it appearing to the satisfaction of the court that the statements in support of the petition are true, now, therefore, it is hereby ORDERED, ADJUDED AND DECREED that the name of Everett John Weather be changed to Edward Christopher Weatherup.

"Well, hello there, Everett," Renee whispered.

CHAPTER 15

Early the next morning, the devices in the household chirped and warbled with an all-family notification from the online calendar.

> Everyone—Final podcast taping at house @ 9:00AM

"Will I get to do an interview?" Oliver asked over breakfast.

"Sure thing, son!" Ed said. "We'll each get to do one."

"I feel like this is something we should discuss," Kim murmured. "We did say we wanted the kids out of the limelight."

"It's fine," Ed said. "His voice matters."

"I want to be a podcaster!" Oliver clanked his spoon against his cereal bowl.

Kim rolled her eyes behind his back.

Mariah and Danny arrived an hour later, smelling freshly showered and carrying their recording equipment in black cases and bags. Renee made another pot of coffee while they set up in the family room, Ed following with the eager energy of an intern on his first day.

When she carried mugs of coffee to them, she found that they had erected a pair of standing microphones in front of the couch and armchair, and Danny was wearing headphones and adjusting things on a laptop.

"The acoustics are terrible in here," he said. "So echoey."

"This is the most private room, though," Ed said. "I think we'll feel really able to open up in this space."

"Thank you," Mariah said to Renee, accepting a mug. "I suppose Caz won't be joining us today?"

Ed shook his head. "At a friend's house, I think. But I know Oliver is eager to make a statement."

Renee retreated, wondering if Mariah had any idea what animosity the girl held for her. In the kitchen, she put in her earbuds and relistened to the episode of *Innocent Blood* where Julie's law school friend Alan Cabot described the first months of Ed and Julie's relationship.

> ALAN: Julie and the rest of us were all there for undergrad, and then Ed came along in 2001 when we were first-year law students. He had just moved to Williamsburg for law school, and Julie kind of enjoyed showing him around town . . .

Well that just wasn't true, Renee knew now. Everett/Ed had been in Williamsburg, changing his name and getting up to who knew what else, since 1998. Maybe this was the secret Ed had been keeping from Julie: his former name or the date he actually moved to the town in which they met. But those alone didn't strike Renee as marriage-ending secrets, and she didn't know why it would have taken almost seventeen years for Julie to grow suspicious of that particular aspect of Ed's history.

Unless, of course, the name change had been Ed's attempt to hide something much bigger.

As she passed through the front hall with a watering can for the houseplants, a muffled sob cut through the low volume of the podcast, and she jerked out her earbuds, senses vigilant.

"The officers just told us to get a security camera," came Kim's voice from behind the family room door. "We really are alone in this."

Not alone, Renee wished she could say. One person, at least, was trying to figure it out.

A few minutes later, when she was prepping vegetables for dinner, Danny came in looking a little rattled.

"Kim's crying. Mariah gave me the signal to get lost."

"I think she's been having a hard time." She shook water off a handful of carrots and arranged them on her cutting board.

"Understandable. But you've got good insights," he added, brightening. "Would you be interested in doing an interview with us?"

She paused, her chef's knife hovering over the carrots. "What do I have to do an interview about?"

"This." He gestured at the house at large. "You're here. Obviously, we wish we had more answers about what happened to Julie, but instead, we're focusing on the impact a wrongful conviction has on a family, and you're here to witness all of that."

"Let me ask you this," she said, trying to keep her chopping rhythmic. "Do you and Mariah think there's a possibility Ed lied to you about any of this stuff?"

"What do you mean?"

"Well, his parents, for example. Were you ever able to confirm that they had died?"

"Oh." He looked a little abashed. "Well, we were more concerned with the period of his life after meeting Julie. But surely if any of his relatives were still alive, they would have come forward by now. Goodness knows he got a lot of press."

"So you trust what he tells you?"

"We definitely try to be objective, but most of what he's told us so far has been verifiable. Wait," he added. "Do you not trust Ed?"

Under her knife, the carrot chunks disintegrated into their component molecules. "Everybody lies," she said.

Danny tilted his head, his brown eyes warm and sparkling. "You're an interesting person, Renee."

She snorted. "What?"

He grinned. "I'm serious."

She was about to blurt *The last man who liked me died because of it*, but her mental mentor, Enid Salinas in her perennial pearls, wagged a finger and announced, *Play it cool, girl! Don't immediately tell the first man who might be flirting with you about your dead fiancé!*

"Why are you flirting with me?" she asked instead.

Danny's eyes widened, and he stood up a little straighter. "I'm so sorry if—" he said in a rush.

That was when Kim walked in, eyes red and face wet. She stopped in the doorway, taking in Renee's blush and Danny solicitous look before scowling and stomping to the sink. "Excuse me," she said, unnecessarily loudly, as she passed behind Renee.

"Are you done in there?" Danny asked.

"Yes," Kim said, pouring herself a glass of water. "Hopefully for good."

As if church bells somewhere had announced his entrance, Ed bounced down the stairs with Willow. "She's up and ready for the day," he said, holding her out to Kim.

"I've got a migraine," Kim said, brushing past them and going upstairs.

Ed turned to Renee. "Do you mind?"

Renee began wiping her hands, but Danny held out his arms. "I'll take her. You go ahead and do your interview."

"Thanks, brother. Renee will feed her when she gets hungry." And he was off.

Ed's interview went on even longer than Kim's had, and for two hours or so, his voice murmured evenly from the family room. Renee finished prepping the food and made a bottle for the baby while Danny bounced her around the house. They chatted a little more, but he didn't try flirting again, which was just as well. Lunchtime approached, and Renee began to wonder how much longer things would drag on. Willow would need to go down for a nap soon, and Oliver had gotten a whole morning of uninterrupted screen time.

When noon struck, she tiptoed into the foyer and listened to see how the interview was going in the family room. On the other side of the door, Mariah was talking, her voice quiet and casual, suggesting that the microphones were already turned off. ". . . example, Charlie Perkins. He was caught in a bad system, and we kind of threw him under the bus in our episode about him."

"He was a gangbanger, and he came to my house with a gun," came Ed's voice.

"Maybe, but you don't really think he killed Julie, do you? Right, so I feel like we were punching down on that one, and obviously Catherine isn't happy with how she's presented."

"She's a teenager. There's no making her happy."

"But what I'm saying is that we have everyone's attention now, and with attention comes judgment. Whatever story I choose for season two, I want to show that I'm doing as conscientious a job as possible."

Renee raised her fist to knock, but before she could, Ed said, "What do you mean, whatever story you choose?" The hurt in his voice made her pause.

There was half a beat of silence, just enough for Renee to feel a quiver of awkwardness through the door.

"Well," said Mariah, "we told your story, and now it's time to get someone else's out there."

"Someone like me, wrongfully imprisoned?"

"Actually, I was thinking about a different kind of story. There was this fourteen-year-old girl, Claudia Castillo, who went missing from a foster home back in 2008 after she had been improperly removed from her parents' care. It's an interesting story, and I would love to give a victim like her the focus."

There was the sound of denim shifting on leather, and Renee imagined Ed sitting up with new urgency.

"Of course, that little girl's story sounds really sad," he said. "But I don't agree with you that my story is over."

"I didn't mean your story is over, Ed." Mariah said. "You know Marty Vickers? He emailed me the other day to say some very nice things about the podcast. I bet if you reached out to him, you could do a collab."

"Vickers," said Ed. "He's the one who killed the boy at his school."

"Well, no," said Mariah, slight annoyance in her voice. "He was convicted of that, but he didn't do it, obviously. Since his exoneration, he's been a big advocate for people who are wrongfully incarcerated. Wouldn't it be cool if you two could work together? Give me a hand with these cords, will you?"

Renee caught the dragging sound of a power cable being pulled across the floor and the zipping of equipment bags.

Ed sighed. "I just don't trust anyone with my story but you, Mariah."

"I appreciate that, but there comes a time when you have to tell your own story. Like in your book, for instance. You're still going to write that, right?"

"Absolutely," Ed said. "You think it'll command a good advance?"

"I do. I've already floated it to somebody who knows the industry, and they think they can get you a six-figure advance."

Ed gave a hoot. "Hot damn, baby! That's what I like to hear."

"But we can't get ahead of ourselves. You need to write a proposal, get an agent on board, and get a contract with a publisher. They'll give you some of the money up front, but it might not be a lot. And you will have to write that book, Ed. It's going to be really time consuming. We're talking at least six months without steady income and with a family to take care of, a house, a housekeeper."

Renee grimaced, wishing Mariah wouldn't bring her into it.

"Do you and Kim have a plan for how you'll pay the bills in that time? The insurance money was what, a hundred grand? It won't last forever."

"Don't worry about that. Kim can get a job if she needs to. And I can produce that book. I'm telling you, Mariah, I'm uncovering some things that you're not going to believe."

"What are you talking about?"

"I'm talking about Melanie Hofstadter, Liz Moffet, and Vanessa Dolittle, three Richmond women who were killed by home invaders in the middle of the night the year after Julie died. They were all mothers, all around Julie's age. Mariah, I think I've discovered a serial killer. I think Julie was his first victim."

The packing sounds paused. "Huh," said Mariah. "That is a pretty interesting theory. I'd be curious to see your research on that."

"I can get my notes for you now," Ed said, his footsteps moving toward the door.

Renee's hand jerked up, and she hastily knocked before she lost her chance.

Ed pulled open the door, looking energized. "Er," he said. "What is it, Renee?" Behind him, the tall black skeletons of the recording equipment still stood, partially assembled, as Mariah bent to load microphones and cameras into the pouches of a duffel bag.

"It's time for Willow's nap."

"You go take care of Willow," Mariah said. "You can email me your notes, and I can look at them later. Danny and I should be getting out of your hair, anyway. Renee, maybe you could give me a hand with these?"

Ed seemed annoyed, but he headed toward the kitchen to retrieve the baby, and as Renee began to slowly wind up power cables, she couldn't tell if the other woman was disappointed or relieved to have been interrupted. Maybe Kim wasn't the only one who was ready for the Weatherups and the podcasters to have some time apart.

Renee broke the silence by clearing her throat. "So this was the last episode," she said. "Crazy."

"Yeah," said Mariah. "It's been a wild time."

"If you had to guess," Renee said, hoping she sounded more like a fan than someone who had been listening at the door moments ago, "who do you think killed Julie?"

Mariah didn't pause in her zipping and clipping. "I don't think we'll ever really know," she said. "It's sad, though."

"So you aren't going to investigate anymore?"

"I guess Ed has a theory, and we can look into that, but it's been years since we had a big lead. Lots of tips come into the podcast inbox, but they've mostly been speculation or pure delusion. People just want to involve themselves in the drama, sometimes."

If this was shade being cast in her direction, Renee didn't appreciate it.

CHAPTER 16

Renee's next day off fell on a Friday, and though she woke early, she stayed in her room until the morning hubbub had subsided and she could slip out of the house without speaking to anyone. Odds were good that no one would bother asking her what she planned to do that day, and even if they did, she had no qualms about lying, but she felt nervous about what her day held and paranoid someone might sense she was up to something.

After a quick bite, she got in her car and turned toward the highway, merging into the traffic headed west toward Cumberland and her parents' house—or, rather, a spot just a few miles from her parents' house. An hour or two of web searching the night before had revealed that while Ed didn't have any internet footprint under the name Everett Weather, there were property records for a house on Old Forest Road in Cumberland purchased by Angus T. Weather in 1967.

Following directions to that address, she exited the highway onto the endless, unremarkable roads traveling farther west, and from there onto a narrow curving road that led her into trees and farmland and finally onto a long hummocky driveway that was so similar to the track leading to the Christmas tree farm that she had the brief irrational thought that she had been duped into coming back home.

While Ed had moved through the world telling people his parents were dead, Angus and Gert Weather had lived the whole time in a four-room home surrounded by heavy oaks. The little house was still covered in the nubbly brown asphalt siding that had probably been installed at some point in the mid-century to protect exterior walls that were already old and deteriorating, and now, the house seemed to sag in place, as if very tired but still game to keep on.

The yard was full of lawn mowers, push tillers, and other small machines: hundreds, of all ages and conditions, lined up in neat rows according to some organizational system that would only be obvious to an expert. A sign announcing small engine repair hung from a post amid the parking lot of machines. The sign struck Renee as more of a title on an art installation than an advertisement for a business. After all, the house was so far back from the road that anyone who made it this far already knew why they had come.

For her part, she had come because she really wanted to know what Everett Weather was hiding when he'd become Edward Weatherup.

She parked carefully and approached the house. The door opened before she could knock, and a woman who appeared to be in her seventies with white hair and a heavy gray sweater said, "You Patricia?"

"No, I'm Renee. I'm a housekeeper for Everett. I think he's your son?"

The woman's brow lowered. "And?"

"I'd like to talk to you, if that's okay."

The woman, Gert, stared for a moment longer and then gave an enormous sigh before turning and walking unevenly away from the door, leaving it open behind her. "Angus," she yelled into the house. "You better come out here. A girl from the news come asking about Everett."

"I'm not from the news," Renee said as she stepped gingerly over the threshold, feeling neither quite invited nor uninvited. "I'm your son's housekeeper."

"Oh." With a gruff gesture, Gert directed Renee to sit at the kitchen table, which was just a few feet away. "Thought that was just something you said to get in the door."

She opened the fridge and poured Renee a very tall glass of Pepsi, giving her a chance to take in the room. The short curtains on the one window were a faded floral print, probably handsewn in another decade. The taps on the sink didn't match one another, and the light switch on the wall was a very old push-button model that she'd never seen in real life. The rectangular white refrigerator was probably twenty years old, and its power cord, which snaked along the wall to one of just two outlets in the room, was elaborately bandaged with electrical tape, a fact that didn't prevent the machine from humming along vigorously. This was a house in which, when they broke, things were repaired and sent back into action. By the multimillion-dollar standards of the Fan District, this place might have looked like a dump, but to Renee, whose grandparents had lived in a house much like this, it reflected the spirit of ingenuity and perseverance that could get a family through a Great Depression or two. These were the people Ed was planning to characterize in his autobiography as too lazy to work.

The main decoration was an array of framed photographs on the wall above the table. On the side nearest the stove, they featured baby and toddler pictures of four boys, close in age and appearance, all with straw-blond hair that darkened over the years as they became elementary school aged, with glasses too big for their faces, and then middle and high school aged, with arms too long for their bodies. One was clearly Ed, though his hair was floppier and his features more rounded than now.

As the photos ranged across the wall toward the door, the boys became men—or at least three of them did. While his brothers posed with their arms around each other, then around their brides, then around their children, Ed had vanished from the wall. The last photo of him was at, Renee guessed, sixteen or seventeen, in his baseball uniform, a teenager smiling under the sun for the camera, a bat slung across his shoulders.

A man with grizzled stubble shuffled into the kitchen then, his worn jeans, probably the same ones Daddy purchased at the feed store, held up by suspenders.

"You with the newspapers?" Angus demanded, semicollapsing into a chair opposite her.

"No." She explained herself a third time. "Has the media been here a lot?" she added when he looked disappointed.

"No," he said. "Keep expecting them, but they never come."

These people didn't strike her as attention-hungry types eager for their fifteen minutes of fame, but all these questions about the media were making her wonder. "Well, I'm not from the news, but I can tell you about your grandchildren."

Gert's eyes widened, and she joined her husband at the table. "All right," she said. "All right."

Renee gave a brief report of the children's ages and interests, and though she was sure it crossed a professional line, she showed the Weathers a picture of Willow that she had taken on her phone one day at Kim's request.

Gert held the phone with both hands, gazing into her granddaughter's face with misty eyes. "Sweet little thing."

"Why don't you tell me about Everett?" Renee suggested quietly.

Gert was ready. "He was our youngest," she said. "Just a year and a half younger than his brother Lester and always real smart in school."

"Too smart," Angus interjected.

"He grew up faster than his brothers," Gert went on. "He wanted things we couldn't give him here. He always wanted the new tennis shoes or the new car. He wanted to travel the world and work on Wall Street. We didn't know how to help him do those things. Weren't raised like that, you know. Everett always had a scheme for making money. He was going to sell this or that, or he was going to go in on a business opportunity with a friend. Even when he was in high school, it was like that. He went with girls sooner than his brothers did." As she talked, regret played across Gert's face like a shadow, but Angus just seemed to be getting angry. His eyes found a spot on the table ahead of him, and they fixed there with smoldering intensity.

"He liked them young," he said.

"It wasn't like that," Gert interjected. "It's just that the girls his age didn't like him much. But Ella was young," she added sadly to Renee. "Ella was from a rough background, but what a sweet girl with just the prettiest curly hair. We just thought they were friends, but one day he brought her over to dinner, and it was clear what was going on. He was twenty. She was fourteen."

Renee's stomach turned, and Angus seemed to know what she was thinking.

"I took him aside," he said gruffly. "Told him no son of mine would be carrying on like that."

"That's when he left," Gert said. "Didn't even say goodbye. Ella had a baby after that. Her folks put it up for adoption, and we never heard about it anymore. They weren't the kind of people . . ." Her voice trailed off.

"We taught our boys to do the right thing," Angus mumbled. "But Everett always wanted another way."

"He went to law school, I know that," Gert said, almost defensively. "We found that out when we read about him in the papers later. When I saw those news articles about him and his wife, I thought she looked so pretty and smart. I thought . . ." She took a deep breath, as if the next words were too thorny to speak. "I thought, when a man does something like that, everyone wonders what a terrible person his mother must have been to make him turn out that way."

Angus couldn't pull his eyes away from the table, but he put one hand on Gert's arm and squeezed tightly.

Renee discovered she hadn't taken a breath in a while, and she forced herself to inhale unsteadily. "Did you come forward?" she asked. "Did you tell people what he did to Ella?"

Gert shook her head slightly. "You just can't do that, not to your own child. But also . . ." Her voice faded, and her husband took up the sentence.

"Nobody asked."

Renee felt tears burn the backs of her eyes. This couple definitely hadn't been interested in notoriety, but if they had been waiting for the press to come to their door, perhaps it was because they were hoping to have their hand forced, to be made to tell the story that would betray their son but which they knew, deep down, needed to be told. She felt proud, in a way, to be trusted with the thing. But even more, she feared what they were telling her.

"And Ella? What happened to her?" she asked, her mouth almost too dry to work.

Gert shrugged. "She left at some point too. Can't blame her." There was a long pause, and then she said quietly, "How's Everett?"

"I think he's happy," Renee said, which was the truth. "You probably know that he did get exonerated and let out of prison. Technically, he's innocent of killing his wife."

Angus made a huffing noise. "We read about that too. The new guy let Everett out to prove he was different from the guy before him. All politics. Don't mean anything."

The air in the room felt heavy, and she wanted to escape, to be anywhere else, but she was also afraid of letting the moment end. As soon as she left, she would be alone with it all.

"So," she said slowly. "What do you think of all of it?"

"Well," Gert said. "I don't know what I didn't witness myself, but I do know that when a man thinks he can get away with things, with hurting a woman, he'll keep trying until someone stops him." She pushed herself away from the table suddenly, and Renee knew this was her invitation to leave.

She rose and moved to the door, but something was making her heart knock like a trapped thing in her chest. "Ella Barnet?" she asked as she stood in the front doorway. "Is that short for Elizabeth?"

Gert nodded. "You know her?"

Renee took the fifty miles back to Richmond faster than was safe, her hands clenched on the wheel to stop them from shaking. She listened again and again to the third episode of *Innocent Blood*, in which Mariah outlined her own motivations behind becoming a journalist. As Mariah talked about the expectations society places on the behavior of women, Renee listened for every detail about the graduate student Elizabeth Barnet, who was murdered on the Richmond University campus just four months before Julie died. Elizabeth had been thirty-four in 2018. That would have made her fourteen when Ed was twenty.

If her mind was racing down the right path, Kim and the children were living in a house with a man who'd killed. Twice.

She leaned on the gas pedal.

CHAPTER 17

Renee couldn't focus on anything over the next few days. She monitored Ed's whereabouts at all times and planned her errands so Kim and the children weren't alone in the house with him, if she could help it. She alternated between telling herself she was paranoid and telling herself that paranoia was made for times like this: times when you find yourself living in a house with a murderer.

At night, she would lie in bed, take her phone off the household Wi-Fi, just in case Ed had some way of monitoring that, and scroll for hours, searching for everything she could find about Elizabeth.

As Mariah had mentioned in the podcast, there had been a media storm when Elizabeth was murdered in January of 2018, but speculation was plentiful and details were few. Much was discussed of the cash deposit Elizabeth had made to her bank account a month before her death in the amount of $1,700.

"It's my sincere personal belief that Elizabeth was involved in a notorious porn ring at RU," wrote one confident blogger. "I have reason to believe this because I dated a guy who was in this porn ring, and it was a really bad scene."

"Countless graduate students turn to sex work to support their education," wrote another. "It's simply tragic that Elizabeth couldn't pay for school without turning to an illegal trade."

Her roommate at the time, Daisy Richards, had given one interview a few months after the murder, in which she'd praised Elizabeth's resilience and self-sufficiency. "Elizabeth came from a really tough background, and she didn't talk about it much, but she was determined to make something of herself and show the world that she was worth something. She worked so hard, and I miss her so much."

Only two pictures of Elizabeth were available online, an RU ID photo, and a snapshot of Elizabeth with a few friends at a club. In both pictures, she smiled at the camera, with an open expression, her curly red hair tumbling over one shoulder in what must have been her signature style. *What a sweet girl,* Gert had said, *with just the prettiest curly hair.*

Renee's chest felt hot looking at the pictures. It wasn't proof, but the coincidences were sure adding up.

After Ed left home, he would have gone to Williamsburg, changed his name, and gotten himself into law school somehow. In the interim, Ella would probably have been doing her best to grow up after, if what Gert and Angus had said was true, being sexually abused and giving birth to a baby she was forced to give up. Ed would have moved to Richmond with Julie, settling down at 1125, just a pleasant walk from the Richmond University campus, where Ella would eventually find her way to graduate school.

From there, it was easy to imagine that Ella and Ed might run into each other by accident one day, and it was hard to imagine they wouldn't recognize one another.

During Ed's first trial, lawyers had argued whether money and prestige was a good enough motive for Ed to murder Julie, but they didn't know about Ella. They didn't know that even Ed's mother believed he was the type of man who would keep hurting women until someone stopped him.

But now Renee knew, and she had to figure out what to do about it.

Caz's eighteenth birthday dawned on a gray October Saturday, but Renee didn't feel the holiday spirit.

In the kitchen, Kim had enlisted Oliver's help in making blueberry pancakes. She set the dining room table with bright-blue napkins, a little jug of warm maple syrup, and bowls of whipped cream and strawberries. She even tied a cluster of silver and gold balloons to a seat of honor. It was a commendable effort, and Renee hoped the newly minted adult would be appreciative.

When Caz came downstairs, she was freshly showered, her asymmetrical bob carefully blow dried, and she had an air of deliberate calm that Renee couldn't quite interpret.

Kim went to get Ed from his study, and the family gathered to sing—Oliver making sure to be loudest—around a single birthday candle in a stack of pancakes.

"These are delicious," Caz said. "Thanks, Kim."

"What do you want to do today?" Kim asked. "Go shopping? Mani-pedis? Fancy dinner? Anything you want."

"Actually," Caz said, laying down her fork. "There's something important I have to tell you all."

Renee, observing from her place by the kitchen island, clenched. What had the teenager learned?

"I'm moving out of the house today," Caz went on. "Natasha's parents have invited me to move in with their family through the end of the school year."

"That's ridiculous," Ed said, as though he really thought it was a joke. "How could that possibly work?"

"I've already figured everything out," Caz said. "I've gotten a part-time job after school to pay for expenses. After I graduate, I can work full-time, at least until I start taking college classes. Grandma and Grandpa already said they would help me with tuition. I've done all the math."

"I don't understand," Kim said. There were tears in her eyes. "This seems like such an extreme choice."

"There's nothing to understand, because it's not going to happen," Ed said, his voice strained. "It's just ridiculous."

Caz met her father's eyes with a steady, dark gaze of her own. "I'm not asking permission."

From his chair between his parents, Oliver began to sniff back tears. Caz held out her arms to him, and he ran around the table to fall into them. "It'll be a change," she said. "I know that, but we'll still get to see each other. We'll do Ollie-Caz hangouts, just the two of us. Right?" She gave Kim a sharp look.

"Of course," she murmured, casting a deferential glance at Ed. "If it's all right with your father."

He returned her gaze with a scowl but said nothing.

"Yes," Caz said sardonically. "We'd hate for Ed to be inconvenienced in all of this."

"That's it!" Ed snarled. He slammed a hand on the table so that the flowers and maple syrup Kim had so carefully laid out trembled. "Go to your room, Oliver, right now!"

Oliver's eyes grew huge and his face grew pale as he whipped his head around to look at his father. There, in his sister's lap, he looked much younger than ten years old. Without a word, he jumped up and scuttled out of the room.

Ed turned his glare back to Caz. "This little stunt is over," he said between his teeth. "You've managed to ruin a perfectly good birthday with your selfishness, but I'm not going to let you tear this family apart."

"This isn't a family!" Caz shouted back.

Kim recoiled as though someone had kicked her in the stomach.

"You don't even know Ollie and me anymore, Dad! You never even asked if we wanted to come live with a bunch of strangers in the house where our mom died. You certainly never asked if we wanted to just pretend like nothing happened, because I can tell you, we don't. We want to remember our mom—like, you know, talk about her sometimes!"

Ed shot to his feet, taller, suddenly, than Renee had seen him before. His eyes and lips tightened, and he leaned over the table toward his daughter as if he wanted her to feel the physical threat of him.

Renee reached for her phone. In all her time monitoring his movements, she hadn't come up with a plan for what to do if he actually turned violent in front of her.

"I am your father!" Ed shouted. "I decide where you live!"

But Caz wasn't cowed. She stood, too, leaning forward until her posture matched her father's, her mascara-rimmed eyes locked with his. "Aren't you listening? This is about you acknowledging the shit that Ollie and I have been through these past few years. If you won't ask me what I want, I'm going to have to take it, and that's what I'm doing. I'm leaving, and you can't stop me!"

Ed's hand darted out, cracking across Caz's face with a sound that finally unglued Renee's feet from the kitchen floor. She charged forward, not sure what she was going to do but ready to do something.

Before she could make it to the table, however, Kim was on her feet, her hand on Ed's shoulder. *"Stop!"* she shouted, her voice reaching a volume Renee had never heard from her before. "That's enough," she went on, gathering herself a little. "None of us are happy with what's going on, but you both need some time apart."

She turned to Caz, who had a hand pressed to her cheek and flames in her eyes. "If you have a safe place to go, for right now, I think that's a good idea. We can talk about this more in a few days, when everyone has calmed down."

Ed sucked in a breath to shout again, but Kim turned him toward herself and looked into his face. "You have to get it together," she said. "You're going to wake up the baby and scare her."

Caz looked as though she would like to respond to this, but instead, she turned on her heel and went upstairs, blowing out a long breath as she did so.

Renee followed, not caring that Ed saw her do it, and found the girl in her bedroom, grimly tucking a few last things into a large suitcase that was open on the floor. She had begun packing the night before, it seemed, and the room, which she had moved in to not long ago, was already looking empty again.

"Are you okay?" Renee asked from the doorway.

"No," said Caz curtly. "But I will be when I get out of this house."

"Can I help?"

"I've pretty much got it." Caz swept her retainer case and hand cream off the nightstand and into the suitcase. "Just gotta get this over with." She picked up a framed photo of herself as a baby in her mother's arms, a keepsake brought with her from her grandparents' house, and looked at it before packing it safely between a pair of black sweaters. She made a humphing noise. "Who knows what she would think about all this."

"I think she would think you were a strong girl and it's important to look after yourself."

Caz smirked. "I hope so, especially after that showing from Dad. She would probably say 'This is all *CAB*!'"

"What?"

Caz gave a wry smile. "She was always in a hurry, so she had these acronyms she would use to supposedly save time, but hardly anyone knew what they meant. *PUD* was 'pick up dinner.' Her favorite was *CAB*. It stands for 'completely atrocious behavior.' Who knows, maybe she'd agree that I'm just acting out. But then again"—she waved her hand at the house—"none of us would be in this situation if she were here." She zipped the suitcase and stood it on its wheels.

Natasha, who was proving herself to be a young lady of great generosity and impeccable timing, was just pulling up to the curb outside, and Renee helped Caz carry her suitcase and backpack out to the car.

"Can you keep an eye on Oliver?" Caz asked when the trunk was loaded. "I'll be checking in, but it's not the same."

"Of course," Renee said. "I'll do everything I can to be there for him."

"I know you will. Thank you for everything." Tears welled up in Caz's eyes, and as if to control them, she rolled her whole head to look at the sky, which was overcast and lumpy with clouds. "You know, that night, I was so excited to be out of the house. I'd never had a sleepover with Hadley before, and we weren't, like, best friends or anything, but I was so happy to just get a break from my parents. They'd been fighting a lot back then, often about money and how much my dad was spending. They weren't even bothering to hide it from us anymore.

"That night, right before bedtime, I found out that I hadn't packed my pajamas in my schoolbag like I meant to." The words were rushing out of her now. "Mrs. Kowalski offered to drive me home to get them, but I had been looking forward so much to being away from home that I said no. I borrowed some of Hadley's pajamas. Sometimes I think that if I had . . ." Her voice collapsed into a whisper, as if she couldn't muster sound for the next words. "That if I had gone back to get them, it wouldn't have happened." The tears were falling now.

"You don't have to say anything. I totally know that my mother's murder didn't have anything to do with my pajamas or whatever. But the house just feels so tense, and I'm afraid Dad and Kim are going to start fighting any day. God knows they're burning through money. I mean, like, I don't really think the fighting had anything to do with my mom's death. It's not that. I just remember what it was like to live with all that anger as a kid, and I don't want Ollie and Willow to feel that. Sorry." She met Renee's eyes with a crinkling of her face. "I know that was way more than you asked for."

"You're a good person," Renee said. She couldn't think of anything else to say, but she also thought it was true.

Caz slumped into her arms, an unsolicited hug that made Renee's heart swell.

They said goodbye, and Caz climbed into the passenger seat beside the patient Natasha. Together, the two girls pulled away, departing slowly down the street.

Overhead, a wind rustled the drying leaves in the treetops, and Renee thought about Ella Barnet. Maybe Ella had been looking for Ed all those years but didn't know he'd changed his name. Maybe a chance encounter in this very neighborhood was the opportunity she'd been waiting for, to finally hold him accountable. Maybe she would have asked for money—call it blackmail or call it an off-the-books civil settlement, but it would have been the tiniest way of getting back some of the power that he had taken from her all those years ago. Maybe he'd paid her once, thinking he could get away with one two-grand withdrawal from the marital bank accounts—"walking-around money," as Conrad Harrington had described it. Two thousand dollars had gone out of Ed's account, and then seventeen hundred had gone into Ella's. That was two grand minus, Renee assumed, a nice dinner and a new pair of shoes.

Ella's roommate had described her as "wound up" during that time. Maybe that was the heightened emotion of a woman who was finally confronting what had been done to her in the past, what she had been taught to be ashamed of but what was actually Ed's shame to bear. She hoped there was triumph for Ella there.

But perhaps Julie had been more aware than Ed had given her credit for—Julie, who had loved talking about what she made, who had tracked every expense and receipt. She'd become suspicious of Ed's cash withdrawal, and when Ella had demanded another payment, Ed had known he couldn't risk it. He'd gone to meet her in a cold, secluded part of the campus, and he'd killed her. Maybe it had been an impulsive decision, or maybe he'd planned to get away with it because the link between him and Ella was so far in the past, had been kept so secret under a blanket of disfunction. And he had gotten away with it, as far as investigators were concerned. They had blamed Ella's murder on an ex-boyfriend and called it a day. Another win for old Ed.

Or it would have been, except Julie was on edge at that point, watching his spending, asking questions, realizing that she didn't actually trust the man she'd married.

Renee turned back to the house and was startled to see Ed himself standing in the front window, his expression hard, his eyes following her as she climbed the porch steps. He'd been watching everything, had seen the connection she'd shared with his daughter and the long moment of thought that followed, and he met her eyes through the glass, making sure she felt his displeasure.

Renee paused on the doorstep and, trying to keep her face as neutral as possible, raised one hand in a still wave. *I've got my eye on you, too, buddy. And unlike Julie, unlike poor Ella, I'll see you coming.*

By the time she made it through the door, he'd gone upstairs.

The good news was that one of the children was safely out of the house. Now she just needed a plan to get the rest out too. Worst-case scenario, she thought sarcastically, was that it would only be eighteen years before Willow graduated.

That night, Renee lay in bed, skipping through episodes of *Innocent Blood* until she got a crick in her neck. The later episodes of the season didn't interest her. They discussed the downfall of prosecutor Raymond Prescott and Ed's feelings about his appeal being granted. Episode seven made a lot of hay out of Ed's second trial, despite everyone agreeing it was pretty perfunctory. What Renee cared about, however, was the episode with Julie's last voicemail. She tracked to the spot in the audio recording and played it once, twice, three times.

> JULIE: [voice on tape] What are you doing here? We already talked about this, and there's nothing more to say. [slightly muffled] It's over and I'm empty. [sound of another muffled voice] What are you talking about? What have you done? [muffled noises] This is *CAB*! Stop! [sharper] Just stop! *No!* [swishing noise, thud]

Everyone had thought she was saying "I'm empty," the words of a woman who was fed up with an extramarital affair that had run its course, as Mariah had opined. But now Renee heard differently. Perhaps Julie was saying "I'm *MP*," an abbreviation she used to mean "mid-paperwork." Mid-paperwork on a divorce filing, perhaps.

And then, what had that other person said? She couldn't make it out. Maybe that was the moment Ed told Julie that the only thing that mattered to him was keeping his lifestyle, the status that set him apart, in his own mind, from his parents. Maybe that was the moment he told her that he'd already killed to keep that lifestyle and he would do it again.

What have you done? This is completely atrocious behavior.

She lay back in bed, her neck sore and her heart certain that it was time to tell someone everything she knew. Someone official.

CHAPTER 18

The next day, Renee seized a moment when Ed was at a dentist appointment to dart out of the house on the vague excuse of picking up some dry cleaning she knew full well was already in the back of her car. She wanted to be home before Ed got back, and she didn't want Kim to ask any questions, not that Kim was paying much attention to what Renee did these days.

The fifth precinct of the Richmond Police Department was a large brick building, austere except for a pediment over the entrance that achieved nothing in the way of flair.

"I have information related to a crime," Renee said, approaching the reception desk.

"What crime is that?" the desk clerk asked, as if she had never heard of such a thing.

Renee lowered her voice, feeling suddenly embarrassed. "It has to do with the Weatherup family?"

"Weatherup?" the clerk repeated at full volume. She typed a few things into her computer. "We have a report of some vandalism in September. Is that it?"

"Sort of."

The clerk gave her a narrow look. "I think we have someone who can talk to you about that."

After a few moments of waiting and shuffling, Renee was brought back into an open office space where people in and out of uniform typed at generic composite-wood desks, talked on phones, and milled around. A man stood up from a desk that was particularly laden with papers and file folders and gestured for her to sit across from him. "Detective Eric Dorian," he said, offering a hand.

Among the people in the room, he was on the younger end, in his thirties perhaps, with a clean white shirt and a neat haircut. She had seen him before, lingering on the edge of the crowd at the press conference.

"Detective?" she said, shaking his hand and taking a seat. "And you've been assigned to the brick-through-the-window case?"

"Well, not technically," he said. "I'm actually a homicide detective, but I'm available to talk to you, so I thought I would."

She smiled politely, but she wouldn't buy this story if it were on deep discount.

"In that case, thank you in advance for your time. My name is Renee Beale, and I've been the housekeeper at 1125 Linden Avenue for about a month."

Dorian pulled out a notebook, flipped to a clean page, and wrote down her name. "Do you know who threw the brick?"

"No. But I'm actually here to talk about the death of Julie Weatherup."

"Okay." Dorian's forehead wrinkled slightly.

She took her time, laying out the pieces she'd assembled in her mind: the nondead Weathers, the brand-new steak knife, Kim as Ed's alibi, Julie's acronyms, and Ed's hack cabs. "You've heard of hacking?" she asked.

"I'm familiar."

"I just—" she said, uncomfortable now that it was time to speak the words aloud. "I just think it's possible that Ed killed Julie."

Dorian's jaw muscles clenched one time. "I will say that we didn't know Mrs. Weatherup purchased a knife of that description before her death, so thank you for bringing that to our attention."

"What about the rest of it?"

"I don't know." He closed his notebook. "It's not illegal to lie about your parents being dead, and we were aware that Mr. Weatherup went on to marry Ms. Duvall. As far as Julie Weatherup, officially, I can't comment on what is, once again, an unsolved case. I'm sure you understand."

"Sure." She took a deep breath. "The thing is, I think Ed killed someone before Julie."

Dorian's brow lowered in an expression Renee couldn't interpret, and she charged ahead. "His parents told me that when Ed was twenty, he sexually abused a fourteen-year-old girl named Ella Barnet, and she became pregnant right before he moved away. I think that's the same Elizabeth Barnet whose unsolved murder occurred in 2018. I think—" She felt breathless and incoherent, suddenly, as she realized how much she sounded like the internet opinion-havers who wrote about Elizabeth online. *It's my sincere personal belief*. . . "I think that she found Ed and approached him for money. I think he paid her about two thousand dollars at the end of 2017, but Julie noticed that money going out and got upset. She'd just gotten a promotion and a big raise. Ed was looking at a life of leisure, but only if he stayed married to Julie. He couldn't let Ella ruin that. I think they met somewhere dark on the campus and he killed her."

Dorian started to speak, but she rushed on.

"And then, just a few months later, Julie said she was divorcing him anyway. It was all going to be for nothing. I think he had already gotten away with murder once and figured he could do it again."

Dorian held up a hand. "Miss Beale. I appreciate that you took the time to come in today. We're always interested in hearing from members of the public about potential safety concerns. But you should know that Mr. Weatherup was acquitted of murdering his wife, and that's the end of that. Double jeopardy attached with that second verdict, and now, no matter how much evidence we might find in the future, he can't be prosecuted for that crime again."

Renee became aware of how sweaty her hands were as she clenched them in her lap. "You'll look into everything he did to Ella Barnet?"

He gave a noncommittal grimace. "I'll be sure to discuss it with my superiors."

She gathered herself and gave him the firmest stare she could muster. "I know Ed killed Julie, Detective."

"You *think* he killed Julie."

She saw where this was going, but she couldn't stop. "No, I *know* he killed Julie, and I *think* he killed Ella."

"And do you have any information about the brick incident?" Dorian asked, giving her a pointed look. "Any idea who might have taken a loose brick from the Weatherup property, painted *Killer* on it, and threw it through the window?"

She sighed. "At least think about what I said."

Outside, she sat in her car for a few minutes, the autumn sun glaring on the hoods of the other parked vehicles. She was fully aware how unhinged she sounded, linking tenuously connected facts and creepy feelings like a conspiracy theorist. How easy it would make her life if she just let all of it go, as Dorian clearly wanted her to do—just turn her back on all her conjectures and focus on making money and doing her own thing. Why did she have to put herself in the center of this when all she'd wanted was a clean start and a chance to get to know herself away from home?

Then the scariest thought of all: Maybe this *was* who she actually was without her parents or Brandon to ground her. Maybe she was the person Detective Dorian had seen, a rabid busybody with no boundaries or sense, no purpose of her own outside ruining others' lives. Maybe she was doomed to be like this forever.

Then she remembered the look on Ed's face when Caz had challenged him, when he had slapped her at her birthday breakfast. Would Ed look at Oliver like that if he ever got in the way of Ed's happiness? At Willow?

She put her key in the ignition and started the car. No, people had been ignoring Ed's bad acts for too long. She wasn't going to be one of them.

That night, she opened up a new email account under the name throwaway5555 and composed a message:

> Dear Innocent Blood,
>
> I want to beg you to keep investigating Ed Weatherup. He's been lying to you about some important things, and he's not as innocent as he wants you to believe . . .

She wrote out everything she'd learned, everything she'd told Detective Dorian, and signed it *Sincerely, A Concerned Party*. She read the email over and, feeling like she was taking a page out of Andrea's playbook, clicked send.

CHAPTER 19

One morning at breakfast, Kim announced that she'd been talking to a counselor.

"Her name is Dr. Wanda, and she specializes in reunifying families after incarceration."

Oliver and Ed, who were eating cereal at the dining room table, both gave her a blank look. Everyone had been on their best behavior since Caz's birthday, and the house had a stilted, edgy quality that made it quiet, if not peaceful. Maybe Ed regretted slapping Caz—Renee wasn't sure about that—but he was making a point to be gentle with Kim and Oliver, and they were making a point not to upset him.

"Is this one of those things where everything is my fault?" he asked dryly.

Kim held up a hand. "No, no. I've been doing a lot of reading, and people who have been in prison often have what they call *postincarceration syndrome*."

She read from her phone. "It's a collection of symptoms including difficulty with trust, emotional outbursts, and feelings of anxiety. Family members may also experience feelings of uncertainty and vulnerability as they watch a family member suffer with postincarceration syndrome. This is all from Dr. Wanda's website."

"And how much does Dr. Wanda charge for her services?" Ed asked.

"It's very reasonable, especially if she helps us work together better as a family, don't you think? If it goes well, she's also open to doing a collab on my social media. I think I'm really finding a niche as, like, a prison-reform wifey."

Renee, who was sanitizing bottles in the kitchen, grumbled inwardly. A family counselor would have been such a good idea if the Weatherups could have brought themselves to do a single thing without an audience.

While Kim was thinking about prison reform and social media collabs, Renee was turning the house into a surveillance state. With the help of the online calendar, she kept track of Ed's activities.

Today

Ed—personal trainer @ 10:30AM

Tomorrow

Ed—haircut @ 2:15PM

Kim and Ed—video call with Dr. Wanda @ 4:00PM

When he was home, she avoided him by taking Willow out for long walks and trips to the park that the infant could only enjoy in a limited way. When in the house, she would leave Willow's monitor turned on all day, whether she was with the baby or not, and carry the receiver in her pocket with the volume dialed way down. Since she was doing most of the baby care these days, no one noticed that the monitor battery was constantly running low.

She put 911 on her phone's speed dial and kept it in her pocket at all times. As she moved around the house dusting and tidying, she mentally inventoried things that could be used as a weapon. Ed might pick up that lamp, but if he did, Renee could grab this coatrack.

"Is it illegal," she asked the internet, "to put a nanny cam in someone else's house?" It was, of course, but was it immoral in this situation?

The web couldn't help with that, nor could it tell her whether Mariah had read her email.

Meanwhile, Ed turned to working on his book full-time, spending most of every day shut in his study. He had a good excuse, of course. After all, the theoretical book deal was the only source of income on the family's horizon, and he did seem to be putting in a commendable amount of effort, filling up one legal pad after another with handwritten chapters. The pads accumulated in a pile on the floor beside his desk, and anyone looking at them would assume he was making real progress toward something that would be, if not great literature, at least a salable book that could effectively cash in on the notoriety of the podcast.

But Renee knew otherwise.

Each day when Ed went to the gym, she would slip into his study, ostensibly to collect old coffee cups and run the vacuum, and each day, she would flip through pages to check on his progress. The truth was that each morning, Ed started writing at the beginning of his life's story. He would be born to parents who he would characterize some days as harsh adherents to an abusive religion and other days as too lazy to feed their children. He would grow up struggling as a smart child in an inadequate public school system who wanted better for himself than to be the agricultural drones he believed his schoolmates to be, and then he would emerge from home at seventeen (not twenty, as his parents claimed), a rakish and clever young man who got through college on his wits and ingenuity, slid into law school to rub shoulders with the offspring of the rich, who barely believed he hadn't gone to the same prep schools they had. There was, of course, no mention of Ella.

And then, in law school, Julie would enter the scene. The exact circumstances of their meeting would change from day to day. Sometimes Ed was a bartender at a local joint patronized by Julie and her friends. Sometimes Ed's friends would bet him that he couldn't get the phone number of Julie, the prettiest girl at the party, and he proved them wrong. Sometimes he was just smoking a cigarette on the quad after an exam and Julie wanted to bum one. In every iteration, however, beautiful, feather-haired Julie gravitated to him, lured in by the blue-collar charm that the boys in her elite circle couldn't compete with, though they often tried.

And then the chapter would conclude, and the next day, it would begin all over again. After two weeks of steady work, Ed had accumulated a dozen versions of the first chapter of his life and not a single chapter two. Renee wasn't an expert, but she didn't think that was the way to get a book finished.

She started to wonder what she'd do if Mariah never acted on her tip email. She could try taking the podcaster aside in person and sharing her concerns, but she worried Mariah would be even less receptive than Detective Dorian had been. She would assume Renee was a fame-seeking wacko who'd sniffed out a chance to claim the story as her own. One day when she had a few precious hours alone in the house, she photographed each of the pages of Ed's many first chapters. With these, she could show Mariah that a man who was incapable of telling the truth about how he and Julie had met couldn't be trusted to be honest about other things.

And if Mariah didn't listen to her, then what? Would she wait until Ed published his book and then take to the internet with her photos and accuse him of misleading his readers? That would only get her fired, separated from the children.

There was also the option of just telling Kim what she knew, but she wasn't sure that was even safe. Mariah herself had said that the most dangerous day in a woman's life is the day she leaves a dangerous man. She couldn't send Kim into a tailspin unless she had a plan for how to deal with it.

Just be patient, whispered Enid Salinas of *Today's Housekeeping Essentials. Daily hard work will pay off in the form of strong strategies for exposing your employers' criminal misdeeds.*

One day in late October, Oliver came home from school and headed straight for the kitchen, hoisting himself up onto a stool at the island, letting his backpack slump on the floor. Now that Caz wasn't around to take him to and from school, his parents had decided that he was old enough to walk by himself, and he was a bit sweaty from the five-block hike, his hair sticking in loops to his forehead.

"How was school?" Renee asked. She'd made a batch of pumpkin muffins from a recipe Kim was "testing" that had applesauce instead of sugar, but she'd sneaked some chocolate chips into the ones she offered to Oliver now.

"Thank you," he said. "It was okay. Shane got wheelie sneakers for his birthday, but he wasn't supposed to wear them to school and got sent home."

"Wow," Renee said, unsure what the import of this news was supposed to be.

"Everybody's having birthdays but me," he added glumly.

"You know you're going to have one soon enough," Renee said. "When is it? We can plan something special."

"March twenty-third," Oliver replied as he finished the first muffin and started a second. He didn't sound excited, and Renee couldn't fault him for that. They both knew how birthdays went in this household. After a while, he said, "Dr. Wanda says we should do fun things together as a family."

"Okay, sure."

"Do you think I could have a sleepover at Caz's new place?" he asked. "That would be fun."

"That does sound like fun. How about you ask your dad?"

"Actually." The boy wiped crumbs from the front of his shirt, but he didn't meet her eyes. "Can you, like, set it up? I don't really want to ask my dad."

"Oh." She did her best to keep her expression neutral. "Why not?"

"I don't know," he mumbled. "I just don't want him to get mad at me."

She felt like crying, but that would have been unfair to the hunched child in front of her. She had no idea what Oliver did or didn't know about his father at this point, but he could sense the conflict in the house, and he was scared. She put her arms around him, smelling the still-childlike sweat in his hair, and hugged him tight.

"I'm glad you told me what you're feeling," she said. "And I will always do whatever I can to keep you safe." She just wished she knew what exactly to do.

"We've got to get Willow back into day care," Kim said one morning as she and Ed went over the calendar at the dining table. "I cannot get anything done around here." Willow's teeth had begun emerging one at a time in a slow, painful march that made her fuss nearly constantly, and the short naps, the crying, and the clinging were beginning to wear on Kim and Renee, though the latter knew better than to complain about it.

"We're both here all day long," Ed said. "And we have a housekeeper. Isn't that enough?"

Renee, washing vegetables in the kitchen, slowed her work ever so slightly.

"You're in your study all day long," Kim said. "You don't even know what goes on in the rest of the house."

"I'm writing my book; you know that."

"Yes, but . . ." Kim's voice trailed off, but Ed was already on the offensive.

"My book is a real thing," he snapped. "Even if you don't respect it."

The temperature in the room rose. Kim exhaled harshly and made a sharp gesture for Ed to follow her. They got up and moved to the family room. Renee waited for the door to slam behind them and then crept after, barely breathing.

"I know you're writing this book, okay, but I have things to do too," Kim said, her words muted but still quite audible. "I want to get a website launched, and I need time to take a food styling class online."

"You're the one who wanted to take her out of day care in the first place," Ed said. "And quit your well-paying job."

"Yes," Kim said with dangerous enunciation. "Because I thought at least one of us would have an income. You used to be a lawyer, for God's sake. I thought you could just go back to that. But whatever. If this book is going to be so successful, at least it will pay for us to be comfortable, right?"

"That's not even a question," Ed said. "Mariah says she can get me six figures, easy, and then the royalties will just roll in, which you should be happy about, since dollar signs are all you see when you look at me, apparently."

"That's not fair, Ed!" Kim cried. "You were in prison when I married you. I waited for you!"

"Did you? I don't know if I want to spend that money on day care for a baby I'm not sure is even mine." The words hung in the air, poisonous.

"How could you say that?" Kim hissed.

Renee hovered, unsure whether her first move should be to rush into the room or stay safely out of reach where she could call 911. Either action would have consequences she couldn't undo.

She found herself drifting to the dining room wall like she imagined young Caz might have done in the weeks before Julie's death, listening to her parents argue with 10 percent voyeurism and 90 percent self-preservation. Surely Ed wouldn't do anything when he knew someone else was in the house. That wasn't his MO.

"You could have forged those documents from the IVF clinic," he said, as if everyone would know how to do this.

"That's ridiculous! What's wrong with you?"

"I found your condom, Kim." Disgust reverberated off the walls. "In my study, no less. How many boyfriends did you have parading in and out of my own house?"

"I can't take this," Kim said. "You're being an asshole. If you really think she's not yours, we can get a paternity test done, but otherwise, I don't want to hear anything about this again."

Renee's lips made an involuntary ooh of surprise. Kim could issue that challenge with confidence because she already knew what the paternity test would reveal, but even she had seemed to need confirmation at some point.

"I don't hear you denying that you slept around on me," Ed retorted. "That condom had to come from somewhere." He was fully shouting now.

"It's not mine! It's probably Catherine's!"

"She's gay!" Ed snarled. "Everybody knows that."

"Whatever!" Kim shouted back. "Then it's Renee's!"

Renee tried to take a breath and discovered a sharp metal taste in her mouth. She should have thrown away that condom. It was the only time she had ever decided to butt out, and this is what it got her.

"Whatever you say," Ed growled. "You were never planning on actually having to be married to me."

"Were you ever planning on supporting your family?"

There was a slamming noise, and then Ed's shoes stomped up the stairs, the cue for Renee to scuttle back to the kitchen and begin vigorously scrubbing potatoes at the sink. Up in the nursery, Willow started crying, roused from her nap by the noise. A second, electronic version of her voice echoed from Renee's back pocket, and she changed course, drying her hands and hurrying up the stairs before anyone else could go to the baby.

"I'm sorry you had to hear all that earlier," Kim said later in the day, when Renee brought Willow upstairs for a bottle and bath. Kim was sitting in bed, propped up on all sides with white pillows like a consumptive Victorian lady with a morose look on her face and Instagram open on the tablet in front of her. "It's all very unpleasant," she said glumly.

"No need to apologize. Fights happen," Renee said, as though the argument earlier in the day had been anything like a normal household spat.

"I just thought we were on the same page about how things were going to be, you know? Maybe I didn't know anything," she added, detangling herself from the bedclothes and holding out her arms for her child. "It's not like anyone showed me what a good marriage was supposed to look like."

They moved into the nursery, where Kim sat down to feed Willow, and Renee began piling balled up socks and folded sleepers into the appropriate spots. She wondered if it made Kim uncomfortable to see someone's hands moving so close to the secret envelope with the DNA test at the bottom of the drawer, but the other woman's mind seemed entirely elsewhere.

"It's a weird thing," Kim went on, "to have someone tell your story for you while it's happening. When Ed and I first got married and Mariah was investigating and recording those first few episodes, it felt like she really got us, really understood what an unfair situation we were in and could make other people understand us. I think I just assumed that once her podcast was over, we would have our happily ever after, and we could just ride off into the sunset. That doesn't feel like it's going to happen anymore."

Renee, finished with the clothes, turned and leaned her hips against the dresser to listen, unsure where Kim was going with this train of thought.

"I shouldn't complain, obviously," Kim said. "Mariah did an amazing thing for us, but inside the house, inside the story, Ed and I are alone in this."

"You have me," Renee said, softly chiding. Despite the fact that Kim had used her as a scapegoat mere hours ago.

"And I'm so grateful for that," Kim rushed on. "But at soccer games or school drop-off, people don't take an interest in us; they just care about Mariah's *version* of us. I don't want that to be our lives. I don't want that to be Willow's life. Which is why," she continued with the air of someone deliberately steering into optimism, "I want to give her the chance to play with other kids. That's what day care is for."

Renee nodded, thinking of Caz's words: *They're burning through money.* "I'm sure that'll be possible soon," she said, hoping she sounded encouraging but not too encouraging.

"Oh, it's gonna happen," Kim said, gathering strength. "And I know Ed was all pissy about it today, but true crime books are all the rage, and according to Mariah, he'll get the first installment of that six-figure advance as soon as he can sign with a publisher. For that, he only needs an outline and a couple of chapters, and I know he's working hard on it. It'll come together fast."

"Sure." Renee thought of the many universes of Ed's "Chapter One" littering the floor of the study just below them.

"And, you know," Kim went on. "Every marriage has problems. He's my husband, and I just have to trust him. That's why I'm just going ahead. I found a really nice day care near here—it's pricy, but the best ones are—and I'm going to put Willow's first month on the credit card and just pay it off as soon as the money starts coming in."

A pit opened in Renee's stomach, and her few remaining boundaries fell in.

"I've got to tell you something." She knew it was a bad idea, but if the family went bankrupt, they would all be in trouble. "I think Ed has been struggling with writing."

Kim looked up so fast she jostled the bottle in Willow's mouth, and the infant reached out reflexively. "What are you talking about?"

"He's just been rewriting one chapter for the last two weeks, and the facts . . ." She fished for a politic way to say it. "The facts of the story keep changing."

Kim's eyes widened. "What do you mean?" she asked, a fearful note creeping into her voice.

"It's his early life, mainly," Renee said quietly. She was opening a door that she couldn't close by talking to Kim in this way, revealing that she knew things about the woman's own marriage that Kim didn't know herself. "He changes details about his parents and how he was raised. He changes the story of how he met Julie."

"Oh, dear." Kim gave a nervous titter. "Maybe he's just struggling with writer's block?"

"I'm sure," Renee said. "Maybe I just assumed it would be easier if it's just describing the facts of your own life."

Kim's expression morphed from uncomfortable to pained. "Sometimes it's not that simple," she muttered, looking down to fumble with Willow's burp cloth. "I'm sure he's trying his hardest."

In the past few weeks, Renee had been withholding a lot from Kim, keeping the other woman in the dark about things that directly affected her life and safety. It had been well meaning—or she'd meant it as well meaning, anyway, an effort to protect Kim, to keep her from inadvertently making things worse. But that was wrong, she saw now. It was infantilizing, and she was never going to be able to keep Kim safe if she couldn't contain even a little skepticism about Ed. But when and how did you throw a grenade like that into someone's life?

As carefully and kindly as possible.

"I think," she said slowly. "I think it's okay to still have doubts and complicated feelings about everything that happened with Julie."

Kim looked down into Willow's face as the baby sucked placidly, meeting her child's round brown eyes. When she looked up again, there were tears on her lashes. "You know," she whispered. "I don't think I give myself the space for that."

It was an opening. Renee put down the basket. "How about you tell me."

"It's always been hard," Kim said with a sniff. "When I first met Ed at the law firm, I was twenty-eight, fresh out of a bad relationship, and he was everything I wanted in a man. He was handsome, professional. He had this beautiful home and family. Point is, I would have never tried to break up his marriage, but I just sort of put a pin in him, you know? I wanted someone *like* him and a life *like* his."

Maybe that explained why Kim never seemed to have advocated for selling this massive house with its dark past, Renee thought. The house represented the achievement of what she'd wanted all along, a life as close to Julie's as she could achieve.

"The Friday we all went to the conference, there was this celebratory energy. People wanted to let loose. I wasn't much of a drinker, but I had a few drinks at the hotel bar, and I was enjoying the spirit of the evening. A couple coworkers were flirting in a corner booth, and I saw them kiss. Ed was being really nice to me on that trip. He was always a gentleman at work, but he was sort of looking out for me like a big brother, making sure I didn't have to walk around the city alone, that kind of thing. I felt flattered that he wanted to sit beside me at the bar, that he bought me a drink and laughed with me even though I was a more junior member of the staff. I got tipsy, and I started to think that maybe if I waited my turn, sort of, I could earn him and all the good things he brought with him. It all sounds stupid now, but it felt like something was opening up between us."

Renee held her breath and her tongue. *Tell me,* she willed, nodding her head.

"I had more to drink than I was used to. Our coworkers were drinking even more. People started dancing, and Ed asked me to dance. I felt giddy and nervous, but I was wrapped up in the moment, and I didn't want it to end. Finally, a few people started going to bed, but other people said they were staying. Ed said, 'How about we get you up to bed,' and I just let him lead me away to the elevator. My head was spinning, and I thought there was a moment where he might kiss me, but he just grinned as he got out. He said, 'Drink some water. You've had a late night.' He might have said something like, 'It's getting on toward midnight, believe it or not.'" Kim squeezed her temples for a moment, as if feeling drunkenness surge over her again. "I thought, *He's right; this is the latest I've ever stayed out in my life.* I went straight to bed and woke up late with a horrible hangover and the feeling that something big had happened.

"That morning, I heard from some people that Ed had a family emergency. I was the first one to hear specifics when I got a call from Detective Evans. Ed had given him my phone number to confirm his alibi for the night before, and I was shocked. It was crazy. I told Evans about the whole night, the bar, going up in the elevator. He asked what time we went upstairs, and I said it was late, probably eleven-thirty." Kim looked up at Renee with a strange, tearful expression and made a noise between a hiccup and a laugh. "You know," she said, "even with all the media attention, there's one thing about Ed's case everyone gets wrong, even Mariah." She made the laughing noise again. "After I made the statement to the police, I overheard some coworkers talking about how the hotel bartenders got pushy and made them all close out at eleven-thirty, and I started reconsidering my answer. I did a little math and realized how stupid I'd been, blinded by alcohol and what I thought was romance. I was an idiot."

Kim was crying again, and Renee realized that tears were running down her own face too. Perhaps, on some level, even her tear ducts were trying to ease Kim's words along, urging her to say what she should have said all those years before.

"It was like nine thirty," Kim gasped, every surface of her face wet. "I was so drunk and stupid. I think I went to bed at like nine thirty and thought it was the latest night of my life."

Renee couldn't speak, but it didn't matter, because the other woman couldn't meet her eye. "The thing is, nobody in the group offered a different story. They were all too drunk or involved in their own drama to remember exactly who left when, and once my version of the night was out there, people assumed it was right. Later, the defense attorneys asked me to sign a sworn affidavit, and I realized how critical my testimony was to his defense. I was too embarrassed and afraid of hurting his case, so I signed it."

She scoffed. "It had all gotten so massive and scary, but then it didn't matter anyway, because he didn't do it, and he still got convicted anyway. So what if I put my thumb on the scales for him a little? Goodness knows the media put their whole foot on the other side of the scale.

"I was devastated, but Ed was so nice to me. He sent me a whole gift basket before he went to prison with a card talking about how good a friend I was and how special he thought I was. It meant so much that he wanted to stay in touch with me despite everything he was going through, and I'll be honest, I did feel special to be on the inside of such a big news story, to have that private insight into him and his character." She smiled a little through her tears. "There was a moment where every woman who followed the news wanted to see inside Ed Weatherup's head—whether they hated him or loved him, they wanted that, and I was the only one who had it."

Renee wiped her eyes on the cuff of her sweatshirt and tried to catch her breath. There was a lot she could blame Kim for in this moment, for wasting everyone's time and helping Ed escape justice. But the one thing she couldn't blame her for was wanting to be on the inside of the story. After all, somewhere along the line, Renee had wanted that too.

"We kept talking and writing back and forth," Kim was saying. "Our relationship grew, and I realized he could still offer me many of the things I wanted. He still had this amazing house; he could still father children, even from prison, and I knew he really was a decent man. He didn't kill Julie," she said, meeting Renee's eyes. "I know in my heart that he didn't, and I know my mistake doesn't matter anymore now that he's been convicted and exonerated again. But I've just held so much shame in my heart." She paused and stroked a finger across the wispy hairs along Willow's forehead. "Thank you for letting me tell you all this. I know I can trust you not to tell anyone, not that anyone would necessarily care at this point."

Renee wasn't so sure about that.

"I'm just so grateful that we're on the other side of all that," Kim said, wiping her eyes and smiling damply. "We're on a good path."

It was denial doing its oppressive work, Renee thought. Kim had barely heard the new information about Ed lying in his manuscript pages before she'd crammed it down into whatever mental hole it was in which she carried all her doubts about him.

For the rest of the day, she mulled over what to do with the news of Kim's alibi mistake (Kim's word) or lie (Renee's word). With two hours tacked onto his window of opportunity, Ed's movements on the night of Julie's murder finally made sense. He would have had more than enough time to hail a hack cab, drive south, murder Julie, and drive back again. With this damning information and a little stroking of Mariah's ego, she might now be able to nudge the podcaster into reinvestigating Ed's story. If *Innocent Blood* changed its tune about Ed Weatherup, she was sure popular opinion would shift as well, and that would mean no book deal and no more fawning soccer moms. Maybe Kim would finally realize she needed to leave him, and maybe the Lauderbachs would have grounds for reclaiming custody of Oliver. Maybe, just maybe, there was a route out of this house for all of them.

The house was dark, and Renee was in the second-floor bathroom brushing her teeth when the sound of tense voices coming from the third floor told her that Kim had brought up the topic of the book.

She turned off the light and eased open the bathroom door, the better to eavesdrop.

". . . depending on you," Kim was saying. "It doesn't have to be perfect. We just need the money."

"You don't get it," Ed snapped back in the strained tone of someone who wanted to yell. "The whole world is going to be reading this book, and I have to do it right. This is my life just going out there for everyone to see."

"*Our* life, Ed," Kim said in a muted wail. "It's *our* life now, even if you don't seem to get that. I made *sacrifices* to be here, and I want to be here, be married to you, but not if you keep making me look like a fool who's just along for the ride."

"What sacrifices would those be?" Ed snarled. "Getting to live in a nicer house than you've ever seen? Having the baby you always wanted? Being waited on by the household help? You want attention for your little Instagram account, but you're already a celebrity. I gave you that."

Renee sucked in her breath, but upstairs, Kim's laughter came quick, harsh, and a little too loud. She froze in the hallway, hoping Oliver, behind his closed door just a few feet away, would sleep through all this.

"You have no idea what I've given up, Ed. My freedom and my privacy for starters, and other things you could never understand. But I wanted to do it because I thought we had something real, something mutual. I thought you wanted that, too, but if that's not the case, maybe I should reevaluate."

Ed scoffed. "Reevaluate what? You need me, and that's not going to change."

"Maybe I do," Kim said. "I don't think that's a bad thing, to need your husband. But you need me too. We both know this whole happy-second-chance narrative doesn't work without me."

Silence fell over the house, a silence so ominous that it seemed to rattle against Renee's eardrums. *No, no, no, Kim,* she thought. *What are you doing?* The last thing they needed was for Kim to remind Ed that she held a precious two hours of his life in a secret place in her heart.

"What have you done?" Ed's voice was low and thick with menace.

"What do you mean, besides helping your son with his homework and hiring a therapist so you can work out your anger issues?"

"Did you email Mariah?"

"What are you even talking about?"

"She called me yesterday. She said someone sent an anonymous tip to the podcast about how I'm really guilty and I've been keeping a bunch of secrets."

Renee's face felt suddenly cold. Mariah had gone straight to Ed, even though Renee had handed her the Weathers on a silver platter.

"Of course it wasn't me!" Kim's voice was shrill with righteous indignation. "You know the last thing I want is more drama. I'm not an idiot! It was probably the same wacko who threw the brick through the damn window."

There was a pause, and when Ed spoke again, his voice was too low for Renee to make out the words.

"I know it doesn't have to come to that," Kim snapped. "That's what I've been saying."

Ed spoke again, still quietly, but at more length this time, and when he was done, Kim responded, her voice softer, calmer. "Of course I do," she said.

Just like that, it seemed, the fight was over. As Renee crept into her room and silently readied herself for bed, she could hear Kim and Ed talking, muffled voices back and forth, but no more snarling and snapping. Eventually, as she shut her door and lay down, there was quiet.

It was getting colder outside. She could tell by the way the floors creaked and the furnace kicked on. It would have been a perfect night for a deep hibernation, curled in the warmth of her bed, but she didn't fall asleep for hours.

CHAPTER 20

The next morning, Kim arrived in the kitchen looking a little bleary eyed, and Renee felt a lot bleary eyed, but the atmosphere was easier than it had been for a while. When Ed brought Willow downstairs clean and ready for the day, Kim received them with a big smile and a kiss for each.

It would have been normal and nice, Renee thought as she poured coffee and helped Oliver get his breakfast, if she didn't know that it was all teetering on a stack of lies.

Even the boy seemed to sense the easing of tensions. "Can I visit Caz this weekend?" he asked. "She said she'd take me for ice cream."

"Sure, bud," Ed said. "I'll help set that up."

"What about having a sleepover?" Oliver asked, emboldened.

"I don't think we need to do that. How about you have a sleepover at one of your friends' houses instead?"

"I don't have any friends," Oliver muttered.

"Enough." Ed squeezed his son's shoulder. "Get your shoes on. Kim and Willow are dropping you off today before they go shopping."

"I can do the shopping," Renee said, but Kim, who was pulling on sneakers and scooping up the baby, waved her off without meeting her eye.

"I got it."

When they had gone in the requisite whirl of lunch box, backpack, bib, and baby toys, Renee found herself alone in the kitchen with Ed.

He sat at the island, his eyes slowly following her as she moved around from sink to fridge, cleaning up the breakfast things. Her skin crawled, but she couldn't just walk away from the pile of dirty dishes.

Finally, she said, "Should I put on another pot of coffee?"

He set down his cup. "You're fired," he said.

Her arms dropped reflexively, and the coffee pot in her hand drooped, leaking dregs onto the floor. "What?"

"You're fired," he repeated, his voice neutral as though the conversation meant nothing to him. "We'll give you two weeks' pay in cash, but you have to be packed and out of here by ten o'clock."

"What?" she said again, but when Ed raised an eyebrow, she rephrased. "Why?"

"You don't know?" he said. In another context, with other people and other topics, his tone might have seemed flirtatious.

"How about you tell me?" she said dryly.

"Renee, we both know you've begun crossing some professional boundaries with my family. You've been talking to my wife behind my back, turning my children against me, generally taking it upon yourself to meddle in our business, and we can't have that." He raised one brow. "And then there's your cute little email."

She tried to keep her face frozen, but he must have seen a traitorous muscle twitch, because he seemed gratified. He waved a hand. "But I think we both know that no one's going to listen to silly little you."

"Does Kim know?" Renee said, trying to stay on the offensive. "About you firing the only person around here who makes things run smoothly?"

He gave her a disbelieving scowl, and she felt like an idiot. Of course Kim knew, she of the I-got-it and the no-eye-contact. She rolled her eyes. "Whatever," she said, a childish response for a situation handled childishly. Fear was inching up inside her, but something told her it was safer to show anger than fear in this moment. She plonked the coffee pot down on the counter and stomped upstairs to pack.

Tears came as she jammed clothes and toiletries into her suitcases, angry tears that made her angrier at their existence. This is what she'd been afraid of the whole time, that she would be cast out of this horrible house before she was ready.

An hour later, she stomped down the stairs, letting her suitcase bang the woodwork a few times. If anything, the show seemed to please Ed, who stood in the foyer with his hand out.

"Keys?"

She relinquished them, getting in exchange an envelope full of cash, which she stuffed in her pocket, uncaring.

"You're making a mistake," she said, letting every ounce of the aggrieved housekeeper show. "It's all going to fall apart without me."

"I don't think so." Ed gave her a wink.

Disgusted by his smugness and her own helplessness, she turned and ran out of the house, out of the life she'd been so desperate to start.

It wasn't until she was buckled into the driver's seat of her car on elegant Linden Avenue that she realized she had nowhere to go and no one to blame but herself.

"You're an idiot," she said aloud in the calm, clear tone she imagined Mrs. Salinas using if she were sitting in the passenger seat. "You're a damn idiot." How dare she believe she had a handle on the situation?

Her phone pinged with an alert that Ed had added a new agenda item to the shared calendar. It was a task color-coded pink to indicate it was Kim's to handle.

Oliver—drop-off for sleepover at Caz's @ 3PM

So little Oliver had gotten his wish, a chance to spend the night with his big sister and her hopefully very normal host family. She was happy for him. It was odd, though. An hour ago, Ed had gruffly dismissed the proposal of just such a sleepover, and now . . .

A cold feeling caused her to click on the calendar app and check the rest of the day's events. There was only one other item on the agenda:

> Ed—Pod-A-Thon overnight, carpool w/
> Mariah @ 11:00AM

The wind was kicking up, pressing against the car and warning of a clear, bitter night to come, the first really cold one of the year. She imagined Kim going to bed that night, alone with her baby for the first time since Renee joined the household, since the children moved back, since Ed came home from prison. Kim was probably looking forward to a peaceful evening on her own as soon as Willow went to bed. No night terrors from Oliver or fights with Ed. Ed, who was starting to feel the pressure of bills and expectations, who didn't like it when women made demands on him.

She thought about one of the things Stephanie Kowalski had said on the podcast. *I can't forget that Julie was alone in her own home, too, when someone attacked her.*

Renee's hands were shaking. It was all happening again.

She drove for a half mile and then pulled into a shopping plaza, where she parked and scrolled through the list of important contacts Kim had given her when she first started the job. Her initial thought was to call Mariah, but she discarded that idea out of fear that Mariah and Ed might already be together, preparing for their trip. Danny was the safer choice, and after all, Danny liked her.

"Renee, hi!" His voice sounded clear, almost close.

"Hi," she said. "Sorry for the random call. Is this an okay time to talk confidentially?"

"Sure, I've got a few minutes. What's up?"

"Here's the thing," she said, trying to summon whatever vein of previously undiscovered calm she could. "I'm actually a little concerned about something I noticed, and I wanted to give you a heads-up." She was a lot concerned, but that wasn't the place to start.

"Oh?" he said with placid interest.

"Well, first up, I've got to tell you that Ed's been lying to you about some things." As factually as she could, she recapped everything she knew. Again.

"Oh," said Danny, this time with a note of reservation. "Renee, did you send the podcast an anonymous email recently, by any chance?"

"Yes." It was awkward, but it was truth time now.

"You could have just told us your suspicions, you know."

Debatable.

"I'm telling you now, and there's more. Kim and Ed have been fighting about the family and his book, and last night, she reminded him that she has a piece of information that he wouldn't want publicized."

"And what's that?"

She explained about Kim's hazy memory of the elevator ride. "Bottom line, he had two extra hours in his timeline, and nobody knows but her."

"Huh." His tone was too reserved to read, but she hoped that was a sign he was focusing, not retreating from her words.

"Now Ed's setting up a situation where Kim will be alone in the house tonight, just now that he's feeling threatened by her."

She paused for him to fill in the gaps himself, but he said nothing.

"I'm afraid Ed is going to sneak home from Pod-A-Thon and do something to her," she went on. "Just like last time."

There was a long pause, and then he said, "Well, that's all very interesting. I can't speak to anything about Ed's actions on the night of Julie's murder."

No, Renee thought, *you can only do that on a national platform.*

"But I hear your concerns about the fact that there is currently tension in the house here when Ed's about to be gone for the night. I don't understand what you mean about Kim being alone, though. Can't you just kind of keep an eye on her? Just, like, turn on the security system if she feels nervous?"

She had been hoping, somehow, she wouldn't have to say this part. "Actually, Ed fired me this morning. I think he wanted to get me out of the way."

There was a soft noise on the other end of the line, and she imagined Danny rubbing a hand across his face with the resignation of a man who has found himself too close to a crazy woman. "Well, look. I'll take what you say under advisement, but Kim's a big girl. She can take care of herself."

"What about Ed? Can you keep an eye on him this weekend? Just, like, make sure he's where he's supposed to be?"

"Look, Renee, I know you've come to really care about the Weatherups since you've worked for them, and that's commendable. But this thing happens a lot in the podcast world, where people listen to the story and then they feel intrigued and want to, sort of, solve it for themselves. But that's not really how it works. It's just a good story, not part of some bigger conspiracy. Maybe you've gotten too close to everything and it would be good to move on with your life and let them take care of themselves from here on out."

Renee drew a deep breath and looked up at the linty ceiling fabric of her car that was beginning to bubble with age in places. It was over. She couldn't expect any more from Danny now. Maybe she'd completely misjudged his interest. "Okay," she said. "I guess . . . just think about what I told you."

She hung up before he could respond.

Debating what to do next, she sat in her car for a long while. She thought about visiting Detective Dorian again, but she already knew he wouldn't be receptive. No, there was really only one person who needed to hear what she had to say, and while that was also the person least likely to believe her, she had to try.

She waited around for a few hours until she was confident Ed and Mariah would be on the road, according to the schedule. She could only imagine that he was eager to get there early to glad-hand around the convention, hoping someone would ask for an autograph. He would want to dress to impress before his panel, soaking in a hotel hot tub, perhaps. Renee, by contrast, killed time by gassing up the car and checking the tire pressure and then, in the parking lot of the gas station, repacking some of the items she'd hastily stuffed in her trunk, planning a script for herself as she did. *Just hear me out . . .*

Finally, when she thought the coast was clear, she called Kim. Maybe it would be best if her call went to voicemail, where she could respond to Kim's chipper "Can't take your call!" with a succinct warning. Then she would have done everything that could be reasonably expected of her.

The phone rang once, and then an automated voice said, "The person you are calling is not available. Goodbye." A loud beep sounded in her ear, and she pulled the phone away to look at it. Kim had blocked her number.

"Goddamn it!" she snapped, loud enough to attract the attention of a couple of teenage girls, not unlike herself and Sarah May had once been, old enough to be out on their own but startled by the sound of blasphemy.

Kim wasn't going to make this easy.

Renee had left Linden Avenue so recently that her parking spot was still available when she slowed to a stop in front of 1125. *This is so stupid,* she berated herself. Maybe it would be for the best if Kim called the cops on her.

On the porch, she gathered herself, trying to look as normal as possible, and then knocked.

Kim answered almost instantly, a smile on her face that warmed Renee with the feeling that maybe her former employer was happy to see her—maybe she, too, had been eager for a private talk. But Kim sobered when she saw Renee, and she narrowed the door on herself as though expecting Renee to try to barge through.

"Everything's okay," Renee said, holding up her hands. "I don't want anything, and I don't want to come in. I just want to talk for five minutes, and then I'll leave forever."

Kim checked her watch. "Okay," she said guardedly. "You can't have your job back."

"I don't want it back, but if we're never going to see each other again, I owe it to you to tell you everything I know."

Kim said nothing, her eyes searching Renee's face for a sign of something, maybe instability, drunkenness, or anything else that could cause someone to behave like this.

"I know this is hard to hear, but I think Ed killed Julie, and maybe another woman too. And I think you're in danger tonight."

Kim scoffed. "Give me a break, Renee!"

But Renee bowled ahead with the story she'd become very practiced at recently: Ella, Ed, Julie's suspicions, her divorce filing. "He had already gotten away with one murder, so he came back from Baltimore that night and killed her. He had just enough time to get back, and it all worked out for him because when you were in the elevator—"

"Is everything cool here?" A man's voice and a firm footstep on the porch came from behind Renee, and she whirled.

It was Danny, dressed nicely in a linen shirt and smelling of aftershave.

She gaped at him, trying to reconcile his presence when she'd been sure he was on his way to DC. She looked for parallel surprise on Kim's face but saw none, even as Danny joined her in the doorway, placing himself ever so slightly between the two women.

"What are you doing here?" Renee demanded.

"I could ask you the same thing," Danny said sharply. "Is everything okay?" he asked, turning to Kim.

"It's not okay," Renee interjected. She had to get back on track. "But my bigger point, Kim, is that you might be in danger tonight!"

"Is this all because you got fired?" Kim asked. She gave Danny a helpless look, and he put an arm around her.

Renee rolled her eyes, nearly straining an optic nerve. "Look. I'm just trying to do the right thing, here. Everything I've told you is verifiable."

"Okay," Kim said flatly. "Is that all?"

"I've just told you that your husband is a murderer, and you're the only one who can prove it to the world," she said, her voice rising into unfortunately plaintive territory. "You have to know that Ed feels vulnerable now, and he's creating a situation where you're alone and he's out of town. To him, that's an opportunity."

Kim shrugged. "I'll be safe tonight," she said flatly, stepping back across the threshold and letting Danny pass her into the house. For the first time, Renee noticed he was carrying a small duffel bag in one hand.

Then it all made sense: the DNA test in Willow's onesie drawer, the overheard breakup call, Kim's displeasure when she saw Danny flirting with Renee, and Danny's continued flirting just when Kim might walk in.

"Damnit!" she said, raising a palm to block the closing door. "You blamed that condom on me!" In a clearer moment, she would have chosen to handle it differently.

Through the crack in the door, Kim glared at her with cold eyes. "You need to go," she said. "We Weatherups aren't your business anymore."

The door snapped shut, and Renee gave a frustrated wail that hurt her throat and undoubtedly alarmed a few neighbors. She was so annoyed at all of them.

She stomped back to her car with the aggrieved refrain of every woman who has ever run a household. *Do I have to do everything myself?* As the sun slid behind a cloud and passing pedestrians pulled their coats tighter around them, she took her phone back out and searched up the web page for Pod-A-Thon.

> All your favorite podcasters live in one place for a weekend of events and conversations about pop culture, wellness, and, of course, true crime!

With a general feeling of foreboding, she navigated to the shop tab and bought herself a ticket.

CHAPTER 21

The *Innocent Blood* panel was scheduled to begin promptly at 8:00 p.m. in the Premier Auditorium of the Century National Convention Center just south of Washington DC, to be followed by an after-party with a cash bar and a DJ in Ballroom C. By 7:30, Renee had already taken her seat. She'd been at Pod-A-Thon for a few hours at that point and had already eaten an overpriced burger from the food court and toured the main concourse as much as she dared, not wanting to be spotted by Mariah or Ed before she spotted them.

From what she gathered, Pod-A-Thon's attendees fell into two categories. There were the actual or aspiring podcasters, who dressed the part in jeans and muted colors and who slouched around, shaking hands and exchanging tips in front of booths that advertised **Beyond Rate and Review: How to Generate a Following for Your Feed.** Then there were the fans who clustered around booths belonging to their favorite podcasters to get books signed and take selfies in their colorful T-shirts repping slogans that made no sense to the uninitiated.

Thanks, Whatever Your Name is!

Murder Doesn't Pay the Bills

Don't get Me Started, Ashley . . .

Tired from the two-hour drive (plus the extra half hour getting lost in Alexandria traffic), and eager to start her surveillance of Ed, Renee was relieved to leave the clamor of the main concourse and take her place in an unobtrusive side seat in the auditorium. She knew this might all be pointless. Maybe she was wrong about Ed's intentions for Kim. Maybe he was just planning on being a shitty husband but not a murderous one. Maybe she was here, still casting herself as the hero behind the scenes because she couldn't bring herself to go home, go back to being Sad Renee, whom no one relied on for anything. She shrugged this thought away. It didn't matter. She was here now, and nothing bad was going to happen tonight on her watch.

The attendees who filled the seats around her were disproportionately women in cheerful pairs and rowdy small groups. They held cans purchased from the in-house bar, and many wore merchandise with the official *Innocent Blood* logo. She felt a burst of revulsion at the celebratory atmosphere. Didn't these people know they were giving Ed exactly what he wanted, confirming that he was exactly as special as he thought himself to be? Though she couldn't really judge. She, too, had felt the allure of almost-fame back when she'd sat just inside the window at 1125 Linden Avenue while the Weatherups had held their press conference. Yes, she'd reveled in it then, but she now knew that Ed was to be feared, not celebrated.

"Excuse us! Sorry!" She rose to let in a foursome of middle-aged women, who squeezed into the row beside her with their bags of merch purchases and matching homemade shirts that said **I'VE GOT QUESTIONS FOR ARLO**. When they were all settled, the nearest one turned and extended a hand. "I'm Terri! Are you here as a singleton?"

"Renee." She accepted the handshake. "Yeah, it was a spur-of-the-moment thing for me."

"Welcome!" said Terri's neighboring friend. "You can hang with us if you ever get lonely!"

"So," said Terri with conspiratorial intensity. "Who do you think killed Julie?"

"Well," Renee said with a dry smile. "So far today no one has wanted to hear my theories."

"That's so not true!" crowed Terri's neighbor.

"Girl," Terri reproached her. "We'll listen. This is a safe place. It's a community, really."

"Oh?"

"Absolutely," Terri went on. "*Innocent Blood* got us through Leslie's chemo treatments."

Leslie, a few seats down, raised her arms and let out a whoop. "Seven cycles, seven episodes!"

The rest of her crew echoed her cry, and one of them said, "Ooh! We should make that shirt."

"We'd listen to the episodes together," Terri explained to Renee. "And then we'd get on the message boards and exchange thoughts with the other listeners. We turned into quite the little team of web sleuths, honestly. We were on Facebook and everywhere looking at whatever we could find. We even sent some tips into the podcast email address."

"We found a house-painting company that had done work across the street from Ed's house around the time of the murder," Leslie said. "We thought Mariah should ask them if they saw anything."

"Did you ever get a response to your tip?" Renee asked.

"Not yet," Terri said. "But she has to look into it, right?" The group enjoyed a self-deprecating giggle.

"We're going to get white-girl wasted at this after-party tonight!" one of them announced to the laughter of the others.

"So what *do* you think happened?" Leslie asked, leaning forward to see Renee.

She basically had the speech about Ed's lies memorized, but she couldn't say these things now. She didn't care about protecting the Weatherups' reputation anymore, but she couldn't dampen the pleasure these women were taking in the day. They had been through something horrible together and had made it to the other side united. Their celebration wasn't about Ed or the podcast as she'd first thought; it was about their love for each other and their own resilience. "You know," she said finally. "I think I have some questions for Arlo too."

As Terri grinned and clapped her on the shoulder, the houselights dimmed.

A pompadoured young man emerged onto the stage and introduced himself as Andy, the event host. Next, Mariah appeared, dressed trimly in black as always, alongside Ed, also in black jeans and a black sweater, though only Renee knew what an obvious affectation this was. At first glimpse of him, the crowd erupted in screams and cheers fit for a rock star, and he turned to them and gave a jaunty tilt of his salt-and-pepper head that caused a few shrieks from around the room.

Ed and Mariah took their seats beside Andy and exchanged pleasantries, after which he said, "So your podcast has been a true sensation in the last year. Everyone is buzzing about it. What do you think it is about your story that people are responding to so strongly?"

Mariah raised her microphone, but Ed made it there first. "I think people love the mystery element. It's a whodunit with all kinds of suspects, and people also love to see a story where the underdog hero gets victory in the end."

Mariah smiled coolly in Ed's direction, and Renee wondered if his showboating was finally starting to wear on her. When he was finished, she raised her microphone again. "Well, Andy," she said. "True crime has always had a place in the public consciousness, whether we realize it or not. I think talking about crime helps us understand ourselves and a side of humanity that we know but have trouble grasping. We want to know why people do terrible things, and we also want to prepare ourselves or protect ourselves somehow, through knowledge. In *Innocent Blood*, I also make the case that true crime storytelling is particularly interesting to women because it's a lens through which we can better understand the inequities and the dangers women face in a world that views them as vulnerable, as victims, as Madonnas and whores, so to speak."

Andy nodded enthusiastically. "Obviously, all of us here today just really want to know one thing." He paused for effect, priming the crowd to cheer when he said, "Who do you really think killed Julie Weatherup and why? Let's hear from you first, Mariah."

She raised her microphone with a polite smile. "I can't accuse anyone without cause, of course, but I can tell you that whoever it was committed a grossly criminal and antisocial act, and his motivations might ultimately be nonsensical to us as rational people. And in a way, Julie wasn't the only victim. Ed, of course, wrongfully served time in prison, and Julie's children lost their mother. But there were also ripple effects in the community compounded by the media attention. After a murder, everyday citizens feel a tangible loss of safety, and I think that really happened in the city of Richmond after Julie's death."

If there was to be any applause after her response, Ed preempted it. "Of course, we can't say what was going through the killer's mind, Andy, but I'll say one thing for sure. Once a person kills like that—purposefully, methodically, and gets away with it—they'll probably do it again. At least that's what I've gathered from my reading into criminal psychology."

His words were so close to what his mother had said that Renee, in the dusky auditorium, felt a chill.

"I can tell you that our audience is so excited to have you here," Andy said, "and we already have some participants ready with questions." He turned toward the crowd, where people had lined up behind a staff member with a microphone. "Let's get those houselights up a little so we can have a chat."

"Hi, everybody," said one woman, breathless with the pressure of being the first. "I just want to say congratulations to you, Ed, on your freedom. We all love you so much, and we've stood behind you. And, of course, Mariah. My question has to do with what kept you going while you were in prison. What kept you sane and grounded that whole time?"

"Give me a break," Renee muttered.

"Thank you for that question and for all your support," Ed said, grinning into the lights. "I can't say that prison was easy. Obviously, there were a lot of tough times, but I tried to just stay focused on the truth and on hope. I knew I was innocent, and I was going to stand up for that even when no one else could."

"Another question for Ed," said the next audience member. "When you got out, what was the first thing that you were most excited to do?"

Ed chuckled, "Go for a long jog outside and then get dressed up and go out for a steak dinner. Fresh air and creature comforts. I'm a simple man."

"You had three kids," Renee growled. "Don't want to give them a mention?"

She'd said this louder than she intended, prompting an odd look from Terri.

"What has it been like, settling into regular life again?" asked the next participant.

"I'd be lying if I said it was simple," Ed said. "There's a lot to adjust to—but Kim is the light of my life, and she puts up with all the postincarceration syndrome and everything else." Coos of sympathy from the audience. "But we're working it out, and we're all looking to a bright and beautiful future."

The Q and A continued with one marshmallow-fluff question after another, and Renee became bored. Mariah seemed to share the feeling. She sat onstage, legs crossed, lightly kicking one glossy boot while Ed answered questions about what TV shows he'd missed most while in prison.

Finally, the host took back the microphone to ask about season two of *Innocent Blood*, and Mariah sat up straighter. "We, Danny and I, are so excited about what's coming up next in the show," she said. "We're going to tell the story of Claudia Castillo, a teenager who disappeared from a foster home in 2008. It's a fascinating and heartbreaking story about the roadblocks systematically placed before families living at the poverty line and young girls of color."

"Amazing," Andy said amid enthusiastic clapping. "And this is a great time to give a shout-out to your producer and podcasting partner, Danny Dudek. I think we all remember his sonorous voice from the truly iconic car-trip episode."

There was cheering.

"Is Danny here tonight?"

"Danny likes to stay behind the scenes," Mariah said smoothly, "but he's never very far away." Renee suspected Mariah knew exactly where her producer was that evening, but as the crowd cheered for Danny and his sexy voice, Ed glanced instinctively off stage, as if he really did expect to see the other man in the wings. When he didn't, he scanned the crowd with the slightest frown. Was he thinking back over the day and realizing he hadn't seen Danny at the convention at all? Then, for the briefest moment, his eyes narrowed and his lips pressed together. It was a fleeting look but an ominous one.

"And what about you, Ed," said the host, oblivious. "What comes next for you now that your saga is finally over?"

Ed recollected himself in an instant. "Well," he said, with a rakish smile, "I wouldn't say my story is over, in fact. I have so much more to tell. I'm writing a book about my experience, and I think you will all be shocked at some of the details that've never been heard before."

"Oh? Are there still more twists and turns?"

"Absolutely," Ed said, looking carefully back over the crowd as he spoke. "I've been working on my own theory of who killed my wife, and it has taken me down quite the rabbit hole. It's more complex than I ever expected. I see this as my chance to finally get justice for Julie, you know? To be, sort of, her angel of retribution."

The crowd cooed their approval. All of them would probably buy his book, if it ever got written, to watch him spin some poorly reasoned theory about the sinister forces of which he was the true victim. Angel of retribution indeed. One of the anonymous internet users who had threatened Mariah at the beginning of her investigation had been called angelofretribution. Perhaps Ed was so absorbed in his own story that the phrase was at the tip of his tongue. Or it was he who had cyberthreatened Mariah, just enough to pique her interest.

"I can't wait to share all the details with you," Ed went on, and his roving gaze paused. He'd seen someone who interested him in the audience, but it wasn't Danny. It was Renee. He held her eyes for a full beat. "But I'll give you a hint," he went on. "Julie was not the killer's only victim."

The crowd gasped, and Andy transitioned to concluding the panel and reminding attendees about the after-party, but Renee barely heard it. She felt pinned to her seat, unable to breathe. There were three hundred people in this room; how on earth had he picked her out? And what was she supposed to do now?

As the crowd began to stand and gather their things, she saw Ed lean in for a private word with Mariah and Andy. He might have meant it to look like the sort of collegial whispering shared by a TV host and guest before a commercial break, but a look of concern crossed Andy's face, and Mariah's eyes snapped to scan the room.

Renee scrunched down. She was hemmed in on every side by Ed's allies. Were any of them following Mariah's gaze to identify the interloper? The room suddenly felt very hot. She had to get out of here.

That was easier said than done, however. Panel goers were already clogging the aisles, and many were still chatting with their friends and new acquaintances. Renee weaved between them, excusing herself and trying not to look too urgent, but it was already too late. When she finally emerged from the back exits of the ballroom, two uniformed security guards were waiting for her.

"Excuse me, ma'am," said the taller and burlier of the two very tall and burly men. "We'd like you to come with us."

Technically, they weren't cops, and she could have run from them, but as they flanked her and other terrified-looking convention attendees parted ways to let them through, it was hard to focus on technicalities. She found herself walking between the two men through a staff door in an otherwise blank wall and down a corridor that smelled faintly of onion rings.

"What's happening?" she said. "I don't think I'm agreeing to this."

"Sorry, ma'am, but you have to speak with our head of security for a moment," said one of the guards. "It won't take long."

She hoped it wouldn't. She had bigger things to worry about right now.

Seconds later, she was escorted through a door marked **Security** into a bland room with a bank of monitors on one wall, a few desks, and a minifridge. The guards closed the door behind her and indicated one of the plastic chairs. "Our boss is on her way," he said. "Please have a seat until she arrives."

"I need to get out of here," Renee said, refusing the chair. "I've got somewhere to be."

"Sorry, ma'am, but we have been alerted to possible criminal activity, and we have a duty to protect the safety of the people at this event. That means we can detain you until we have ascertained the circumstances."

The circumstances were that while everyone else had been watching Team *Innocent Blood* having a nice chat, Renee had seen the moment when Ed noticed Danny wasn't there. He'd put two and two together, she was sure of that, and she'd seen the flash of rage, the kind of rage that would only further motivate a man who had already decided to be violent. She had to wrap this up ASAP and figure out a way to keep a very close eye on Ed tonight.

Just then, a wiry woman in a heavy-duty security uniform jacket strode through the door and held out a hand to Renee. "Hi, Miss Beale, I'm Cameron. How are you doing today?"

"How do you know my name?"

"Well, one of the convention attendees told us that you've been stalking him. He said you're a former employee who was let go and you've been paying too much attention to him and his family. Do you know what we might be referring to?"

She felt her face growing red against her wishes. "That's not how I'd describe it," she said.

Cameron pulled one of the other plastic chairs uncomfortably close to Renee and sat down, their knees almost touching. "Miss Beale, our main priority here is that everyone stays safe at this location. Can you see where I'm coming from?"

Renee rubbed her eyes. This was so stupid. "I understand," she said flatly.

"Now, our protocol is to ask one of the parties to leave the premises, and because the other party in this situation is one of the event participants, and people have paid to see him, we have to ask that you leave the convention center and do not return to this event."

"I bought a pretty expensive pass," Renee said, already knowing this tack wouldn't work.

"You can contact customer service at another date, but that's not something we can help you with," Cameron said calmly. "Now, we do have to confiscate that pass, and I'm going to ask these two gentlemen here to walk you off the property. Do you think you can go calmly so we don't have to get the police involved?"

"Maybe you *should* get the police involved," Renee said, a hopeful thought occurring to her. "If I'm such a big threat to safety, I'm sure they'll want to take statements from me and whoever this other super-important guy is."

"Now, I know none of us want that," Cameron said, glancing at the other two guards for confirmation. "And I think once you have a chance to calm down, you'll be happy we didn't go that route." She read Renee's scowl and added, "What if the roles were reversed here, and the event participant was a woman and a man was making her nervous? Wouldn't you want us to escort him out of the location?"

Renee had hit her limit. She needed to get out of here before she smacked one of these people.

"Fine," she said, throwing her event-pass lanyard down on the table. "Let's get out of here."

The security guards led her through the internal halls of the building and out a side door that exited onto a deserted cross street. It was fully dark now, except for the blue glare of LED streetlights, and anyone who frequented the business park for work had already gone home long ago. It was quiet enough that she could hear traffic sounds from a distant highway and the muted music from some after-dark event happening in some other part of the convention center.

Not ones to be accused of not taking their jobs literally, the guards hustled her across the road and down to the far corner, where a stoplight silently changed colors for no one.

"This is as far as we go, Miss Beale," one of them said. "Please continue exiting the area, and have a nice night."

"You're just going to leave me out here by myself?" she asked. "My parking lot is like half a mile from here."

"Our jurisdiction ends at this corner," said the other as they turned to go.

"It'll be so embarrassing for you if I get murdered out here!" Renee yelled after them, hoping those wouldn't be her last words.

Exasperated, she checked her pockets for wallet, keys, and phone and started walking in what she hoped was generally the direction of her car. She had to figure out a way to get back inside and into that after-party without a pass. Maybe there was a staff entrance? She would just hang out inconspicuously at the party with a drink in her hand and pretend to be on her phone or something. As long as she could keep eyes on Ed, she would know that Kim was safe, and that was all she could focus on right now.

She was still considering one unrealistic plan after another when she realized someone was following her.

Her first indication was the sound of brisk footfalls in the otherwise quiet street. Sneaking glances in her peripheral vision, she saw a dark-clad figure half a block back. They had hands in their pockets, and they were moving at a rapid clip, their shadowed eyes seemingly fixed on her.

There were a million reasons someone might be out on the street at what was really only 9:30 p.m., but to Renee, no innocent explanation could account for the intentness with which the dark figure appeared to be tracking her.

Clutching her jacket, she was torn between pretending everything was normal to avoid antagonizing the stranger or just admitting her fear and running for it. She was walking along the blank side wall of the convention center, and there was nowhere for her to turn, no more populated area in sight, no place to go except straight ahead. Unhelpfully, her mind conjured the image of Ella Barnet, on her nighttime stroll years ago. She quickened her pace.

Behind her, the footsteps broke into a run, and a familiar voice shouted, "Renee, stop!"

Turning and giving her pursuer a full look, she confirmed it: the black outfit, the long black boots, the wavy dark hair. It was Mariah.

"What are you doing here?" Renee snapped as her heart fluttered with adrenaline and relief. "Why are you following me?"

"What the hell is wrong with you?" Mariah closed the distance between them at a march. "Ed told me what you did, and I can't believe you would betray him and all of us like that. Hasn't this family been through enough?"

Renee took a step back. "Well, I can't wait to hear what Ed's version is."

"He told me everything. You drove a wedge between him and Caz and tried to make Kim backtrack on his alibi. You snooped through his papers, and you were the one who sent that psycho tip email to the podcast with all that made-up stuff. Seriously, Renee, what? Do you think you'll be famous? Or do you just want to make his life worse? Do you realize how hard all of us worked to get to this place?" Mariah was yelling now, and Renee found herself impressed by how much fierceness the other woman had mustered.

"Ed and Kim have kept secrets from you," she said, forcing calm. "He's going on the defensive now because I know things that can hurt him."

"Well, I know he fired you and then you stalked him here. Do you have any idea how threatening that is? You almost ruined the panel; he was so shaken."

"I gathered that when security kicked me out."

"This isn't funny, Renee!" Mariah leaned in close.

"It's not funny. In fact, I think Ed is going to sneak back to Richmond tonight and murder Kim because he's losing control of her, and to top things off, he just realized she's been sleeping with Danny."

Mariah's eyes widened, but she gave a derisive snort. "Even if any of that was true, how would he get there? I drove him."

"And has he been on his own at any point today? Long enough to make a deal with a driver? Long enough to buy a stolen car with cash? He knows how to do these things. He's been in trouble since he was a teenager."

In the sickly glow of the streetlamps, a furrow formed on Mariah's forehead. "That's such bullshit. Ed isn't going anywhere. You scared him so much that he had to skip the after-party and go back to his room. He's a wreck."

"Shit!" Renee cried. Ed was already off the map. She wheeled, intending to charge back to her car, but Mariah caught her arm in a surprisingly firm grip and held her in place.

"What do you think you're doing?" she snarled. "I'm not going to let you harass him anymore. I'll call the cops."

She paused, taking in Mariah's wide dark eyes and the alarm on her face. On stage, the podcaster seemed so self-assured, but she was still so young, just starting out in many ways.

"I talked to some of your fans in there," she said softly. "You made something that touched people. You did that, not Ed, but he's still happy to hog the spotlight. You don't need him. Don't bind your future to his."

Mariah looked as though the sidewalk had jolted under her. She opened her mouth to say something else, but even as she did, her grip loosened on Renee, who ran without another word.

CHAPTER 22

As far as she knew, Ed had left the convention center up to half an hour ago. Even assuming he needed a few minutes to exit the building and locate his illicit ride, whatever the specifics on that were, he still had a solid head start on Renee, who pelted, breathless, the half mile to her car and navigated the spiraling garage ramps with shaking hands.

He'd slipped away from Mariah and his fans with a plausible excuse, an excuse Renee herself had given him. Now, all she could do was race him back to his ultimate destination.

Once on the highway, which was sparsely trafficked at this time of night, she took out her phone and began dialing numbers. Kim still had her blocked, and Danny's phone rang quickly through to voicemail. She thought about calling Caz, but she couldn't ask the teenager to discover a murder scene. She could call the police, but tell them what? A man who had never made any explicit threats was on his way home?

Clamping her hands on the wheel, she aligned the car in the precise middle of the lane and put her foot down on the gas. She had to arrive quickly and safely and hope she wasn't too late.

Two hours later, Linden Avenue was quiet, dark between the streetlamps, which created stick figures out of the trees that had finally lost their leaves. Elsewhere, the murmuring of a city at night went on, but here, no one came or went from the stately houses. The neighborhood residents were home for the evening, happy to have snapped up all the street parking with their BMWs and mini SUVs, and Renee had to settle for a spot well away from 1125. She parked where she could, zipped up her coat, and jogged toward the house on stiff legs.

The porch light was on as usual, but the front windows were already dark for the night, with lights off and curtains drawn. Silently, she climbed the front steps and tested the doorknob. It was locked. She'd been so focused on getting here that she hadn't considered what to do next. Uncertain now, she sat down slowly, her back against the cold painted brick of the house.

Maybe she'd gotten here ahead of Ed, somehow. It would be a miracle if she could catch him going into the house. It was genuinely freezing, and the wind was brisk, blowing any heat her body generated away from her before she could enjoy it.

Moments ticked on, however, and she began to wonder exactly how long she could wait after all. An hour or two, maybe, but as the night got deeper and she grew more tired, she would be increasingly at risk for hypothermia. How embarrassing to die and be discovered the next day like some creepy adult version of the Little Match Girl.

Even if she didn't die on her former employer's porch, what then? How long would she feel responsible for what happened inside this house? How many years would she spend watching the Weatherups' movements and racing, uninvited, to guard Kim and the children at any perceived murder opportunity? She'd been played, sucked into the drama Ed, Kim, Mariah, and Danny had created around themselves. She'd bought what they were all selling, and here she was, still subscribed.

She imagined the story as her parents would know it: Their daughter had become so damaged and delusional that she had stalked a family just so she could be a part of something only she believed to be true. That's the story people would whisper at church and at the feed store. Just as Andrea had foretold, she would become the kind of woman no one wanted, the kind who could nurture nothing of her own, who could only latch on to someone else's family, someone else's life, someone else's man.

She cried, long silent sobs that curled her whole body as they came out of her, concentrated and roughened by just how unfair the whole situation was. It had been a long time since she'd wept like that, maybe not since those first chest-crushing weeks after Brandon died. And maybe that had been the problem all along. Trying to protect the Weatherups wouldn't win her any awards, but more importantly, they couldn't free her from her own grief. It had been a mistake to give them that power.

And then, from inside the house, she heard a scream.

CHAPTER 23

It was Kim's scream, coming from somewhere deep inside but still audible in the chill night. Renee was on her feet in an instant, phone in hand.

"I'm calling to report a violent domestic disturbance at 1125 Linden Avenue," she gasped when the 911 dispatcher answered. "There's screaming and sounds of a struggle."

"Are you inside the house now?" the dispatcher asked in a methodical tone.

"No, I'm out in the street, but I can hear it. It sounds bad."

"All right, I'm putting out a call to dispatch right now, but I have to let you know: We've already had two shootings tonight, so the response time might be up to fifteen minutes. I promise that someone will be on their way as soon as possible. Tell me your name, honey."

But Renee, who was already leaping down the porch steps, hung up.

Anything could happen in fifteen minutes.

In the weeks after Brandon had died, she'd replayed his last day over and over, changing one thing each time. What if they had scheduled their rendezvous earlier, later, or not at all? What if she'd gone with him to tell Andrea about the divorce? If she could have done anything to save him from dying alone on that icy, dark road, she would have. At times, she prayed for the chance, not even to save him, but to go back in time and be in that car when he spun off the road. Dying beside him would have been preferable to being forced to do nothing.

If I could have done something. . . It was the refrain that had tortured her in grief.

Whatever else happened, whatever other pain it caused her, she couldn't let herself feel that helplessness again.

It took her less than a minute to sprint around the block of houses and into the back alley. The high wooden fence behind 1125 was as impenetrable as she remembered, and the gate was locked, but the household's trash bins were still standing in the alley, contrary to city ordinance, their lids dangling indecorously.

Not caring if anyone saw her, she flipped closed the lid of one trash can and boosted herself onto it with a series of grunts and thumps. She straddled the wooden slats, teetered there for a painful moment, and then flopped across and down into the backyard. She landed harder than she wished on the brick pavers, twisting her ankle and triggering the motion-sensitive lights, but she couldn't worry about that now. Heaving herself up, she hurried to the back door, where a touch of the knob told her that it, too, was locked.

She was gambling that Ed and Kim had forgotten one pretty important thing, though.

It was easy to locate the loose brick in the west corner of the yard. Despite having been warned to move the spare key by officers of the Richmond PD, none of the Weatherups had gotten around to doing so. Maybe everyone had assumed it was Renee's job. Regardless, the key was a little cold and muddy but still right where she needed it to be.

Another scream and a heavy thud echoed through the house as she unlocked the back door and pushed inside. The big old Victorian smelled of Chinese takeout and scented candles with just a whiff of Ed's silver-fox cologne. It was dark except for the winter moonlight gleaming through the slatted blinds, and the security panel by the door was silent. Someone had already turned it off. The noises were coming from above, raised voices and the sound of sharp, uneven footfalls. Kim was sobbing something unintelligible in a heartbreaking half scream.

Without pausing to consider if this was really what she wanted to do, Renee was on the move, taking the stairs two at a time despite her painfully clumsy ankle. The second-floor landing was dark except for a moonbeam that crossed the hall from the window of her former room, spartan now, the door hanging open.

She pressed up the next flight of stairs toward the sounds of a struggle and a white glow emanating from the primary bedroom. "Stop, stop!" Kim was wailing. "Please, please, please!"

The scene in the bedroom was worse than she'd imagined.

Danny was face down on the floor, dressed in boxers and nothing else. His arms and legs were sprawled and still, making angular shapes in the blood that pooled under him.

Ed stood with his back to the door, a black-clad shape silhouetted in the gleam of his phone's flashlight, which he aimed down at Kim, who cowered in the corner closest to the nursery. She was dressed in a silky negligee, and she gripped her own forearm with the opposite hand, trying to stop the bleeding from what must have been a bad cut there. Her hair was wild and her eyes swollen with tears as she looked up at her husband, who raised the slim, gleaming knife in his right hand.

Renee did the first thing that came to mind. She yelled, "Hey!"

CHAPTER 24

Ed whirled, his flashlight blinding Renee until her groping hand connected with the light switch. Kim scrambled to her feet, blinking in the unexpected illumination, clutching her injured arm and panting, primal eyed, staring at Renee as if she wasn't sure whose side she was on.

Renee focused on Ed. "The cops are on their way," she said, raising her hands, either to defend herself or calm him, she wasn't sure.

"Meddling little bitch!" he barked, advancing on her.

As soon as his back was turned, Kim made her move, darting into the nursery and slamming the door.

Enraged at having lost one of his targets, Ed lunged forward with unexpected speed. He dropped his phone and grabbed a handful of Renee's hair, clenching it close to the scalp, and pulled her toward him. White pain made her muscles go slack for a moment, and before she knew it, he had her back pressed to his chest, his knife at her throat.

"If you leave," he bellowed through the nursery door at Kim, "I will kill her, too, and then no one will help you!"

But Kim's decision was already made. From the next room, Willow whimpered sleepily as she was scooped from her crib. Then the door onto the hallway opened, and bare feet pounded down the stairs.

In the bedroom, Ed's breath scorched Renee's neck and cool, brand-name steel nipped under her chin. She was alone with him now, gripped by the monster she'd been imagining for weeks. Her heart pounded, and her muscles, electrified to fight or flee, twitched, looking for a way to move that wouldn't get her throat sliced open. But inside her head, all she could do was think angrily about how foolish she'd been, foolish to have thought she was in control of anything, foolish to think she could stop the inevitable fact that someone would die tonight. Her mother would be so disappointed in her.

"Bitch!" Ed shrieked after Kim, and then he murmured, almost intimately, into Renee's hair, "Never mind her. What's she going to say? Obviously the three of you were carrying on some kind of disgusting love triangle and she killed you both. No one will believe her. By the time the cops come, I'll be gone. And I have an alibi." He clamped her tighter, his arm across her collarbone making it hard to breathe.

"Is that all you want?" she gasped. "More stories about you?"

"No," he said, a smile in his voice. She felt him press his pelvis against her. "I also want you to struggle."

Once, when she was too young to know most things, including the effect of hot sun on a car door, Renee had burned herself grabbing the door handle of her parents' station wagon. "Why didn't you let go right away, baby?" Mama had lamented.

"It felt cold at first," Renee sobbed.

That was how she felt now, as rage flashed ice cold through her body. But it wasn't ice. It was fire. Ed Weatherup was no enigma. He was just trash.

She snapped her head back, connecting with something hard. He grunted, and the knife blade slipped on her throat, searing her. It might have been a bad cut, but she didn't know and didn't particularly care. His grip had loosened, and she wrestled free, spinning to face him. At least it was going to be a real fight.

His nose was bleeding, and he wiped tears of sinus pain from his eyes, but he was already moving, lunging toward her again, knife first, uncaring what he connected with this time. He was backing her into a corner of the bedroom, his taller frame and longer arms blocking her exit.

"I know you killed Julie," Renee hissed, as her options narrowed.

"You don't know anything," he snarled.

"I know everything." She met his eyes as they each shifted, jockeying for an opening. "You let me into your life, and now I know everything."

He jolted forward, grabbing at her, but she made it to the door of the rooftop deck and, with a flailing arm, opened it and stumbled through. Her ankle didn't even hurt anymore, as though her body knew worse pain was possible now.

The night air had only been growing clearer and colder, and sweat and blood steamed from the neck of her winter coat as she emerged onto the deck, which was almost as empty and unused as when she'd seen it last. There was no evidence of Kim's aspirations for the space except a six-pack of tiki torches leaned against the railing, still in their wrapper.

It was a bleak place to die. But she wasn't the first person to learn that.

What would her odds be if she jumped from this third-story roof, she wondered as she ran toward the railing. She didn't want to jump—everything in her body told her to stay away from the edge. But Ed was pounding behind her, and at least the pavement below wouldn't derive pleasure from killing her.

But Ed seemed to be making the same calculation, and before she could reach the edge, he dove, catching the hood of her coat and yanking them both to the wooden planks.

They rolled and struggled for control, their gasps rasping in the night air as blood and sweat made any exposed skin slippery. Renee, dizzy and winded from her sudden change of direction, bit, gouged, and bicycled her knees in an attempt to nail Ed where it would hurt. But he was bigger than her, and she was getting tired. While he had been going to the gym and eating Kim's healthy grain bowls, Renee had been ironing his shirts and cobbling together a grilled cheese for dinner. She wished she could scream, alert the neighbors that there was a fight happening, but she barely had enough breath to power her struggle, and what noises she could produce sounded more like random quacks than cries for help.

And still he had the knife.

He jerked her up, and with a thud that made her ears ache, slammed her against the brick wall of the house, well in the shadow, where no neighbor who happened to look out an upper window would see them. One arm was trapped behind her, and he leaned against her, disabling her free wrist with a crushing grip. He pinned the tip of the knife to her throat. "I'm going to impale you," he said in a harsh whisper.

Renee's brain, exhausted and oxygen deprived, seemed to calm itself even as she felt the frigid steel burn her throat. If she were a bystander, a spectator watching coolly behind a screen, she might assume that the victim in the case might be racing to strategize her next defense. Or maybe the victim knew her time was over, and her life was flashing before her eyes.

But that wasn't really what was happening. Like a mind tired from the day and ready to rest, her brain drifted idly to the Pod-A-Thon panel. Mariah said that women follow true crime as a way to understand the flaws in culture and humanity. Ed said that anyone likes a story with an underdog hero. She thought he might be right.

He was just wrong about who the hero was.

"I know you only got away with it by accident before," she said, quietly, trying not to flinch as he leaned close. "I know you had to trick Mariah into even caring about you in the first place, just like every other woman in your life."

"You're full of shit," he snarled, spit flecking her face. He was in pain; she could see that. She must have gotten him somewhere good, but it hadn't been enough.

"I know about Ella. Your mother told me."

This got a reaction, a jolt of surprise that gave her the inch she needed to pull her arm out from between herself and the wall.

"Shut up, shut up," he hissed. "You have no idea what life I've led, what I've accomplished. You're nothing! You're a child!"

"Why don't you tell me how you killed the others, then?" she said. "Because it seems to me like you just got lucky."

He sneered at that and adjusted his grip on the knife. "Why are you obsessed with me, then?" he said. "Why do you care so much?"

It occurred to her that if she died, her body would lie up here for hours while police and investigators worked their way through the crime scene. After that, it would be a very long while before anyone would want to spend time out here again. One murder a house could almost survive, but two on the same spot? She thought about Kim's visions of patio cookouts and romantic sunset gazing. Those dreams would never come to pass. Not for Kim anyway.

Ed's snarling face was very close to hers now, and some cold part of her observed that was a good thing. It meant he might not notice as she slid her right hand up the surface of the wall, the brick scraping against her palm. She prayed that Kim hadn't gotten around to nailing anything down out here.

Her fingertips connected with rough, rusty metal, purchased by Kim at a yard sale for eight dollars. And maybe Enid Salinas was smiling down upon her that night because the metal rattled loosely in her hand. "I guess," she said to Ed. "I guess I don't care about you that much."

In her grip, the corroded iron sunburst slipped from its hook, and she swung it as hard as she could, ramming one spiky sunray into the side of Ed's throat.

He staggered back, gurgling and sputtering. The sunburst fell with him as he collapsed backward and lay, gagging and squirming, on the boards at her feet.

Not stopping to investigate, she slammed back through the door into the expansive bedroom, past Danny's body lying grimly still, and pounded down the stairs. Somewhere in the house, Kim and Willow might have been cowering, afraid for their lives, but she was bleeding from the neck and didn't have time to look for them.

So she thudded down the next flight of stairs and skidded across the parquet of the grand foyer. There was so much pounding—her feet on the floorboards, her heart in her chest and ears—that she didn't hear the pounding on the door, didn't process it at all until she flung open the front door and barreled out into the startled arms of Richmond PD, late to the scene, as promised.

CHAPTER 25

Ten minutes later, or a year, Renee lay handcuffed to a gurney in the back of an ambulance. An EMT, who smelled like a long night running on coffee alone, leaned over her, sanitizing and bandaging Renee's neck in two places. The flyaway hairs that had escaped the EMT's bun surrounded her head and created a halo in the gleaming LEDs of the ambulance.

Renee couldn't be angry about the handcuffs or the mumbled rendition of her rights that came with them. When she had charged out the door of 1125, her first words had been "I killed him."

"Good lord," said one of the officers, shining his flashlight in her face. "Killed who?"

"The killer," she said, and then she either collapsed or tripped.

Later, as she lay in the ambulance wondering what would become of her, she learned that no one had, in fact, died. At least not yet. The first ambulance to the scene had whisked away Danny, who was immobile on his stretcher and straddled by an EMT desperately administering chest compressions. The next stretcher out of the house held Ed, attached to IV fluids, with one paramedic holding pressure on his neck and another shoving him into the back of the second ambulance.

She knew Danny was in critical condition, and she was sure she'd feel very sad about what happened to him at some point in the future when her emotions had returned to a more normal rhythm. For now, all she felt was relieved, relieved to be alive, to know that, while she'd done some real damage to Ed, she was not, herself, a killer. She felt herself drifting, exhausted, euphoric from adrenaline and survival. Still, she knew she was in trouble. Somewhere Kim was talking to the police, recounting whatever version of reality she had pieced together in her panic. Renee knew better than to depend on her for an accurate retelling. Kim had chosen Ed over the truth before.

"Am I going to jail?" she asked, unsure who she was even talking to.

"Hush," the EMT admonished her. "The detective is going to ask you a few questions, and then we'll take you to get some stitches."

The aforementioned detective, who climbed into the ambulance and sat beside her a few minutes later, was Eric Dorian, looking a little rumpled and bleary in a fleece jacket, as though he'd either gotten out of bed for this or hadn't been to bed in days.

"Hi, Renee," he said. "I'm here to find out what happened tonight. Can you tell me?"

She nodded, causing a jabbing sensation in her neck, and the EMT glared at her. "I knew Ed was going to kill Kim. I came to stop it. He was already here. We fought. He tried to kill me, and I hit him with a sun thingy."

"Why did you think Ed was going to kill someone?"

Adrenaline was draining out of her now, and she could feel her nervous system crashing, her brain becoming foggier by the second. "Long story," she muttered. "What did Kim say happened?"

"Kim wasn't there," Dorian said. "No one else was in the house besides you and the two men."

"Well, I don't know what to tell you, then."

Outside, a car pulled up and jerked to a halt. Doors slammed, and Renee could hear a woman's voice asking urgent questions of the uniformed officers outside. Dorian looked out. "Do you know who that is?" he asked.

"It's the podcaster," she answered without looking.

"I should go talk to her." He rose to a stiff hunched position.

"Better you than me," she muttered.

To her relief, the EMT slammed the ambulance doors then, and they rode off to the hospital, where she was rolled through the loading doors like so much cargo.

The emergency department was busy. There had been two shootings, after all, and Renee had plenty of time to lie handcuffed on a too-small exam table in a too-cold curtained compartment somewhere near the lobby. An officer stood outside her curtain, waiting to make sure she didn't run away, she supposed, as if she would have had the energy to plot an escape.

Eventually, a resident who looked no older than Caz came in and gave her a few stitches in her neck and handled her ankle for a moment before pronouncing it "minor." Renee spent the whole time wondering what the doctor thought of the restrained suspect in her ER. What would anyone think of her now?

She thought about asking to call home, but Mama and Daddy would be asleep. Better to let them live in ignorance a little longer.

Sometime around 3:00 a.m., the officer entered the curtain area and cleared his throat. "We verified some parts of your story, so I'm going to take these back now," he said, unlocking the handcuffs and putting them in his pocket.

"I'm not under arrest?"

"Not at this time," he said. "You need to make a formal statement at the station tomorrow, but for now, you're free to go as soon as you get discharged."

He left before she could ask any other questions, and she sat, rubbing her arm and wondering why it seemed to be no one's job to talk to her.

When the nurse came in with the discharge paperwork, she asked, "What happens next?"

"You go home, baby," the nurse said. "Your ride is waiting in the lobby."

She couldn't even say what she expected or hoped for as she walked down the hospital corridor toward the exit. No one knew she was here except the police, and she wondered if there had been some mistake. The ride must be for a different patient, someone who hadn't stabbed a guy in the neck.

But she did recognize the person standing by the sliding glass doors. It was a woman in a large coat over pajama bottoms, a sleeping baby slumped on her shoulder.

It was Kim.

"Are you here for Danny?" Renee asked as she limped over to her former employer.

Kim shook her head. "Mariah and his mom are with him. I'm here for you."

EPILOGUE

Renee spent most of December in her parents' barn, which served as a workshop in the Christmas season. For the first time ever, she found herself taking personal pride in decorating the workshop the way she wanted to, hanging strands of lights and weaving festoons of evergreen to give off what she hoped was a sophisticated mountain-Christmas vibe.

"Where's the inflatable Santa?" Mama asked when she came out to inspect her work.

"He's skipping this year," Renee said, to which Mama shrugged and wandered off to deal with something else. She hadn't given Renee as much guff about things in recent weeks. Maybe the moment her daughter had broken into a mansion and fought hand to hand with a murderer was the rite of passage she'd been waiting for to finally start treating Renee like an adult. Or maybe it was just temporary pity that would wear off as the scars on her neck faded. Either way, she was going to enjoy it while it lasted. She'd earned it, not just the night she fought Ed but in the hours and days after.

The night Kim had picked her up at the hospital, they'd gone together to the same Howard Johnson where they had all stayed after the brick incident. Renee had sat on one of the beds holding Willow, drawing comfort from the small sleeping body against her chest.

"She's getting so big," she said, stroking the child's back.

"You saved my life," said Kim. "I'm so ashamed."

All night she'd been dying for someone to admit as much, but now that it was real, all she felt was the humiliation radiating off Kim, whose eyes were dark and sunken and whose arm was wrapped in a few drugstore bandages. She didn't know if she had it in her to comfort Kim anymore.

"I just didn't want to believe it," she gasped, sitting cautiously on the bed beside Renee.

"He put on a good face," Renee said, unsure what stance she was supposed to take.

Kim slipped under the covers and pulled the blanket up to her chin as if trying to ward off an arctic cold. The words came in a rush. "I thought he loved me. But I was the stupid little goose that accidentally laid the golden egg, and what was a few letters and a marriage license if it kept me quiet? You must think I'm a terrible person getting involved with Danny like that, but we really never thought Ed was ever getting out of prison, and I really liked Danny, and I think being married gave me this safety that let me open myself up to someone real and kind like him. And then Ed got his second trial, and we had to end it, of course. I wanted to really try to make a life with Ed. After all, that's what I thought I wanted way back when. But it barely worked; it was all just—"

"Yeah," Renee interjected. "I was there for that part." She felt very tired then, her body demanding sleep. Even the dim lighting felt too bright, and her eyes blurred when she tried to focus. She slid down the headboard until she was lying down, letting Willow settle flat on her chest.

"I know in a lot of ways I wasn't ready to be a wife and a stepmother, and I know it wasn't a traditional start to a relationship, but all those things we talked about over the phone, family vacations and school graduations, teaching the kids to drive. I thought he really did want those things. I thought he really had gotten attached, you know?"

Renee closed her eyes and felt herself start sinking into oblivion. "Maybe not," she murmured. "But double jeopardy had attached."

The next day, she spent hours explaining and reexplaining what had happened. She called home first, walking Mama as calmly as possible through the circumstances, and then made a formal statement at the police station, which took several hours of repetitive questions under flickering fluorescents.

"Did he admit to killing Julie?" Dorian asked, his brow furrowed with repressed urgency.

"He didn't deny it," she said. "He's got a flair for the dramatic. All he wants is a titillating story."

By far the hardest part of the day was telling the least titillating version of the story to Dale and Debra Lauderbach, who arrived on the scene by lunchtime. They sat together in the Postman, which remained too hip for any of them, and she explained about the online calendar and her sneaking suspicions. The Lauderbachs' faces were tight with swallowed emotion as she talked, and afterward, Dale shook her hand and thanked her.

"I'm sorry," she said, meaning it to cover everything.

"You took good care of the children," Debra said. "We'll never forget that."

They collected Oliver and Caz from Natasha's house and took them both back to Virginia Beach that afternoon.

Things moved quickly then. Ed was released from the hospital after just a couple of days, and based on statements from Kim, Danny, and Renee, he was arraigned on three charges of attempted murder and one charge of child endangerment. The judge, a supremely surly gentleman, who had likely watched plenty of the Julie Weatherup saga, denied bail, announcing sharply that without the skilled work of first responders and surgeons, Ed would have been charged with murdering Danny Dudek, who had suffered some nerve damage but was now safely convalescing at home.

With Ed behind bars, Renee could start breathing again and Kim could file for divorce. They ran into each other once or twice at the prosecutor's office, and Kim seemed harried, a little older or more tired than before. But bolder, too, more businesslike. Renee searched for indications of whether Kim and Danny were still together, but she saw nothing conclusive, and she hoped they both had enough sense to move on to someone who hadn't fallen under the spell of a serial killer.

The trial was set to move quickly, as quickly as such things could. Conrad Harrington was defending Ed once again, but his only public statement on the matter was a couple of platitudes about seeking justice and not wasting taxpayer money. Renee, who watched on the living room TV back in Cumberland, thought he looked like a well-heeled thundercloud in a pin-striped suit. Ed stood beside him, his throat discreetly bandaged, his eyes staring straight ahead. She had the distinct impression that Harrington had threatened to "personally throttle" Ed if he said a word, and she hoped neither man was enjoying this return to the spotlight.

She would have to face Ed in court eventually, and the prosecutor on the case, Jared Deverell, who'd probably thought he'd already put everything Weatherup behind him, warned her that she wouldn't be able to bring up anything related to Julie's or Ella's deaths while on the stand. She could live with that. If the judge's pursed lips had suggested anything about the outcome of the case, Ed would spend more than five years imprisoned this time. The pendulum of public opinion had swung against him again, and no one was on hand to help him spin the narrative.

The narrative spinner in chief had called Renee several times in the ensuing weeks. *Hi, Renee, it's Mariah. I'm calling to see how you're doing. I'd love to talk to you at some point. Please call me back when you're available. Hope all is well.*

She had ignored that message, prompting a much more apologetic follow-up. *Hi, Renee, it's Mariah. Look, I'm sorry for, well, for everything. I obviously misjudged a lot about Ed, and I know the podcast was partly responsible for putting you in a dangerous position. I understand if you don't want to hear from me again, but I still want to talk to you and at least hear how you're doing.*

Renee sat at the workbench in the Christmas barn for a long time after she'd gotten that message, tying red velvet bows and thinking about how much she'd wished for Mariah's attention not too long ago and how, now, she didn't particularly want to talk to her. Still, she and the podcaster had also been through a lot in recent weeks, and it seemed rude to ice her out completely.

"Thanks so much for returning my call," Mariah said when she picked up. "How are you doing?"

"I'm all right. Just working and waiting for the trial."

"I owe you so many apologies," Mariah said in a rush. "I got the whole story wrong, and even afterward, we should have listened to you better. Danny told me about everything you found, and I feel so bad."

Renee sighed quietly. She was tired of patting other backs, graciously accepting concern to comfort the concerned party. "It was a learning experience for all of us," she said blandly.

"It could have been so much worse, you have no idea. He sent me all these emails after he got arrested about how he was tricked into going back home, and he's being targeted by a serial killer who is stalking him and killing the people he loves. He said the serial killer was probably the person who threw the brick that one time."

Renee opened her mouth to inquire how exactly Ed imagined he'd been tricked into stabbing his wife's lover, but Mariah was still going.

"He was even kind of threatening me, saying that I would be a target because people would want to silence me for telling his story but that he could protect me because he 'knows people.' It's so messed up."

"You know," Renee said. "It was probably Ed who threw that brick."

Mariah sucked in her breath. "What? Why would he do that?"

"Anything to stay the center of attention at all times."

"Wow." Mariah was silent for a moment, so Renee followed up.

"Was there anything about me in the emails?"

"Not so far, but that's a good thing, you know. You do *not* want to be in Ed's crosshairs." The excitement in her voice suggested that being in Ed's crosshairs could very well net someone a juicy book deal.

They had both gotten in over their heads when it came to Ed Weatherup, even if only one of them had realized as much. "How's season two going?" she asked, hoping to steer things away from Ed.

"It's going great! We're taking so many steps to be much more victim-focused on Claudia. But we do have to confront what Ed's done, and our own mistakes, and we're planning a special series on the upcoming trial. We'd love for you to be part of that. I want nothing more than to make your voice front and center."

"What good would that do?"

"It would get the truth out there," Mariah bowled along. "Your story is so important."

Renee sighed again. The last thing she needed was to get any more semifamous than she already was. "Notoriety isn't a good thing for people like me," she said. "It doesn't pay the bills. It doesn't get me a job. It doesn't make my life any easier."

"What about the story of *that night*?" Mariah asked with heavy emphasis. "Who's going to tell everything that happened?"

"I'm sure you'll figure it out," Renee said. "Good luck, and don't let Danny sleep with Claudia Castillo's cousin or whoever."

Mariah was right that it was a good thing not to be the object of a killer's fixation, but Renee had her own theory about why she'd been omitted from Ed's persecution fantasies. He cared about people who tried to deny him what he wanted, people who could advance or threaten his own self-aggrandizing agenda, and he simply hadn't thought Renee had any power in that regard. She hoped he regretted that miscalculation now.

She hoped he hated her.

As Christmas drew closer, Renee picked out presents for her parents and for Aaron, who would be home on leave for New Year's. She spent more lavishly than ever before, grateful they were all still alive and that she had a little more money saved than normal. The season had been a good one on the tree farm, thanks in part to how many church friends were in the market for a Christmas tree with a side of salacious gossip. They wanted to hug Renee, see her scars, and ask her if she would be on *Dateline* anytime soon. They were well meaning, and she found the fervor more amusing than annoying. After all, it was better to be Hero than Homewrecker.

Somewhat predictably, Andrea visited the farm in mid-December with Emma and Wyatt in tow. The children looked all right, Renee thought, passing an assessing eye over them from the doorway of the barn. They had new warm coats and boots, and they looked unequivocally joyful as they trotted down toward the rows of trees, ready to complete their holiday mission. She was relieved to see that. There was trepidation, too, though. Last they talked, she'd agreed to give Andrea $500 a month for the foreseeable future, and her second payment was now overdue.

When Andrea and the children brought their chosen tree into the barn for netting, Emma and Wyatt squealed at the sight of Renee, but even as she bent to hug them, Andrea intervened, hustling them back toward the door. "Remember I said there were candy canes in the car for after we were done?" she said. "Why don't you go find them?"

The children ran off, and Andrea turned back to Renee. "It's been a while," she said with a sugary edge to her voice.

Renee resisted rolling her eyes, and with a practiced heave, she boosted the stocky, six-foot Douglas fir onto the chute of the tree netter and pulled it through the hoop of plastic webbing, leaving it compact, portable, and smelling sweetly of pine resin. "I can't give you any more money," she said. "You gotta know I don't have that job anymore."

"I still have bills to pay," Andrea said. "The kids have bills. How about a cut of the reward money?"

"Reward for what?" Renee snipped off the netting and measured the tree trunk with a snap of her tape.

"Catching a killer."

She couldn't resist giving Andrea a pitying look. "There's no reward for getting attempted-murdered," she said. "And you and the kids look just fine."

"You can't just cut us off like this." Andrea drew closer so she could add venom to her words without being overheard by the other customers, who were dawdling by the wreath display. "You have responsibilities to this family."

"I don't know," Renee said, thinking about the last time she'd tried to control a situation that didn't belong to her. "I don't think you really want me to be part of your family, though."

Andrea scowled. "I'll tell people—" she started, but Renee held up a hand.

"Say whatever you like," she said. "We all have our own story to tell in this world."

Andrea was rapidly going from rosy cheeked to red faced, but she had one more dagger to throw. "If I don't get more money today," she said, "I'm going to have to cancel Christmas for the kids."

Renee glanced out the barn door, where she could just make out the children chasing each other around Andrea's car with fistfuls of candy in each hand, and she told herself again that they really did look okay. "You got this, Andrea," she said, trying to let the other woman know she meant it. "I'm sure you'll figure it out." She hoisted the Christmas tree onto its stump and tilted it toward Andrea. "Tree's on the house."

Andrea gathered the tree in a huff and hustled back to the car. Renee felt relieved, but at the same time, it was painful to watch them all drive away and realize that the moment represented just another ebbing away of the life she would have had. Obviously, she hadn't enjoyed being emotionally blackmailed. It had made her feel like people had been right that she did have something to be ashamed about, like she'd somehow been the one to separate Brandon from his children. But in a backward way, Andrea's money demands also had been proof that Renee and Brandon had something real, something worth fighting over, and now that thing was gone. Today represented progress but progress further into a future he didn't inhabit.

But there were other kinds of progress happening, too, kinds that didn't make her ache inside. News of her household successes had made it to the wealthy moms of Richmond, it seemed.

One day in mid-December, she'd gotten a call from a woman who introduced herself as the mother of a baby at Willow's day care. "I want to hire a housekeeper, and I got your number from Kim Duvall!" she'd chattered. "Kim just can't say enough good things about you. She says you're a literal lifesaver!"

Renee had promised to set up an interview after the holidays, but she didn't feel the same urgency she once had to get a job and get out of her parents' house. She'd learned a lot during her first voyage away from home, most notably that she could voyage if she chose to, and of course, she didn't have to take the first job that came along.

The Saturday before Christmas, a minivan full of unexpected visitors pulled down the long drive to the workshop. The Lauderbachs had driven the children for three hours to get their tree at the Beale farm, a gesture so sweet that it brought tears to Renee's eyes. Oliver jumped out of the minivan in his coat and winter boots and ran to throw his arms around her. "Surprise!" he yelled. "Merry Christmas!"

Caz, too, gave her a long hug, though hers felt wearier. Renee didn't know what the Lauderbachs had told the children about Ed's actions and Renee's part in the whole thing, and she didn't envy them the long, painful task of helping the young people understand that their father had killed their mother, that he had tried to kill their stepmother, and that he had done both without regard for his own children's suffering.

She walked the farm with her guests, watching Oliver frolic between trees and listening to the adults update her on their news. Caz and Oliver, whose names had been legally changed to Lauderbach, would spend their lives confronting their father's choices in one way or another. But for now, they seemed to be doing okay. They were happy to be back in the beach town where they had friends, a stable home, familiar schools, and they didn't have to walk each day through the house where their mother had lived out her last hellish moments. Caz had already gotten her first college acceptance letter, and Oliver would be in the school play. They were in weekly contact with Kim, who had sold the house on Linden Avenue as quickly as she could and moved herself and Willow to a more affordable apartment. She was back to working as a paralegal, and she intended to make sure Willow had a good relationship with her half siblings.

Renee was glad everyone was doing as well as could be expected, but as she hugged the Lauderbachs goodbye and watched them bump away down the rocky drive, she thought that it might be nice if she didn't see them for a while. They were good people, and she cared for them, but it was time for their paths to diverge.

Really, their paths should never have crossed in the first place.

A clear, fast dusk was coming on, and the temperature was dropping into the twenties. She closed up the workshop and turned off the lights. She knew that back at the house, Mama was cooking supper and Daddy was stamping the dirt off his boots on the porch. But instead of turning that direction herself, she zipped up her coat and headed down the trail toward the acres of pine. She walked until the ground rose, and she got a clear view of the sky. The moon was half full, surrounded by the glittering stars and the paler swath of the Milky Way.

There, where the signal was better, she lay down on her back, the frosty, long-dead grass crinkling beneath her, and gazed up at the points of light, so bright, so, so far away. She would have a few minutes here before the cold seeped through her clothes and she would go home, but for now, she would rest and admire.

At some point in recent weeks, when she hadn't been looking at it directly, the grief and shame she'd held inside her since Brandon died had evolved into something else. Still grief, of course, but now, when she reached out and touched the place in her heart where that grief lived, the first thing she felt wasn't pain. There was warmth there, now, maybe even strength.

She was surviving, surviving loss and sadness, surviving Ed. But bigger than that, she didn't feel so stuck anymore. Maybe for the first time in her entire life, she could see options, futures. She thought he would be proud of her.

"I miss you, Brandon," she said out loud to the stars. "Things have been wild, lately. Long story."

ACKNOWLEDGMENTS

My heartfelt thanks to my skillful editors, Elizabeth Agyemang and Charlotte Herscher and the entire hardworking team at Thomas & Mercer, especially Jenna Justice and Anna Barnes for their superhuman attention to detail.

So many years' worth of thanks to my agent and thoughtful guide, Amy Bishop-Wycisk, for so much patience and always having the best ideas.

Thanks to my local community for their friendship and support, especially to Jeannie Vanasco for comradeship and professional counsel and to Chris Shannon for unprofessional counsel. Thanks to Taya Graham and Stephen Janis for industry insights and gossip, which I value equally. Thanks to Mairin Barney and the SWAGers for weekly writing solidarity. Thanks to Martha and Tad Glenn for always asking how the book is going and to Kini Collins for always making more art.

Thanks to my long-distance community—I wish I lived closer to all of you. Special thanks to Joe Bechtold for years of reading drafts and good talks. Thanks to Claire Wahmanholm and Dan Lupton for so many magical visits. Thanks to Abby RayAlexander (and her team!) for wisdom about academia and everything else. Thanks to Lufi Paris for talking books and bots and for being so excited. Thanks to early readers, Helen Lauer, Peggy Reding, Joyce Payne, and everyone at Kipland Vale.

Thanks to Aneliese Apala Flaherty for long chats and always putting things so well. Thanks to Johna Strickland for being my cheerleader since our first writing class together. Thanks to Annamarie Pagel for real legal advice about fictional legal problems—all errors are mine, not hers. And special thanks to all three of you for a very particular piece of murder-related brainstorming back in 2023.

Thank you to Jim Peterson, who invested so much in me, and whose advice about writing and teaching guide me every day.

And thank you to my family, especially to my parents, Jean Reding and Franklin Reding, who taught me to make time for stories in all parts of life. Thank you to Io Wolf, my first and best comrade in imagination. Thank you to Thomas Bechtold, partner, first reader, champion.

ABOUT THE AUTHOR

Photo © 2024 Thomas Bechtold

Lauren Reding grew up in rural Virginia. She earned a BA in English from Randolph-Macon Woman's College and an MFA in fiction from Johns Hopkins University. Lauren enjoys planting native perennials, playing video games, going for walks, and shooting the breeze.